# MORE A Cottage Grove Novel

# THAN A

# FRIEND

# Amber Nation

**More Than A Friend**

A Cottage Grove Novel

Copyright © 2015 Amber Nation

Cover Design By Najla Qambar Designs

Edited By Silla Webb

Other Titles by Amber Nation

# *Prologue*

## *2003*

## *Miri*

I clenched my hands around the nylon straps of my backpack and peered up at my new school through my thick lenses. The last month had been complete chaos as my entire life had to be uprooted due to the unexpected death of my parents. So, I had to move clear across the country from Charlotte, North Carolina to Cottage Grove, Oregon to live with my grandmother, Tillie. Brand new town in a brand new state, and now I was standing on the sidewalk staring at my brand new school.

There were swarms of butterflies circling around in my stomach and a tingling in my throat indicating my nausea. That's all I needed to do was throw up in front of my new classmates. It was bad enough that I had to start in the very middle of my freshman year, I didn't need to be dubbed with a ridiculously embarrassing nickname on my first day because I blew chunks. High school was supposed to be fun, finally being in the home stretch before graduating, and I just wanted my mother.

I was still greatly mourning the loss of my parents, who were killed in a car wreck a mere four weeks ago, but Gran insisted that I needed to get my hind end out of bed and start going about my life. She assured me that I would love it here in Cottage Grove, I wasn't entirely sold yet.

Gran owned Tillie's Tavern and still slaved away many hours there even though she was on the upper end of her sixties. It wasn't fair to her that she had to take in her daughter's child, especially when all of her own babies had flown the nest several years prior. She certainly didn't need the burden of seeing me through the age of eighteen now.

I hoisted my backpack up higher on my back and began ascending the stairs to the front door, sliding my massive headphones back from my ears until they were hanging around my neck.

That was one thing that didn't ever have to change, my love of music. My home life and surroundings could change, but the music I held close to me would always be a constant. Several students were still milling about, so I knew I should have enough time to make it to the office and my locker before heading to my first class of the day.

Things took longer in the office than I anticipated. The counselor loaded me down with my course schedule and an extremely vague map that might as well of been written in Italian then sent me on my merry way. I studied the map with a pensive expression trying to figure out which way was up. Someone should have designed this a tad better. I found the giant X that was written in red ink on the position of the office, which also stated "You are here," then decided I should go right to try and locate my locker.

Students were quickly rushing past me in the halls, so I knew that the bell would inevitably be ringing a matter of moments. But looking at the people surrounding me, I also knew that I didn't exactly fit in here. With my coke bottle lenses, frizzy hair, and stick figure, I stood out like a sore thumb which had several kids openly staring at me as they whirled by. Also the fact that I didn't have an ounce of style and apparently had the word 'newbie' written on my forehead didn't help my case either.

It seemed as if I turned down two different long-stretched hallways before I successfully found the freshman hall of lockers.

I normally loved my choice of footwear, but today I wished I wouldn't have worn my old, dingy Doc Marten boots. The heavy sole made for loud footfalls as I clamored down past the long rows of lockers on either side of me.

139…

140…

Locker 141, the perpetual home for my school books for the remaining four months.

I positioned my hand on the dial that awaited the precise twists and turns of the combination before it granted access.

Starting on zero, I turned the knob to the right three times landing on the first number, to the left twice and finding the second number, then back to the right landing on the third number only to lift up on the lever and nada…nothing happened.

*Ok, don't freak out, maybe I did it wrong.*

I frantically spun the dial around and started the process all over again at zero, glancing at the paper held tightly in my clutch to make sure I was stopping on the correct numbers.

Did you ever have the nightmare where you went to school for your first day with your locker combination securely stored within the deep recesses of your brain only to stand in front of your actual locker and have your mind draw a complete and total blank? And of course, you don't have it written down anywhere as a backup because you were confident in your ability to remember. So you have to drag your sad, sorry behind to the office for them to give it to you. And while they're doing so, they're giving you a look as if you're wasting their time because you didn't write your combination down as a backup.

Yeah, this was kind of like that, but you had the paper with the combination right in front of your face and the lever WOULDN'T. BUDGE.

Leave it to me to get a broken locker.

The bell trilled at a deafening volume and I craned my neck to see that the speaker was strategically placed right above my broken locker.

*Great.*

Out of the corner of my eyes, I see a rush of students in a hurried frenzy trying to get to their first class. I could feel the panic begin to sink in as my hands started to tremble. I decided that I was going to try the combination one last time before I spent the rest of the day struggling to carry a backpack full of books around to each and every class.

Slipping my arms out of the straps on my Jansport backpack that I've used for the past three consecutive years, I threw it down on the ground without much thought of the books that were inside until it was too late.

"Fudge!"

If the last twenty minutes was any indication as to how the rest of my freshman year would be, then I'd rather be homeschooled and stay holed up in my new room.

I missed North Carolina.

I missed my friends, and I didn't want to make any new ones. I was socially awkward and my old friends learned to adapt to my quirkiness.

But most of all, I missed my parents and being a family of three.

Pressing on my closed fists, I aggressively cracked my knuckles, blew out a breath, and tried the series of numbers to this piece of crap One. Last. Time.

I was hopeful that this would be the time when it'd open just fine for me and the last few times were just my nerves getting the better of me. All of this anxiety and frustration would be for nothing. Heck, I may even laugh it off.

"Six," I muttered the last number under my breath as if saying the numbers out loud would help any and inched my hand to pull up on the latch.

Again, nothing.

Now, I allowed all of my pent up anger and heartache that'd affected me over the past month break free and took it out on that God forsaken hunk of metal.

Jerking repeatedly on the only way into the locker, I tried using all of my might, which pathetically wasn't all that much, just trying to get it to budge.

The noise alone from my clanking was enough to interrupt the nearest classroom but add in my verbal sparrage against an inanimate object and I could be facing some serious suspension time. I wonder if that's ever happened before. Started school that day and already suspended.

"Seriously, you big hunk of metal. Budge you useless piece of crap." I imagined that if I was one to actually curse, then I was sure that many expletives the vast colors of the rainbow would be flying out of my mouth.

"Dagnabbit." I continued on as if it actually heard me and I could hurt its feelings.

I had just reared my right leg back to kick the darn thing, because let's face it, if anything were going to infiltrate Fort Knox, it would be a Doc Marten boot, when a warm, slightly callused hand covered my own.

"Easy there, killer," a deep voice advised from my right. His tone was smooth and rich and sounded like he was much older than my measly fifteen. My foot slowly lowered until it was firmly planted on the worn tile floor.

My knees felt a bit wobbly just by his voice, if I was already this affected by sound alone, add in a few other senses and I may actually pass out.

I slowly turned my head towards the boy who was leaning on the lockers to my right and just about swallowed my tongue. I was also sure that there was an audible gasp that left my throat without permission.

Correction, this wasn't just a boy, this was a *man*.

If he hadn't already turned eighteen, then I'd be seriously surprised.

He had a mess of shaggy brown hair on his head that laid in numerous wayward directions that looked like he hadn't used a comb in a month. And I bet the ridiculous amount of money that my braces cost, that he actually *meant* for it to look like that.

His equally as brown eyes, which reminded me of the richest of milk chocolates, like the good kind that my dad used to bring back from his business trips to Germany, were twinkling with amusement. He must think that I was a basket-case, but at the moment, I couldn't care less because my sights just zeroed in on his perfect jawline that led me to the whitest and straightest set of teeth under his smile.

I wondered if he'd ever shot a toothpaste commercial?

And he probably didn't even need a mouthful of metal to achieve that flawless smile.

*Lucky.*

Where my knees were just a bit wobbly before, were now full blown feeble, and I was afraid I'd have to grab ahold of his bicep before I threatened to fall back on my behind. He was so dreamy.

*Great!*

And now I was looking at his bicep.

His big, strong arm that I could actually see the muscles rippling underneath his long-sleeved Abercrombie shirt.

*Stop it, Miri!*

I felt the overwhelming need to reach out and touch it just to see if my visual observation was correct, so I quickly brought a hand to my face to adjust my frames instead.

*Real smooth.*

He raised a brow because I hadn't actually said anything. I was still rooted in my spot openly gawking at him. He rendered me completely inarticulate. So I did the only thing I really could, I blinked.

He chuckled lightly and glanced at the handle of my locker that I still had remaining in my grasp. "May I try?" He said in such a polite manner that I decided he must be the nicest person, to actually stop whatever he was doing to come and help me out of my jam.

Someone who looked like him, helping someone who looked like…well me.

I briskly released my grip on the handle and took a step back, gesturing that he was free to proceed. If he thought that he was more than capable of trying something that I hadn't, then I had no direct qualms in letting him step up to the plate.

And I would stand here inspecting him as he did so.

He chuckled again before glancing back over his shoulder at me, "One thing, did you seriously just say dagnabbit? I've only ever heard my grandma say that."

I didn't exactly know how to take that other than his grandma had an excellent choice of wonky words, so I just shrugged my shoulders. My self-confidence had already taken a huge beating of epic proportions, then he had to go pointing out my absurd choice of vocabulary and compare me to his *grandma* without even batting an eyelash.

He flashed me his lopsided cocky grin, one I'm sure was normally reserved for girls who actually warranted that look. I had absolutely no idea why it was directed at me, but his quip from earlier had already been forgotten.

A smile like that must have girls eating out of the palm of his hand.

My own palms were now producing a serious sweat from this close interaction, so I had to wipe my clammy hands down the length of my pants hoping he wouldn't take notice.

"You see, this locker hasn't been used in a while and it tends to get stuck." He slowly ran his rough hand over the exposed metal as if it held his most private secrets. And then startled me when he banged his fist just above the combination.

Perhaps he was scaring away the cobwebs.

"All it needs is a little coercion." And miraculously, he lifted on the lever and it opened easy as pie. "Now that it'll be used more often, it should be a bit more," his gaze traveled the length of my body and I could instantly feel my cheeks heat in embarrassment before he snapped to my eyes with a wink, "pliant for you."

Holy moly, he just checked me out without raising a lip in any sort of disgust. That had to account for something, right?

Not so subtly, I cleared my throat as he started to walk backwards away from me. I found a tiny scrap of courage that was buried down deep and asked, "How did you know to do that?"

He pointed to the hunk of metal as he carefully descended the hall. "That was my locker freshman year." He winked again, something that I assumed happened on a regular basis around him, and turned on his heel as he continued on to wherever he was headed.

I realized that I hadn't even thanked him, how incredibly rude of me. I raised my voice, projecting it down the hall, "Uh...thank you!"

He turned back around and flashed his signature grin once more while holding out his arms, "It's what I do!" before he turned the corner and was out of sight.

I leaned my head against the edge of cool metal from *my* locker and just stared after the empty space the mystery guy occupied just seconds before.

"Wow," I breathed into the void of the empty hallway, "Who was that?" I hadn't even caught his name. Here he came to my rescue and I would undoubtedly replay the entire situation in my head. I could only refer to him as 'The guy with the panty dropping smirk.'

"That's Bentley Jenkins. He's a senior and a serious flirt to boot. Seriously, that guy sees flirting as an extreme sport." Another deep voice startled me from behind. I jerked my head off my locker and turned towards the new male voice.

"Wow!" His eyes widened once my gaze whipped around to his. "You have thick lenses," he surveyed, adjusting his own frames.

I blanched at his words and replied with a high level of annoyance, "Well aren't you Captain Obvious. And to think, we spectacle wearing people tend to flock towards one another. Where is your alliance?"

His mouth opened and closed repeatedly as if he were a gaping fish out of water. His pause allowed me to take in his appearance. With my hands now crossed in front of my chest, I took in his tall stature, like Bentley.

*Bentley...*

I rolled the name around in my head. The name absolutely suited him with his manly good looks and boyish charm and not to mention, his extreme politeness. Unlike this schmuck who's presence remained in front of me.

Whereas Bentley had muscles on top of muscles, this guy was extremely lanky. Sandy blond hair and an awkward posture. What really rounded out his entire look was his shirt that stated, 'Super Jock.' It was an extreme contradiction because he looked as if he only excelled at chess. My mother would have my rear end if she knew that I was judging someone before getting to know him, but he kinda deserved it.

"I, uh..." he stuttered, before readjusting his glasses on his nose once more, "I apologize, I'm a wee bit socially awkward." He held his hand out to me as he introduced himself, "I'm Oliver Tildon."

I openly stared at his outstretched hand and wondered if a handshake was a standard proper form of an introduction here in Cottage Grove. Back in North Carolina, a brief nod of the head was about as far as introductory touching went. But then I thought, what the hey? I had nothing to lose. I placed my palm in his clammy one and instantly wanted to retreat. I bit back my extreme unease regarding his sweat covered hand and clearing my throat, said, "Miri Armstrong."

It was finally the last period of the day, and I managed to successfully open my locker three times now. I guessed all it needed was Bentley's magic touch.

The remainder of the day was pretty much uneventful for the most part. Oliver and I had a few classes together, plus he saved me a seat at lunch. It definitely beat sitting in the girl's restroom, which was where I was sure I would be banished to sit. He introduced me to his friends, and I actually did learn that he was captain of the chess team. He certainly was a bit awkward, so we were pretty much one in the same.

I was now rushing towards my last class which was study hall. The room being clear on the other side of school from my locker. After my embarrassing tardy this morning, which resulted in me having to stand in front of the class and giving them 'my story,' there was no way I'd be late to another one.

My breathing was coming out in large pants as I continued hoofing it in the right direction. Dodging students left and right, my boots made a loud squeaking sound every time I had to stop short so I wouldn't run into anyone. My backpack was weighted down with books and homework and I even had to end up carrying my US History book and notebook in my arms because I had no other choice.

I rushed into the classroom with mere seconds to spare and my eyes immediately locked on Bentley's.

*He was in a class with me?*

My face heated as I took far too much pleasure in knowing that I would actually have the entire study hall in a room with him and I ended up stumbling, tripping over my Doc Marten boots and slammed right into a girl with a resounding 'thud.'

My book clattered to the floor as all my handouts slowly skittered right along behind it.

I threw my hands in front of me to help keep my balance, I was teetering on the cusp of falling directly on my butt. "I'm so sorry!" I tried profusely apologizing to the innocent bystander who was caught in the crossfire of my clumsiness.

Finally making eye contact with the girl after I readjusted my frames on my face only to find her lip furiously lifted in a sneer. I immediately took a step back away from her.

She looked down at me with severe distaste, and I could just imagine her making a voodoo doll with my name on it and hex me to death for actually touching her.

"God, Grace, watch where you're walking," the snooty girl verbally lashed out at me. Talking to me in such a tone that made me feel like gum on the bottom of her expensive shoes. She flipped her hair over her shoulder and stormed off in the direction of her seat.

She was a pleasant ray of sunshine.

I bent to the floor to retrieve my papers, wishing that this entire day was over so I could go home and cry, when a form dropped to their knees beside me and began gathering my scattered papers.

"Sorry about that." It was Bentley.

How about that, my voice lodged in my throat. Him being in such a close proximity messed with my head. I inhaled deep and his heady scent filtered into my nostrils.

The man wore cologne.

I was tempted to ask what it was just so I could beg Gran to buy stock in it. If I could actually speak.

"Lana can be a bit of a bitch," he added. I didn't know why he was apologizing to me for her behavior.

*Unless…*

Unless Cruella Deville was his girlfriend.

It was proven that opposites do attract; kindhearted, beautiful guy with rude and conniving girl.

Stranger things had happened.

I quickly admonished all thoughts of Lana and Bentley together.

"Here's your papers, Grace." He held out my History papers in a nice pile in his hand and I reluctantly took them out of his grasp, hoping he didn't notice my hands trembling.

He smiled and winked at me as I was barely able to croak out the words, "Thank you."

Once I finally felt like I got a handle on my voice, I whispered to his retreating back, "But my name is Miri…"

I hesitantly went towards the back of the room and took my seat in one of the empty chairs, careful not to meet anyone's eyes. The swarm of butterflies continued battling it out in my stomach due to Bentley's presence. As I slid into the cool tan chair, it dawned on me that he came to my rescue once again.

Opening up my notebook and finding the correct page in my History book, I came to the conclusion that there may not be much to me now, but one day I would be worthy enough of Bentley Jenkins.

# Chapter 1

## December 2014

### Miri

As I stood in front of my full-length mirror, fussing with my wayward hair that just wouldn't cooperate, the thought of shaving my head completely bald crossed my mind. I tried putting it up into a twist at the nape of my neck with some wispy tendrils framing my face, but I couldn't get the bobby pins to cooperate enough to make my hair stay in place. It definitely had a mind of its own and there would be no doubt that by the middle of the evening it'd be falling down as if I were a drunk rowdy female.

So I tried the next option, wearing it down. This would suit just fine except the fact that I lived in Oregon. And it rained all the time. Even though it was the middle of December, you couldn't count out the fact that it could rain at any point. Thus resulting in a rather unattractive frizz ball.

I didn't even know why I was going, it wasn't like the actual bride invited me. It was her maid of honor…

Julia, the MOH, came into my work, Cottage Grove Massage Specialists, purchased an hour long gift certificate and then just casually invited me before she all but rushed out the door. When I asked Gran if she wanted to come with me, she was already attending so it actually made it kind of perfect.

I grabbed my curling iron off of my desk and wrapped a strand of hair around the burning contraption. I needed to be extra cautious, just knowing my clumsiness, not to mention my luck, I would no doubt burn a portion of my flesh.

Releasing the handle, making my hair fall out of the iron's hold, it fell against my face like a limp noodle.

"Ugh," I stomped one of my bare feet on the carpet of my bedroom, "I don't even know why I'm going." This time I voiced my frustration out loud.

"You know good and well why you're going." Oliver, my roommate, came up behind me, his handsome face reflecting in my mirror. It was a darn good thing that I had already released my hair, being startled like that was a finger burn waiting to happen.

I turned towards Oliver, who had a steaming bowl suspended in midair, close to his face. Taking a heaping forkful of ramen noodles in his free hand, he brought it to his lips to blow away some of the heat before shoving it into his mouth.

"Ollie, you do know that you can afford more than ramen noodles now, right?" I said trying to get my mind off of exactly *why* I was sucking up my lack of self-confidence and attending this wedding. Oliver was a veterinarian, just graduating this past May. Upon his graduation from veterinary school, his grandparents surprised him by paying off all his loans. All, however, many hundreds of thousands of dollars that it was. Without having any college tuition repayment looming over his head, he was able to start securing a nice little nest egg once he began working at Cottage Grove Veterinary Clinic.

He shrugged a shoulder before shoving another bite into his mouth, making me physically gag, "I know. Just bringing things back to my youth. Back to the good old days of college when neither you nor I really had a pot to piss in. Back to the simplicity of life when we weren't technically an adult."

I wanted to delve deeper into his meaning, but with Oliver it most likely had nothing to do with anything in particular. He was the strangest person that I had ever met, but he's been my very best friend since I moved to Cottage Grove ten years ago. So dealing with Oliver's unique personality was small in comparison to his wonderful friendship. I don't know where I would honestly be without my Ollie.

And ever since that first day we met, he always wore t-shirts with wonky sayings on it. Case in point, the shirt he's wearing right now says, 'Veterinarian by day. Deadly ninja by night.'

He's a mess. But he complimented my mess perfectly. We were a match made in awkward heaven.

Turning my attention back to my hair in the mirror, I picked up a silver barrette and tried pinning just a portion of my hair back away from my face.

Again, nothing was working right. I wasn't one of those girls who enjoyed dressing up. My usual attire consisted of black capri pants or slacks and a form fitting v-neck t-shirt. Pieces of clothing that were appropriate for work yet still casual. And nine times out of ten, my hair ended up in a ponytail that trailed down the middle of my back. If I were feeling super bold on any particular day, I would braid my hair to switch things up.

I was boring.

But yet, here I stood, trying to fancy myself up for the second time this week.

In a dress no less.

It was a simple gray A-line dress that hit mid-thigh and I paired it with a black three-quarter-sleeved cardigan since it was mid-December. It wasn't that it looked bad on me, on the contrary, it actually looked good on my slender frame. I just felt out of place.

"I'm not going." I tried to sound like my statement was final. As if there was absolutely no room for argument.

"I don't know why you didn't just bid on him at the auction," Oliver stated in between another bite as he walked over and leaned against my desk.

And there was my reason for doing all of this.

Bentley Jenkins.

I had been half in love with the man since he helped me my first day of school. He was the brother of the groom, so he inevitably had to attend the wedding.

I wasn't just boring, I was also pathetic.

"Oliver, I told you I don't want him to go out on a date with me because he had to. Because I paid for one."

Every year for as long as I could remember, Gran would put on a bachelor auction at her Tavern. It was a bit archaic, but it was all in good fun. Each year the proceeds would benefit a certain aspect of the community, this year being the public library. The library was near and dear to my heart because I worked there throughout high school and college. Even though I wanted to donate, and I did just by writing a check, I couldn't go through with bidding and trapping Bentley into a date with me.

He didn't even know who I was and if he did, he'd think I was some headcase who was tripped up on him from ten years ago. No matter how truthful that statement was.

It was a comical event, though. My cousin, Maisie, thought she was going to bid on and win a date with Dean Parker, the new town divorce lawyer and best man to the groom today, Baylor Jenkins. There was almost a knock-down drag-out brawl against Maisie and Julia, the maid of honor as they bid against one another. Being that Maisie worked for Gran at the Tavern, she saved up as much money as she could for this date but even her savings couldn't beat the five thousand dollars that Julia bid. From the tension that quickly rose in the Tavern after Eden declared her the winner, I didn't think that Dean took too kindly to Julia interfering. Maybe he wanted Maisie to win the bid...Nah.

My cousin, well she's something else.

She tried to attach her claws into any eligible bachelor she came in contact with, but to no avail actually landing one.

That was the difference between men and women. Maisie would throw herself at anyone and everyone, but any well-respected male would just simply toss her aside. Declare her as pathetic, needy, and a stage five clinger. That wasn't to say she never got a man, quite the contrary. Just not the ones with loaded down pockets and their priorities straight.

Then there were men like Bentley Jenkins, who just had to show a simple flash of his grin and he had women falling at his feet.

*Would I ever be one of those women?*

The actual day when Bentley noticed me and found me attractive would never come, so the point was moot.

*So why was I even trying so hard?*

I slipped my feet into my favorite hot pink flats and finished lightly curling the ends of my hair, hoping some of the curl would take hold. A few swipes of my mascara wand and a light application of shimmery lip gloss and I was ready...to sit in the corner and not be noticed.

The ceremony was beyond beautiful and the bride, Eden, was utterly breathtaking.

It made me long for the day when I'd get my chance. Once upon a time, I thought it would've been a possibility with my boyfriend of four years, Travis. From the age of seventeen until we turned twenty-one, he was my whole world. I was just stupid enough to think I was his.

But the only difference between Eden walking down the aisle to her prince charming and me walking down the aisle towards mine, she had her daddy holding her hand the entire way. What I wouldn't give to have my daddy be able to witness me on my big day.

That's neither here nor there. He wasn't able to grace this earth any longer and I don't have an eligible suitor lined up to whisk me away.

Pulling my thoughts from my melancholy state, I took a seat at one of the available stools at the bar.

Eden's family pulled out all the stops, even springing for a bartender. The gentleman, who had an air of familiarity about him was dressed in a white button-down shirt with a black vest, sidled up in my line of vision asking, "What can I get ya?"

I felt as if I was thrown into the movie Steel Magnolias. Me being Annelle, the one loner invited to the wedding out of sheer pity.

The only thing missing was the bleeding armadillo groom's cake and the lady out on the dance floor who didn't wear a girdle and it looked like two pigs were fighting under a blanket in her skirt.

My back was to the dance floor, so I wouldn't exactly single out that last scenario. But who wore a girdle? Nowadays, it was all about the Spanx; keeping things tucked in appropriately since 2000.

"Miss?" The gentleman muttered, making me realize that I was lost in my own head.

"Oh uh," I tapped my fingernails against the smooth wood of the bar. "I'll have a beer, whatever dark ale you have in a bottle will be fine."

Being that I was raised from the age of fifteen on by a woman who owned a Tavern, I was a lover of all beers. It was definitely an acquired taste for some, but I came out the gate loving the stuff. Didn't hurt that Gran only stocked the best. I preferred a good brew to any other frilly drinks.

Except for wine.

There was no match for wine. Wine always won. Hands down.

Speaking of Gran, I had absolutely no idea where she ran off to. I twisted my body in my seat to either side trying to get a glimpse of her silver, high piled hair on top of her head, but it was no use. Knowing her, she's off sneaking candy from the chocolate bar when she knew good and well that she wasn't supposed to.

The bartender brought back my beer and sat it down on a paper napkin that had Eden & Baylor embossed on the edge.

I placed a five dollar bill on the counter, slid it towards him before settling back in the seat and lifting the beer to my lips. The bitter taste of the liquid that invaded my mouth told me that the beer was either skunked or cheap. The lack of a label on the bottle led me to believe the latter.

Strike my earlier statement about loving all beer. I'd like to amend it stating that I loved all *good quality* beer.

Water it is then.

I crossed my legs under the lip of the bar, if I was going to stick around, then I might as well make myself comfortable. Which led me to my next thought, how long should I stay? How long is customary? I didn't want to appear unappreciative and skip out early. Not that anyone would notice anyway.

In the next moment, someone came up next to me, standing so close that his suit jacket brushed the side of my arm. Was I *so* invisible that the guy didn't even see me sitting here? If the mostly empty bar was an indication, then there certainly was enough room for him to scoot over a bit. I almost had half a mind to look up at the guy and ask him if he's ever heard of personal space and that he was invading mine a little too intimately.

I brought the beer bottle to my lips thinking that I would do just that. I took another swig, ignoring the taste in order to coat my dry throat. I didn't want to get onto the guy and have my voice lodge a bubble in my throat that I couldn't speak around.

The bartender approached with a broad smile towards the rude guest and a bit too enthusiastically said, "Hey Bentley! How the hell are ya?"

*Bentley?*

I jerked my head in his direction as my putrid beer traveled down the wrong tube. The sound that erupted from my throat was a mixture somewhere between a cough and a choke.

Entirely unladylike.

The bartender, who I now remembered as Bentley's friend from high school, Kyle, gave me a strange look as I felt the sensations of someone's palm rubbing across my back.

As embarrassed as I was, I repeatedly chanted, "Please be Bentley" in my head.

I knew that most likely this wouldn't be the case, but that didn't detour me away from profusely wishing it. I imagined that if one day, by some miracle of fate, that Bentley would have his hands somewhere on my body. I envisioned that his hands would be big and strong and he'd have to concentrate on having the gentlest of touches.

Not once did I ever think he would have a delicate touch with small, nimble fingers like the hand that was currently rubbing circles on my back.

That meant that it wasn't Bentley and could only really be one other person…

"Now deary, I thought you knew how to swallow," Gran casually said with a bit of amusement as she appeared directly to my right.

I sucked in a breath and started coughing all over again as my cheeks continued to enflame from my everlasting embarrassment.

*God, if you're listening, I think it's time to beam me up!*

The two men to my left chuckled, no doubt from the double entendre from my lovely, old grandmother, in which I duly thought it was time to start checking into Nursing Homes for. Her ability to speak her mind astounded me. Doesn't matter if what came spewing out of her mouth was offensive, no one commented on it.

It was almost as if people assumed it was acceptable whenever you reached a certain age point.

Bentley picked up his shot glasses and walked away without another word or a backward glance, his suit jacket brushing against my arm again as he turned around.

Once he and Kyle, the bartender, were out of earshot, my voice became unhinged from my throat as I whipped my head around to Gran to give her a pointed stare.

"Really, Gran?" I admonished. "I'm thinking one more mishap and I'm going to be forced to put you in a home."

She smiled brightly, her hot pink lips curling around her teeth. She knew that I was joking even though my expression stated otherwise.

"Sweetheart, with the way I age, you'll be in a home before me."

I rolled my eyes and turned my attention back to my rank beer bottle.

She was right, though, for being on the upper end of her seventies, she was remarkably agile and mostly had her wits about her. *Mostly*.

Even though my granddad passed before I was born, and then her daughter, my mother when I was fifteen, she's always remained positive about the outlook on life. I've always known her to be a free-spirit, dancing to the beat of her own personal saxophone, she was a big fan of jazz. Getting up each and every morning to run the Tavern and really living has kept her embracing her youth.

She sees what she wants and goes for it not worrying about the repercussions.

I wished that I had a measly ounce of her courage and determination.

"Miri, I really wish you'd quit pining over that Jenkins boy…"

"Shh.." I released in a low and hurried breath. "Please keep it down."

Gran perched her elbow on the counter and cradled her chin in her hand. "I'm just saying that you're worthy of a man who knows how to keep his pecker in his pants."

How could I take her seriously when she referred to it as a pecker?

I chuckled lightly because I couldn't even say the correct word in my head, which earned me a raised brow.

"I'm serious, Miri. You aren't your cousin Maisie. You aren't built for a one-night-stand and that boy isn't made for a relationship. Hell, he probably thinks a commitment is some kind of disease that he doesn't want to contract."

Casting my gaze away, I picked up my bottle and took another drink. I haven't become numb to the taste, but I needed to do something with my hands. I knew that Gran was right as she most of the time was, but it didn't hurt hearing the truth any less. Just because I thought he was the epitome of male gorgeousness didn't mean that I wanted to be in a relationship with him. I perpetually knew nothing about him, except his social standing with the ladies.

I was only twenty-five years old, still in the prime of my life. What harm would it do to let myself go and take charge after what I wanted for a change?

I could give up all my inhibitions for one night of no-strings-attached sex. I could be a one-night-stand type of girl.

Slamming my hand on the bar, grabbing Kyle's attention, I decided that I would carry on the night with an open mind and hopefully everything would fall into place the way it should.

"I need two shots of tequila, please!" I pointed and hollered towards the bartender.

If I was going in with guns blazing, then I needed something to help loosen me up. My trigger finger was mighty stiff.

Ha! Loose, that would be a term directly identified with Maisie. And stiff, yeah, we won't even touch that one.

"Miri," Gran warned from her seat next to me. I was so in depth with concocting my plan that I almost forgot that she was there. But the not so subtle warning in her tone told me she knew exactly what I was conjuring up.

She was like the Miri whisperer. Always two steps ahead of me, reminding me that I've always been the good girl. The one who doesn't sleep around, the one who wouldn't even allow a curse word to slip from my lips, even in the buildup of a furious or intense situation.

Kyle sat down two individual shot glasses filled to the brim with the crystal clear poison. I primed the flesh above my thumb before grasping a lime wedge between my fingers. Lifting the shot glass in my free hand, I brought it towards Gran as I gave a brief nod of my head.

"To spontaneous decisions in hopes that they don't become the worst of mistakes."

"Oh Christ," I heard Gran mutter right before I tossed the shot into the back of my throat, immediately feeling the effects as it lit a fire trailing down its path.

"Hey!" Julia appeared beside me as one of my new favorite songs came on from the DJ table.

"Hey!" I responded, not really knowing what else to say.

She glanced back out onto the dance floor, then back to me with a wry grin before gripping my hand in hers. Tugging it towards her, she forced me to pull myself out of the comfort of the barstool. "Come dance with us," she hollered back over her shoulder to me. My brain was misfiring signals to my feet and I had to physically make myself quicken my steps to keep up with her. This was a good sign that the alcohol was already taking effect. Julia may have short legs, but she walked with a purpose and she walked briskly.

I could only imagine who *us* was in reference to whom she was dancing with.

"Miri, this is Dean Parker," she came to an abrupt halt and first introduced me to the tall drink of water lawyer that seemed to have captured Julia's attention if the twinkle in her eye was any indication to go by. Of course, I knew of him because of Maisie's obsessive infatuation towards him.

Not saying I didn't have an infatuation situation of my own that I was dealing with, but I knew how to control myself. And I wouldn't be caught trying to ever proposition someone.

*But wasn't that what I was all gung-ho about just minutes ago?*

I decided that what I was doing couldn't be described being nowhere near the same category of Maisie and her over-redundant sluttiness.

I shook Dean's massive hand as it engulfed mine right before I was directly in front of Bentley. His eyes were transfixed on my own, no signs indicating that he knew the little cough fit from earlier, was me.

As usual I was invisible, until now. The way his eyes flared, there was no denying that he was very much aware of me.

"Bentley, you know Miri, right?"

He took a moment to study me, angling his head, "Miri?" His eyes traveled down the entire length of my body making my heart rate spike and my cheeks flush from his blatant perusal. He almost looked as if he was appreciative of what he saw. Once his eyes were focused back on mine, he cleared his throat and shoved a hand in his pants pocket before adding in a gruff tone, "You've grown into a beautiful woman."

I felt the heat from my body flood my cheeks even more and before I could say a word, Dean and Julia sped off on their own to dance, leaving us alone. Even with the numerous dancing bodies around us, they seemed to all fade away until it was just the two of us standing in the middle of the floor. "Sugar" by Maroon 5 was just now finishing up when the song abruptly changed to "Thinking Out Loud" by Ed Sheeran.

I immediately panicked at the slow tempo song choice, knowing that there was a good chance that Bentley may not want to dance a slow song with me.

All of my underlying doubt eased away as he bowed in front of me. Like a true gentleman that I remembered him to be, he offered out his hand, and then looked at me with his signature panty-dropping grin, which I knew was on reserve for hundreds of women, but for now, this one was all for me.

"May I have this dance?" After all these years, he was still polite, the earlier rudeness of his close proximity immediately forgotten.

"Yes, you may," I responded before lightly placing my hand in his. The electricity ricocheted throughout my body as he yanked me towards him, closing the gap that separated our bodies and wrapped his free arm snugly around my waist. He began to slowly sway once he felt the tentative touch of my fingertips on his shoulder.

It took me a minute to relax my tense posture, I couldn't actually believe that I was dancing with Bentley Jenkins. Wrapped up in his embrace. After a few beats, I felt his breath on my cheek forcing me to snap out of my lust-filled daydream to look into his eyes.

"I thought your name was Grace?"

A small gasp escaped my parted lips. Never in my wildest dreams did I ever think he'd remember me from High School. "You remember me?" I thought his comment about growing into a beautiful woman was just a line, now that I knew it wasn't, I felt myself melting into his embrace all the more.

His lip lifted in a smirk, "And forget your assault on my old locker? Not everyone tries to take down a locker with a combat boot." I couldn't contain the smile that broke free. This right here, between us, was fulfilling ten years-worth of fantasies.

"Well, I have Lana Malone to thank for that nickname. It kind of stuck, but my severe lack of coordination didn't really help my situation." I shrugged my shoulder because there was no use dwelling on my severe clumsiness.

He glanced down in between us towards my feet. "Is that why you aren't wearing heels?"

I raised a brow, what an odd comment to make. "What does wearing heels have to do with anything?"

He seemed to backpedal on his words, "It's just that most women do. Look around, I think you are just about the only woman not wearing heels. Even Tillie and my twelve-year-old niece are succumbing to the inevitable aching feet in order to wear a heel."

I was still completely lost on the entire conversation. "Do you have a weird obsession with women's shoes or something?" I stopped moving altogether, "Please don't tell me you have a secret closet at your house with various heels stowed away that you take out for special occasions to prance around in when you think no one is looking?"

He abruptly dropped his arms from my body and I immediately missed his lost contact. I was afraid that I had offended him by my failed attempt at a joke, but the slight tilt of his mouth in a grin assured me that I hadn't.

"You caught me," he deadpanned while placing a hand on his chest. "I don't know how you saw through me so easily. But please, let's just keep this secret between us." He added with a flirtatious wink. "No, really, heels are sexy as hell."

If he were to repeat that action to me, placing his hand on my chest, he would find an impeccably fast heartbeat pounding against his hand. Throughout his entire retort, the only thing I could steadily concentrate on was that I wanted to be able to wear heels so he could perceive me as sexy, too.

He took me into his embrace once again, swaying to the beat of the song. Even though by now the songs had switched up, we were the only two people slow dancing to a fast song.

I didn't mind one bit and apparently, neither did he.

"Yeah, well no one will probably ever see me in heels. If that makes me different or not sexy because of my taste in footwear, then I'll gladly embrace it." I waited a moment before casually adding, "Besides, would I want to voluntarily prove to anyone exactly how much gravity hates me? No, thank you!"

"I'm sure you're just being modest," he said, lightheartedly.

"Say that to my extensive collection of broken bones," I immediately replied, my tone amusing, but I was dead serious.

He chuckled lightly before he pulled the collar of his shirt away from his neck and cleared his throat. His subtle brown eyes bore into mine as he briefly cupped my cheek and ran his fingertips down the side of my neck. I could see him visibly swallow before he said, "Don't ever say that you're not sexy, because sweetheart, from where I'm standing I'd say you exude sexiness."

Oh, he was good.

He was *real* good.

If I wasn't so transfixed by his gaze and enthralled by the gruff tenor of his voice, I might have laughed at the absurdity of his statement. Now it was my turn to swallow, but mine was clearly audible and nowhere near as alluring as his.

*Riiight...I was the epitome of sex appeal.*

*Me.*

*Miriam Armstrong.*

He may need to get his eyesight checked.

This was clearly so amusing to me that next I proceeded to release a pronounced snort.

My eyes went as wide as saucers as I slapped my hand over my mouth.

*Yep, real winner right here.*

"Care to share what was so funny that you felt the need to snort?" His eyes twinkled with amusement. But I couldn't just confess that I was laughing at him, so I did what any nervous woman would do in front of her longtime crush. I chose the most inopportune time to profess my undying love to him...

Ok, well, I wouldn't say that I went *that* far because I didn't actually love the guy. That would be a bit obsessive, *right?*

"I had the biggest crush on you in High School." *And ever since*. "When I met you during my 'assault on your locker,' that was my first day at Cottage Grove High. I had just lost both of my parents and had to move clear across the country to live with my Gran. You were the first person who was nice to me."

Now, all playfulness was cast aside and my mood was border lining on somber. All traces of the tequila were gone. I revealed too much and judging by his non-existent reaction, I had scared him away.

"You lost both of your parents?"

I nodded my head before explaining further. "Yeah, a teenager fell asleep behind the wheel and hit my parents' car head on."

He got a faraway look in his eye as he fixated his gaze on something behind me.

"My dad died my junior year of High School. I think in some instances it hit me harder than it did Baylor. No one really noticed, though. Mom was distraught about the plumbing business, then Baylor stepped up and took over. I lashed out for attention which only got me in trouble with the Sheriff or the Principal. It's just hard coming in dead last to everyone. I wish he could've been here to see this today, though." A glimmer of a tear shining in his eye caught my attention. "And I don't know why I told you all of that…" He added, albeit a bit sheepishly.

"Don't worry about it," I waved him off, "you can't always keep everything bottled up inside." I don't know what overcame me, but I reached my hand up to his face and gently wiped away the lone glistening tear from the corner of his eye. The action made him flinch as if I had hurt him and when I removed my fingers, the wetness from the tear revealed some mild bruising.

"Crud, I'm so sorry. I didn't know you were hurt. What happened?"

He glanced around before replying, "This was the result of Dean *not* keeping his feelings bottled up. I thought he broke my nose, but luckily he didn't. I'll be sporting black eyes for a few days, though."

Something tells me that this wasn't the first time he's experienced a punch to the nose.

I didn't realize that my palms were cupping his cheeks until he tried to cover my hands with his. I quickly dropped my hands and began fidgeting with my nails. This was becoming a bit too intimate. "I, uh, have to work early, I should be going."

He shoved his hands into his pockets, "Let me walk you out."

I wasn't expecting that. "Oh, let me just tell my Gran that I'm leaving."

"Let me grab your coat, do you have your ticket?"

Reaching into my clutch, I retrieved the little slip of paper that stated which coat was mine, handed it to Bentley and watched him walk away. I was glad that he remembered our coats because my current frame of mind would've had me walking outside and completely forgetting it. I looked around the room among all the dancing bodies and was startled to see Gran dancing with an older gentleman.

"Gran, I'm taking off," I leaned forward to place a kiss on her cheek. She looked past me and narrowed her eyes.

"Just remember what I told you, Miri."

Bentley appeared at my back, holding my coat by the collar so I was able to slip my arms into the sleeves.

"Bye, Gran."

Bentley's hand settled onto my lower back and he leaned in close to whisper in my ear. "How did I not know that Tillie was your gran? So that means Maisie is your…" He trailed off the sentence, not knowing how to exactly answer.

"Cousin? Unfortunately."

"Your lack of enthusiasm towards her explains everything…" He chuckled as he held open the door leading outside for me.

As soon as I stepped over the threshold, I had to wrap my arms around myself to shield off some of the frigid cold. The temperature seemed to have dropped below what was considered arctic. Once the bustling wind hit my bare legs, I shivered in response. If Bentley hadn't insisted on escorting me to my car, I most likely would've run the entire distance.

I released a breath, which hung like a foggy plume in the air due to the weather, trying to think of how I wanted to go about explaining my cousin. "Maisie is…Well, she's just Maisie. Putting it mildly, she's had more hits to her vagina than Google. Kind of like the female equivalent of you, except she would love nothing more than to tie down some unsuspecting guy. Her talons are always out in full force, ready to dig into someone when he least expects it," I rambled off.

We continued walking through the poorly lit parking lot on the way to my car. He fell into silence next to me shoving his hands into the pockets of his coat. I was surprised that he didn't have any kind of sarcastic remark to what I said about Maisie. He didn't even release as much as a scoff.

I began to feel uncomfortable and self-conscious and started obsessively scrolling back through what I said, taking stock of everything that came out of my mouth. Then it hit me, during my nervous rambling I totally insulted him. I stopped in my tracks, which just so happened to be in front of my car door. "Bentley, I am so sorry. I didn't mean anything by it. I wasn't even thinking and here I basically called you a…" I really didn't want to speak the word out loud. It went against who I was.

"A whore," he replied, no speck of amusement laced in his tone.

"Well, I was going to say a tramp or a hussie, but since you wanted to go for the gusto, yeah." Finally, a hint of a smile flitted through his lips. "Again, I apologize, I have no right to judge your lifestyle and the way you choose to live your life." I looked towards the sky and continued on, "I also shouldn't judge Maisie, but I tend to let that slide since I have to constantly listen to her relive her so-called judgments."

"Miri…"

I snapped my focus away from the lamppost and the flurries that were swirling around illuminated by the light down to Bentley's bemused gaze.

"Yeah?"

"You're adorable."

"Seriously…" I said, expressionless. "I was first sexy, then degraded to adorable by something I didn't mean to say?"

"Miri…"

"Oh crud, I think I just said that out loud."

"Miri," this time he grasped my chin between his thumb and forefinger. If I weren't so cold, you would probably make out the red hue of my cheeks due to my embarrassment.

I really shouldn't be let out in public.

"I think it'll be best if you just stopped talking and maybe even stopped thinking."

"How can I stop thinking?" I quipped.

I must've been late to the show, because his gaze lingered on my lips a second before he dipped his head, closing the distance between the two of us. My breath hitched and my heart rate increased tenfold as he pushed me back against my driver's side door all while his eyes never tore away from my now parted lips.

Once his tender, strong lips met mine, all thoughts regarding my embarrassment or lingering uneasiness of being cold were long gone. His calloused hands cupped my face and his touch warmed me right up. My heart ceased any regular beats when his tongue finally swept into my mouth. He removed his lips from mine as he moved his hands and placed open-mouthed kisses along my jawline as my foot lifted on its own accord and skimmed up his pant leg. I couldn't believe that I was taking part in such a brazen act to where anyone could catch us at any moment.

It wasn't until his warm breath blew on the outer shell of my ear, as he whispered, "Let's get out of here," while his hands curved around to grab my backside, did my heart slam against my ribs to kick start back up again.

Of course, I was just another pathetic woman throwing herself at Bentley Jenkins. No matter how many times I fantasized about this situation, this was never the outcome and it felt entirely wrong. I was nothing but another hookup to him.

Silly me to think I could ever be more.

Men like him didn't settle down.

Men like him didn't want to be tamed.

What had changed in the ten years since my little crush began, I was now worthy of Bentley Jenkins, in fact, I was worthy of anyone.

And even though my little teenage infatuation hadn't diminished over time, it didn't change the face that he now didn't deserve me. I'm not easy and I certainly won't degrade my values for a one-night-stand that will be meaningless to him and everything to me.

I can't give up my inhibitions no matter how hot I thought the sex between us would be.

I wanted more than what he could give to me and I deserved nothing less.

The tables have now turned and how I see it, Bentley Jenkins wasn't worthy of me.

I placed my hands on his coat and even through the thick material I could feel his rock hard abs and briefly wished that I *could* be a casual hookup before I shoved him away from me. I immediately missed the warmth of his touch and the enjoyment of what he was doing to my neck with is teeth and his sinfully delicious tongue.

"Bentley, stop. I can't do this."

"You don't want this?" He gestured to his amazing body and even though his arrogance should have been like a bucket of ice cold water to my libido, I found myself continuing to want him.

"That's not it. I would love *nothing* more."

"Then what's the problem?" He stepped forward once more, attaching his lips to the exposed skin of my neck.

I braced my hands on his chest with the logic of trying to push him away, but my attempt was futile. I loved the feel of his pecs underneath my fingertips. Instead of pushing him away, I felt my resolve waning and wanted to pull him closer to me. I had to get him away with words because clearly my body had other ideas. "Your reputation proceeds you, I'm not strong enough to just walk away afterward and you're not strong enough to stay."

His lips left my skin voluntarily this time, which I knew my comment would make him do, but I felt even more bereft. As he stepped back with a dumbfounded expression, my hands dropped to my sides as he searched my eyes for even the briefest hint that I was joking.

Then I said something so perpetually insane, but like most of the night had gone, it just came toppling out without any heed or warning. The voice didn't even sound like mine, all husky and seductive, which was the exact opposite that I wanted to portray at this point in time. "I think it would be best if we were just friends."

# *Chapter 2*

### *Bentley*

I think something in my brain must've short-circuited during that hot as fuck kiss. I couldn't believe that the beautiful, striking woman standing before me, trying to catch her breath but unable to fully clear the desire from her eyes, was Miri.

Of course, I knew her as Grace, but she grew up nice. *Very nice.*

She had come a long way from the coke bottle lenses and metal mouth shy girl I met in High School.

Miri was a nice added surprise to this bazaar as hell day. My brother getting married, my good deed for Julia, and getting punched in the nose by Dean. She made for the perfect distraction and I actually enjoyed talking to her, it wasn't the typical conversations I had with airhead women who wanted to get into my pants and most often succeeded.

She had substance to her and I thought we were getting along really well. There was no doubt in my mind that she was also definitely into that kiss. Resting my hands on my hips and heaving a long sigh, my breath frozen in the air, I rolled that dirty word around in my brain.

*Friends…*

I can't even think of the word without flinching and wanting to break out into convulsions just to make it go away. And the whole...it's not you, it's me. Except in this instance here it was, it's not me, but it sure as hell is you.

The woman who has openly admitted to having a perpetual lady hard-on for me for almost half of her goddamn life has just shoved me into the bottom of the barrel category. There would be no absolute way of redeeming myself and I felt like a piece of me, most likely my balls has shriveled up and died a most violent death.

We're talking this is cruelty on the same level as kicking innocent puppies.

Fuck me sideways, I've been friend-zoned.

This sucker punch hurt far worse than the cheap shot to my nose from Dean earlier. No sane woman had ever told me no before. Women were a dime a dozen and easily replaceable, but the thought of anyone else besides Miri shut down any and all urges of untamed desire.

What the hell kind of voodoo spell did she put me under? One thought that made itself abundantly known was, why in the world did I care so much that she turned me away?

Squinting my eyes and perching my hands higher on my hips, I looked around the ill-illuminated parking lot. I searched around cars, high and low, but ultimately, I came up with nothing.

Nada.

Zilch.

Zero.

"What're you looking for?" Miri questioned, so pure and innocently as if she hadn't just obliterated an enormous chunk of my sanity.

"Oh, you know, just searching for my ego."

She smirked, "Something tells me that you'll have no problem finding it."

Burn times two.

Here is where I should've taken my losses and walked away, even if it was with my tail tucked between my legs. A better analogy, which is actually the correct one, would be to walk away, readjusting my dick and looking forward to a horrendous case of blue balls.

But I never did anything half-assed and I had to go and add insult to injury.

"Are you a virgin?" I blurted out. That had to be the explanation of what this was about, why she was openly refusing what we both clearly wanted. She was saving herself.

I didn't even see it coming.

She huffed out an irritated grumble, which was in all honesty not very terrifying and if I dared to say, cute as hell. But she didn't stop there, she stepped forward towards me and ground the heel of her foot down on the top of mine.

Not so cute now. Searing pain exploded through my foot and I wanted to shout out a million different indecent expletives. But I hid my discomfort well, if you could call balling my hands into tight fists and clenching my jaw, grinding my teeth together.

"Bet you're glad that I didn't wear heels now, huh? And no, I am most certainly NOT a virgin. I just have more dignity."

She whirled past me and disappeared into her car.

Who would've thought that Miri Armstrong had a feisty side to her?

*I liked it.*

I dusted off what little remained of my pride and went back into the reception, sporting a new limp from my injury. I was definitely looking forward to playing the sympathy card now. There was only one thing that could help me recoup and blow off this entire crazy ass evening, and that would hopefully be in the form of a random and willing warm body, whose vocabulary didn't include the word *no*.

# *Chapter 3*

### *February*

### *Bentley*

I loved my brother Baylor. I looked up to him immensely, just about everyone did. It definitely wasn't his fault that I grew up in his shadow, but it still made me uncomfortable to be around him.

I'd just rather not have his wonderful, put together life thrown up in my face whenever I was around his little family. I was considered the misfit of the Jenkins' and I was reminded of this every time we were together.

*I'm not dependable enough.*

*Apparently, I'm set in my childish ways.*

*Why haven't I found a nice girl to settle down with?*

That last point was the biggest issue with my mother. Why was I the way I was with women? Her underlying feelings always front and center. She may not have said it in so many words, but it was always there. "Why won't you settle down and be a grown up like Baylor?"

All of that being said, I still had to make an appearance at Baylor's house to go over issues and books for our plumbing business. Within the last six months, I've been given the opportunity to step up and be in charge of Jenkins Plumbing. I've been a goof in the past, but just being given this chance showed me that my dad was looking down on me. I wouldn't ever do anything to jeopardize the business that he worked so hard to build.

I think Baylor and my mother were impatiently waiting on the sidelines, just ready for me to fuck something up. It'll just make victory that much sweeter when I prove them wrong.

I walked up the pathway to Eden and Baylor's house, straight to the front door where I proceeded to ring the doorbell.

It has repeatedly been drilled into my head to let myself in through the laundry room if the garage was open, but there was no way in hell that I would be subject to the possibility of catching my brother and sister-in-law in any form of compromising positions.

Eden was hot and all, but I didn't need that image seared into my brain for all of eternity.

Talk about making family functions that much more awkward and agonizing.

The front door was abruptly yanked open and a short blur of a girl threw herself into my arms. "Uncle B!" My niece, Norah hollered as her arms encircled my neck, cutting off all oxygen to my brain.

She was a cute kid, too bad she had to endure the pain I was about to bring.

It was either her or me.

And I wasn't going down without a fight.

I grasped her under her arms and paused for just a brief moment before I went to town tickling her. She tried to kick my shins while she struggled to break free from my hold, all the while squeezing my neck even tighter. I needed to hold on just a little bit more. She was twelve and although tenacious, she wouldn't outlast me.

Within no time at all her hold on my neck released and I was able to finally take a deep, full breath. "Bentley," she scolded, stringing out the middle consonants of my name.

"What?" I shrugged my shoulder as I breezed past her into the house, acting as if nothing just transpired between the two of us, my breathing back to normal. "It was either enduring the annoyance of being tickled or suffer a noogie. You're a preteen, I didn't exactly want to know what came next if I ruffled up your hair."

Making my way into the kitchen I saw Eden leaning against the bar boring holes into her phone. "Baylor miss a check-in?" I teased her as I placed a brief kiss on her temple as a greeting. Something I began doing just to rile Baylor up. It was always amusing to see his eyes flare with jealousy.

That guy was fucking pussy whipped.

"No, I just got off the phone with Julia. She said that she wasn't feeling well. I'm just worried about her, she has no one in Nashville since I moved away."

Julia is Eden's partner-in-crime and her right-hand woman. Jules had a snarkiness to her that I would've been completely balls deep in if it wasn't for the fact that she was trying to cover up her blatant attraction to Baylor's best friend, Dean. I may have been called a lot of things in my life and I wasn't exactly high on Dean's list, but I'm not, nor will I ever be a cock blocker.

"Eden, you know you're worrying will all be in vain. You're a newlywed, let loose a little. You worry way too much." I perched onto one of the barstools across from Eden and leaned onto my forearms.

"I take it that I'm actually early for once since my punctual older brother isn't here?" It wasn't all too often that I didn't get scolded for being the tiniest bit late.

"Bentley...You are far too hard on Baylor and not to mention yourself."

This is what always happens when I'm around family. Maybe this was the way most families were, but I was a bit tired of the same old song and dance, constantly trying to stick up for myself. I leaned back in my seat, "No, Baylor is too hard on me. I've done well with the business for the past six months, he needs to cut me some slack and quit breathing down my neck."

Eden released a long sigh, "He's just stressed."

"And again that all falls on me, right? Make a few mistakes in your life and you're forever making up for it." My voice was now to the point of rising. I noticed her grimace and then frown making me feel even guiltier. The weight was just continuing to stack on my shoulders.

Even the strongest of mountains crumbled when pushed too far.

"I'm sorry, I didn't come here to argue." It seemed it was always me left apologizing.

Same shit, different day.

"Moving on. You brought up the topic of being a newlywed..." My heart immediately sank in my chest. I didn't need Eden on my ass about settling down too. I liked my sister-in-law, but there was only so much pressure I could withstand. I didn't want to have to take her out.

Mob style. The messier, the better.

"Have you used your groomsman gift?"

I gave her a sideways glance as I rubbed the back of my neck and tried to suppress my chuckle. She completely caught me off-guard. In all honesty, I had forgotten about the present. I originally thought it was a stupid gift, but then an idea suddenly hit me…

I was back to leaning forward on the countertop, and I looked her dead in the eye, no sign of amusement in my voice, "Do they give happy endings at this place?"

"Bentley!" She gasped as she quickly retrieved a dishtowel and snapped it against the bare skin of my forearm. She really shouldn't be appalled, this was me we were talking about.

"What?!" I rubbed my arm with the slightest bit of pressure trying to get the sting of the cloth material to subside. "It's a legitimate question. I'm going for a massage, it's for relaxation, sometimes they may help relieve tension in other areas. You know, go the extra mile in the name of great customer service." I ended with waggling my eyebrows, which just earned me a childish eye roll.

*Rude much…*

"This isn't a shady place, Bentley. Maybe for that particular service you'd need to find a whorehouse."

"You kiss my brother with that mouth?" I couldn't believe that I actually heard her correctly. Suggesting a whorehouse. As if I needed to go to that much trouble to find a woman.

*Pfft.*

She smirked, "I relieve your brother's tension with this mouth," and countered with a bright flash of her pearly whites.

I stood from my chair, a shell-shocked expression plastered on my face. Covering my hands over my ears, I yelled, "AH! Abort! I can't unhear that shit! I'll talk to you later." I decided I would take my chances getting choked out by my preteen niece than deal with this shit.

# Chapter 4

*Bentley*

I walked into Cottage Grove Massage Specialist and I put a little more pep in my step once I got a glimpse of the cute little redhead perched behind the counter.

A happily-ever-after didn't seem so far-fetched after all.

The raving beauty looked up from her computer and her eyes locked on mine as I turned on my mega-watt signature Bentley Jenkins panty-dropping smile. This shit should be trademarked.

I slowly approached the counter, adding a little more swagger to my hips and read the knockouts name tag. "Briar? That's an unusual but extremely beautiful name." I added a wink just for a little extra added effect.

Her response, or lack-there-of, befuddled me. She quirked a brow and actually looked bored and less than enthused at my attempt at some charm.

"My name is Bentley Jenkins, I'm here for an appointment."

"I know who you are." Again, no spark of desire blooming in her pools of blue irises.

*It was happening.*

I rubbed the palm of my hand in the middle of my chest trying to get the ache to subside.

I knew the day would come where I would lose my touch, I just didn't think it would come this soon or sting this bad.

She rose out of her chair and in a monotone voice, asked me to follow her.

This was where I would normally take a moment and revel in staring at her ass as it swayed back it forth with each and every step. But with her sunny disposition, I was sure she would feel my wandering eyes. So, I decided to forgo my usual ogling and be a gracious client.

Briar stopped in front of an open door and ushered me in.

"Undress completely, lay on your stomach and cover yourself with this sheet. Miriam will be with you shortly." She braced the doorknob with just a hint of a smile before closing me into the dimly lit room.

My mojo mustn't be completely gone, I did get a bit of a smile out of her.

I couldn't help but think as I unbuttoned my jeans and lowered the teeth of the zipper that Miriam sounded like an old lady name.

Definitely no extra-added fondling today.

I finished following the instructions I was given, taking my time to take in every aspect of the room. There were cool and calming colors painted on the walls and several lit candles scattered about the room. It was actually pretty cathartic and serene even though it vastly reminded me of a chick room.

The effects of this room actually had me feeling as if I could actually relax and leave the weight of my life checked at the door.

48

I barely rested my head down on the face pillow before I heard a soft knock on the door and the sound of the door opening. A small, timid voice filled the room. "Good afternoon, Mr. Jenkins. Would it be alright if I turned on some soothing music to help you relax?"

The familiarity of the voice hit me head on and instantly had my dick stirring against the table.

She certainly didn't sound like an old lady.

Now, being in an uncomfortable position with my hardening dick wedged up against a massage table, I responded to her question with a muffled and gruff, "Sure."

I heard her begin to rustle around the room, not being able to place exactly where she was when a song came on that physically had me cringing. Straight up Enya or some shit. Now, before you get all up in my face, trying to strip me of my masculinity, I do have a mother who enjoyed her music. Being the only reason I would know who Enya was.

But at least it had my erection subsiding for the time being, I would call that a win even if I did have to subject my highly sensitive ears to this garbage.

I sensed her movement before feeling her stomach brush across the top of my head, ruffling my hair. Then the sound of her rubbing her oil covered hands together caused my dick to twitch, distinctly reminding me of an act I've been privy to much more often as of late.

*Down boy*, I will him to listen. *Now is just simply not the time to get all excited.*

Her hands clutched the edge of the sheet that was covering my naked body and the cool air hit my exposed back, sending a chill down my spine as she folded the blanket down, stopping at my waist.

I briefly wondered if it was customary to not have any type of interaction with your massage therapists before they got down to business. You'd think they would at least want to introduce themselves. You know, give us a semblance of a face to go with the expert hands that'll be working on our skin.

But what did I know, I was, in fact, a virgin to massages, well, ones of the professional variety that didn't involve particular appendages. Appendages that were begging for a little massage of their own right now.

I had to stifle a laugh and a groan because *virgin* wasn't a word I've directly identified with in a long ass time.

Once her warm, oily hands tentatively touched my shoulder, a jolt of electricity singed through my entire body, throwing me completely off-kilter and causing my eyes to snap open. Being that my face was scrunched up against this pillow, I barely made out a pair of hot pink ballet flats. On the top of her right foot was a hot ass flower tattoo, a cherry blossom to be exact, that had my breath seizing in my lungs.

My dick, never far from the party, instantly became rock hard because I knew this woman.

It was the same woman who has caused me to turn to my right hand for relief more times than I cared to disclose. The same woman I tried like hell to forget but had trouble getting out of my head since December. I had done so well not actually saying her name out loud, being it never strayed from the tip of my tongue.

"Miri?" I pushed myself up on my forearms and the deer in the headlights expression she was sporting led me to believe that she thought she was working on a different Jenkins brother. That the thought never crossed her mind that it would ever be me.

"Bentley?" she asked breathlessly.

Oh yeah, I was affecting her just as much as she was me.

Then it finally clicked. My dumbass finally put two and two together. "Your name is Miriam?"

She lowered her arms down to her sides, "Gee, nothing can get past you."

There was the feisty girl I vividly remembered.

She released an exasperated sigh, signs of guilt shadowing her face, "I'm sorry, I don't like being caught off-guard." She gritted her teeth, "They told me you were Baylor."

"Sorry to disappoint," I said with an air of sternness. So, that's what must've had Briar smiling. She thought she was the coy one.

*But wait…*

My brows rose, "You were going to feel up my brother?"

"Bentley," she chastised. "This is my job."

"I didn't know you worked here." Really, I didn't know much about her at all. Although, if I had known this was her place of employment, regular visits would've been in order.

"Three years now. Our little chat is cutting into your massage time. May we resume?" She said the words, but she looked pretty reluctant to proceed. "Are you allergic to coconut oil?"

"No. I don't know if I can just lie back and have your hands roam all over my body." I smiled as if I were joking, but it was the God's honest truth. Now that I knew it was Miri performing this massage, absolutely no relaxation would be happening.

"You're exhausting. I'm a professional, there will be no funny business. Besides, we're friends, right?"

I sneered. There was that word again. I was beginning to hate that word, especially when I so desperately wanted the woman standing before me, underneath me for the duration of an entire weekend.

No funny business, HA! Didn't mean that I wouldn't be constantly thinking about it, let alone wishing it with her hands all over me.

*Oh, the torture.*

I ambivalently resumed my position, which in turn was excruciatingly uncomfortable, lying against an unrelenting rock hard cock. This was going to be the longest hour of the entire history of man. Trying to concentrate and keep my wits about me and not break my finely straining resolve, would prove to be one of the hardest things I've ever had to endure in my life.

Her freshly oiled hands began kneading across my upper back. As she rubbed the knots out, I could literally feel the tension ease away. I was surprised that I was actually able to relax a bit. Miri was a miracle worker and my new personal hero.

"Uh, Bentley," Miri quickly removed her hands from their placement on my skin, but I was still able to feel the remnants of her fire in their wake. "I asked this before and I thought you told me no. Are. You. Allergic. To. Coconut. Oil?" She annunciated each word slowly and clearly so there was no mistake of confusion.

"I'm allergic to coconuts, why?"

I leaned up on my forearms again and my back started to feel as if it was actually on fire. Miri's eyes went wide as she ran out of the room and came back several moments later with a small bucket of water.

I tried swatting at my back, trying to alleviate some of the burning sensation to no avail. "What's happening?" I screamed erratically as a sheen of sweat broke out along my forehead.

"I asked if you were allergic to coconut oil and apparently you are!" She dumped the water on my back and frantically began wiping at my skin with a towel.

"I didn't hear you say coconut!" I said agitated, the blistering pain only partially subsiding as she continued rubbing the towel along my back. "I just heard that you were going to rub me down with oil, excuse me that my mind went elsewhere!"

"Unbelievable!" She said exasperated. "Is sex all that you think about?"

After she removed the coconut oil from my skin, the burning sensation seemed to stop immediately, but now my skin itched like crazy.

"Is that a trick question? I am a man."

She stared blankly at me. "Your back is breaking out in hives due to the allergic reaction, you should go home and take some Benadryl and get some rest."

"Will you come with me and be my nurse?" Being knocked out by a heavy dose of Benadryl sounded heavenly, but I had to try to trap her with my charm one last time.

Throwing her hands up in the air, she grunted out an, "Ugh," and stomped out of the room slamming the door behind her.

Clearly she was done and I was left a scratching, horny mess, with no direct signs of relief.

That night I laid in bed, hopped up on Benadryl, which obviously didn't knock me out, and replayed every single movement her hands made for the few minutes of bliss that I experienced.

Scissoring my legs to kick off my sheet that laid over my body, I had never in my life been this sexually frustrated. My dick was continuously like granite with recurring thoughts of her running rampant through my mind. Miri was absolutely everything I sought out in a woman. But to be clear, there was one thing that I didn't do, ever; I didn't chase a woman. I didn't take the time to get to know them. I was a love 'em and leave 'em type and all else was just semantics that would get in the way.

I conjured up an idea as I was drunk on that allergy reliever and I didn't know how it would play out. But what I did know was that I always got what I wanted and I wanted Miri Armstrong in my bed something fierce. I would show her *just friends*. That was the last thought I had as I drifted off into la-la land, where I dreamt that massages had happy endings and Miri dropped her panties without argument or stipulations.

# Chapter 5

## *Miri*

I barely survived with my hands on Bentley, even if it was only for a few minutes and only on his upper back. I think if I had gone further south, my heart would've palpitated right out of my chest and onto the floor.

After I all but ran out of the room from his pure arrogance, I made sure that I knew for certain that he had left the building, meaning I watched from out the window in the break room.

"Briar!" I seethed after I sanitized the room and marched out into the reception area. "You!" I pointed in her direction as I continued stalking her way.

She rose from her chair behind her computer and responded with a smile and a curtsey and said, "You're welcome."

"Oh no," I stopped directly in front of her, only inches separating our faces. I was peeved. "I am not thanking you for that," I thrust my index finger back towards my room. "What in the hello kitty was that?!" And now I've resorted to substituting curse words. I was in a worse place than I thought.

"What?" She shrugged, the least bit unaffected, "he'll go home, load up on medication and be perfectly fine."

"That's not what I'm talking about and you know it! Why'd you tell me it was Baylor?"

I had massaged Baylor Jenkins numerous times. Didn't even think anything of it. Bentley and his brother could definitely be twins from the back. They were practically identical.

"Because I knew you would've been too much of a chicken shit to go in there and deal with it otherwise. I did you a favor."

I turned on my heel and grumbled the entire length of the hallway. I couldn't be near that infuriating woman a second longer. It was so completely unlike me to get so riled up, but I didn't like being lied to. And even though it was seemingly his fault that this situation happened in the first place, I still felt guilty that I used coconut oil on Bentley when he was allergic.

That next morning, I woke earlier than usual. Sleep eluded me most of the night as I tossed and turned worried about Bentley. I knew that most likely my worrying was futile, but it still didn't help the feeling that ran through me.

I couldn't wait any longer, I had to call to check up on him.

I dug around in my oversized purse trying to find the post-it I wrote his number on, finding it crumpled in a ball. As I dialed his number into my phone a thought finally occurred to me that he could still be sleeping and he may not be alone. I walked over and tucked my feet underneath me as I sat on mine and Oliver's couch otherwise I'd be pacing the floor. My stomach was in knots as the line continuously rang. I almost wanted his phone to turnover to voicemail, I could leave a nice short message and feel better about going on with my day.

"Hello?" His voice was raspy, clearly laced with sleep.

I now felt extremely silly for even calling to check up on him.

"Uh, hi, Bentley. I was just calling to check up and see how you were feeling?"

"Miri?" he questioned and I realized that I didn't even tell him it was me. He just automatically assumed.

"Yeah, sorry, it's Miri." It seemed as if I was apologizing to the man at every turn.

"How did you get my number?" he questioned.

"Uh…" I didn't know exactly how to respond. "This was a work related call, so I just got your number from the computer system." There, that explanation should suffice. Besides, it's too early for him to actually take the time to think, right?

"And you're calling me from work this early in the morning?"

*Crud.*

"Uh…" I had nothing. "Shoot."

"Busted!" He shouted into the phone, making me pull it away from my ear. Wow, he had a lot of enthusiasm, he must definitely be a morning person. "But hey, thanks, now I have your number and I only had to have an allergic reaction and break out in overbearing hives to get it." He paused for a brief moment before his voice resumed back to normal, "Something tells me that there should've been an easier way."

"I'm sure my number is one of many in the sea of women's numbers crowding your contact list. Be sure to add in my last name so you don't get me mixed up with another Miri." There was teasing in my voice, but I didn't know when in the world I became so brazen as to actually speak what was on my mind.

He sighed deeply into the phone, "You know what they say when you assume things, Miri…" The way he said my name, even though he was virtually scolding me, sent delicious chills down my spine. It was all because of me, my big mouth, and values that Bentley and I were just friends in the first place. I wished that I could just turn off my attraction to him, it would make things a lot less complicated.

I could just hope and pray that he had no desire to actually fulfill his end of the friendship bargain.

"But you really couldn't be more wrong. I have a total of three women's phone numbers stored in my phone and yours will make four."

I wanted to quickly fire back by saying that I guessed he really wouldn't need a woman's number when he had no intention of ever seeing them again, let alone talk to them, but I took precaution to keep my mouth shut.

Something told me that what Bentley divulged was deeper than even he wanted to believe.

An entire week passed by without anyone needing an emergency dose of Benadryl, which was outstanding, or a word from Bentley. I had mixed feelings about the last one. Life had seemingly gone back to normal. That was until I decided to stop by Richardt's grocery store one weeknight after work.

Taking my time walking around the store, I found it to be a miracle to have a smooth sailing cart, so I reveled in it by making sure I savored the experience. I wanted to tag this cart and store it in the back room so no one would mess with it. This cart virtually ruined me for all of my future shopping excursions.

I was busy in the produce section, deciding on whether I wanted honeydew or cantaloupe for the week. Let me tell you, the struggle was definitely real. I was so engrossed in what I was doing that I was oblivious to other shoppers around me, including my newly dubbed friend when he came up beside me.

It took me a minute, but I finally spotted him out of the corner of my eye. He was inspecting a few of the honeydew melons himself but wasn't even acknowledging that I was there.

Finally, deciding that I would take both of the melons, I placed them next to my purse in the front of the cart to make sure nothing accidentally knocked into them, bruising their skin.

Looking up, I saw that Bentley now had a honeydew in each hand and had them held up in front of his chest. I couldn't even contain my eye roll. He was the very definition of a typical male and growing up for him wasn't even on his radar. Nonchalantly, he locked eyes with mine and said, "You really have to compare and contrast the weight of each melon to see which will taste the best."

He glanced down at my cart and then raked his eyes up my body before landing back on my eyes. "These aren't as nice as your melons though."

I stared blankly at him, and I could just feel my face heating up. He had two levels of flirt, his version of normal and hardcore. They were both always on and both more than I was ever used to dealing with.

"Why do I get the distinct feeling you aren't referring to my fruit?"

"Just stating a fact. What kind of friend would I be if I didn't give it to you straight?"

"A normal one," I replied matter-of-fact.

"Nonsense," he waved me off. "It's my duty as your friend to tell you that you have an extremely desirable pair of melons that are in proportion to your well-rounded…uh, assets."

I had to stifle a grown at his overt pervertness and wished that the earth would just swallow me whole and spit me back out at my house so I didn't have to endured this off the wall conversation any longer. It took me a minute to recover from his statement before I counter argued, "*No*, friends don't come onto each other. They especially don't talk about the other's assets that they desire.

They lend an ear or a helping hand." I started walking down the aisle and Bentley didn't miss a beat falling into step beside me, still holding a melon. "They sometimes even offer to bring the wine when the other had a bad day."

I stopped my cart in front of the wine. I loved that they had such an extensive wine section and a wonderful variety.

"So wine is a good thing for you?" If I didn't know any better, I'd actually think he was taking inventory of certain things that I liked and disliked, but that was more wishful thinking than anything else.

I selected my favorite bottle, "Wine is a great thing."

Having to adjust my melons in the top of the cart, I settled my wine in between my fruit and purse. The bottle was precious cargo and would be riding up front and within arms-reach.

Bentley took it upon himself to place his melon in the basket of my cart.

*Alrighty then.*

I guess we were now shopping together. But the kicker was, it almost felt a bit normal, besides the constant vulgar references from the manchild. My grip tightened on the handle of the cart when he started perusing through my items. I'm talking bent over, personally inspecting each item that I had strategically placed in my cart. He was messing up my well-thought out system, making everything mingle together. Cold and frozen things were now mixed in with regular boxed items, putting them with things that should not be placed together. Such as food and cleaning products. I could feel my blood pressure spike until his eyes skimmed past my box of tampons and I quickly averted my gaze away.

I shouldn't be embarrassed, but there was no doubt that my face would turn beet red.

I wanted to make a remark about his nosiness, but I caught sight of a woman with one heck of a scowl on her face as she looked in our direction.

"Well well, what do we have here?"

*Great.* He was calling attention to my feminine products. He needed to learn how to be a better friend, because his social skills department and dependability was severely lacking. Straightening my posture and squaring back my shoulders, I braced myself to tell him what for. But when I turned towards his devilish grin, it wasn't the tampon box he was waving around, but rather my own personal weakness.

Even more so than wine.

He cocked a brow, causing his forehead to wrinkle the slightest bit as he held the box hostage in his grasp.

"Really, Miri, Ding Dongs?"

I defiantly lifted my chin and tilted my head away from him, "Say what you want about me, but don't insult my favorite snack cake."

When he finally blinked, I darted my hand out and snatched the box of divine confections out of his hold. It now rested safely away from Bentley's clutches along with my fruit, wine, and purse right in front of me. Hopefully, he was done making fun of my choices because this divider part of the cart was getting mighty full.

"I'll drop it for now, but if you think my innuendo of melons was bad, you just opened a floodgate about Ding Dongs."

*Holy cannoli, this man was an absolute mess.*

A gorgeous mess, but a mess none the less. And one that made me smile at that.

I started to walk again, this aisle was becoming a bit too crowded.

When I looked up, I halted in place because at the end of the aisle was that same woman featuring the same irked scowl painted on her face. This time a little boy flanked her side.

She was impeccably dressed in a deep violet wrap dress and a pair of black heels.

*Heels.*

Well I'll be, that was a dead giveaway. Must be one of Bentley's women since he was so obsessed with women's footwear of the heeled variety. That also gave me a pretty good indication as to the scowl that was directed at me.

"Bentley," I swatted at his arm while my gaze never strayed from hers. "Who is the lady who is stewing and conjuring up the ultimate way to kill me, one that is slowly with maximum torture?"

"What? Where?" His head jerked around. Once he noticed who I was referring to, he let out a brief curse, "Shit. That's Talia."

*Talia*, how exotic. Miss jealousy had now dropped the scowl and replaced it with a bright smile when Bentley's eyes reached hers. He placed his hands on the backs of my shoulders and tried to partially hide behind me, problem was he was taller than me and had muscles that extended well past my arms.

His breath tickled my ear as he whispered, "She's one of those stage five clingers. We didn't even share a full night together about six months ago and she's been pursuing me ever since."

Talia was now waving and walking towards us with the little boy in tow.

"Aw how sweet, Bentley has a stalker," I said aloud, trying to sound unaffected but inside I was ready to claw her eyes out. I had about as much claim to the man as she did, none.

"Hilarious. Now be my hero and help me," he pleaded between his clenched teeth.

This entire situation screamed psycho, but I also couldn't deny that it was also pretty comical.

"Now, did we forget our manners?"

His grip tightened on my shoulders causing me wince in pain, "Please."

Talia stopped at the end of our cart and turned her smile up a few notches. "Hi, Bentley," she purred. *She purred*, I didn't know women actually did that. "You are one impossible man to get ahold of."

"Talia, hi…" he muttered a bit too cheerily. He was showing fear to the psycho. Didn't he know that's the one thing you don't do? It's like dating 101. But then again, I don't think Bentley has ever been on a date in his life.

He squeezed my shoulder again, obviously waiting for my cue, but I had absolutely no idea where to take this conversation. I really needed to tread lightly here, there was no indication if this lady would turn psychotic on me if I said the wrong thing.

"Listen, I was wondering if you would want to get together this weekend, my son will be at his father's house."

Another squeeze.

I couldn't actually believe that she had the audacity to arrange a hookup right in front of me, in a grocery store no less. If I didn't witness this firsthand, I'd have a hard time believing the magnitude of absurdity. She didn't know who I was, I could very well be his girlfriend for all she knew. That scenario was laughable because I was nowhere near registering on the spectrum of her beauty, but still.

"I'll have to apologize. He's been hard to get ahold of because I've been taking up all of his free time." I tried to sound the slightest bit sympathetic, but it almost came out as patronizing. "Isn't that right, baby?" I turned my eyes towards him and batted my eyelashes, trying to make things seem a bit more believable.

His throat bobbed as he cleared his throat before he responded, "That's right, *sweetheart*." He let one arm fall from my shoulder and travel down the length of my arm, allowing his fingertips to skim along my bare skin until his hand firmly grasped my own.

*This was a mistake.*

My bad instinct was only further solidified when I saw his face come towards me out of the side of my vision, and I literally melted into a liquid puddle on the floor when his lips brushed my temple for the briefest hint of a kiss. I didn't intend on it, but my eyes closed of their own volition, reveling in the sensation of his lips pressed against my skin.

*Such a bad idea. We were talking a colossal mistake.*

I was a stupid person suggesting that we should just be friends. Pretending to be someone that I wasn't as a façade in front of this woman.

Hearts would end up getting involved. And ultimately, broken.

And the probability wasn't weighing very high that it would be his heartbreaking.

My eyes opened and I was looking directly into a pair of striking chocolate brown ones. My mouth was suddenly dry, like a desert with no sign of refreshment in sight.

Snapping out of whatever the heck was transpiring, I brought my attention back to Talia, who was looking back and forth between the two of us as if she was on the verge of war. I quickly came up with an excuse to get us out of there. I couldn't deal with this any longer. "I'm terribly sorry, Tonya was it?" I knew her name, I just didn't care enough to say it correctly. This was an act right? "But we're in a bit of a rush, so we'll have to be going."

She blinked as her jaw fell slack, it was almost as if she couldn't fathom this would be the outcome of her propositioning Bentley. Truth be told, it shocked me as well. Her head began shaking back and forth, her mouth still agape. She hurriedly turned on the balls of her feet and stormed down and out of the aisle, leaving her poor son rushing to catch up with her.

My first initial instinct was to apologize, I didn't intend on that being the lie I came up with, but I swallowed it back. It wasn't my fault that I was put in that position, so I did the best that I could with what little time I had.

I could sense the tension mounting around us and I needed to form a diversion from our thoughts that surrounded that intimate contact. Pulling my hand from his, I pointed in the direction of Crazy McGee and teased, "Dude, I think it's high time you run some sort of background check on women before you strip them out of their clothes. That woman's crazy was all kinds of exposed. I'm incredibly sad to say that I was embarrassed for her."

He didn't respond, so I decided to drop the whole conversation. We continued to walk around the store, getting the items that we each needed in a comfortable silence. He darted behind me to grab something and I felt his hand brush against my backside. He came back around and threw his item in the cart and gave me a little wink.

When I didn't reciprocate his smile, he held his hands up in front of him, "My bad, it slipped."

Wherever he went before was unknown, but playful Bentley was back.

"Bentley Jenkins, are you using my grocery store as your hunting ground?" Mr. Richardt, Eden's father came up beside our cart.

"Now sir, would I do such a thing?" He smirked.

"Yes!" Mr. Richardt and I said in unison.

Richard's smile reached his eyes when he saw me. He always delivered groceries to Tillie's Tavern for as long as I could remember. "Oh Miri, I didn't realize it was you. Is this troublemaker of a young man bothering you?"

"Young man?" Bentley's brow raised. Nevermind the fact that Mr. Richardt indicated he was a troublemaker, he just focused on the young man comment.

I would never understand him.

"I'll have you know that I'll be thirty in two years." And acted as if he was twenty-one.

"You'll always be the pimply prepubescent teen who bagged groceries and couldn't get a single girl to talk to you until you grew into your good looks."

My eyes bugged out of my head, I had never heard Mr. Richardt talk to anyone like that. You could tell that there was unresolved animosity lurking between the two of them.

The excitement of my awesome gliding shopping cart had long lost its luster. The bazaar situation with Talia and the way Bentley handled it just really set me on edge. Not to mention Mr. Richardt's obvious distaste for the man. This just further reiterated that Bentley Jenkins was pure trouble, and it'd do me some good to keep my distance from him in order to save my heart. My box of Ding Dongs and bottle of wine was screaming my name by this point. It was high time I went home where I could indulge in both with some privacy and replay exactly what in the world went on here tonight.

# *Chapter 6*

## *Bentley*

Today was one hell of a day. If anything could go wrong, it did. Same shit, different day.

The worst part was Baylor yelling at me over the phone while I was with a customer. Belittle me all you want while we are in privacy and I can defend myself, but don't do it where I can't act anything but professional.

My normal solution to a shitty day was to find a woman to get lost in for a few hours, but I found myself wanting to call and talk to Miri instead. She made a point to say that friends offer to bring the wine when the other was down, I wondered if the same applied to me. Hell, after our encounter at the store last week, I wouldn't be surprised if she never spoke to me again.

Having the double whammy of Talia showing up and then Mr. Richardt not being able to hide his true feelings towards me, I actually felt embarrassed for the person that I was. At least Miri didn't dwell on what a monumental screw-up I was. She just joked about the entire situation and moved on. I was almost afraid of what she was actually thinking about. I never wanted her to be embarrassed to be around me.

I won't reach out for her today, because if she refused to talk to me, I just didn't think I could handle another blow on top of the pile of shit I've had to deal with already. But I really didn't feel like going home, I would just sit there and stew more and more about the one-sided argument Baylor and I had. It was over something absolutely stupid too, not even worthy of a discussion. I debated on heading over to Tillie's for a beer until Miri's little four-door Mazda caught my eye.

In the parking lot of the laundromat.

Cottage Grove had minimal crime and for the most part everyone was friendly towards one another, but the laundromat always had sketchy people lurking about. She had no place being there, especially if she was by herself. I couldn't not go check on her, so I jerked the wheel of my work truck quickly to the left so I could pull up and park next to her car.

There she was in the window, Beats headphones over her ears as if she didn't have a care in the world. She was sitting on a metal bench, but her ass was perched on the armrest and her feet resting on the seat. I could just make out through the holes in the bench that she was tapping her Chuck Taylor-clad feet, presumably to the beat of the music. She was so deeply entranced by whatever song she was listening to that she didn't even notice me pull up outside the window.

With the risk of being caught, I killed the engine and just sat back against my seat and watched her. Every so often she would smile and I imagined that the song was at her most favorite part. Watching her feet continuously tapping away, I couldn't help but automatically smile. For as little time as we've spent together she's brought out the brightness in me and I actually liked it. I spent just a minute more basking in her positive aura and her beauty.

Not being one to go all out and over the top with her hair, makeup, and wardrobe choices, her simplicity made me like her all the more. She didn't live to be someone that she obviously wasn't.

She was real.

She was utterly breathtaking.

And now she was staring right at me.

I immediately smiled and gave a small wave before pulling the handle to open my door and jumped out of my truck to head inside. The entire cloud looming over my head from this shitty day faded away when she smiled at me. The closer I walked to her, the bigger her smile grew.

*Just friends.*

It would do me good to remember that. But the more time I spent with her, the more I wanted her. And the reality of things was, I didn't just want to bag her and toss her aside, I actually liked being around her. And friends with benefits wasn't an option she put on the table. She needed the whole shebang, a relationship, and I didn't think that I could be a one woman man.

So friends it was.

My mother would probably endure a stroke if she knew that I was actually friends with a girl. I started out wanting to get her into bed, so I was going along with the friend charade, but my need to be around her outweighed the need to sleep with her.

The wishful thinking that someday I would finally get Miri underneath me would always be in the forefront of my mind. But Miri wasn't the type of woman that would allow us to fall into bed together, and strangely enough the more time we spent together the more I was ok with that.

"Are you stalking me now?" She joked as she pulled her headphones off of her head and hung them around her neck. "First you show up at the grocery store and now the laundromat? Did you hide some sort of tracking device on my car when I wasn't looking?" Her hands flew around animatedly as she spoke.

I released a mild chuckle and sat down on the empty space on the bench and placed my ankle on my knee. "You'd like that, wouldn't you?"

My body jerked to the left as she used her might to shove at my shoulder. "Yeah right. So why are you here? I know it's not because you have fun hanging out with me, I'm a boring person." She spread her arms wide, "Case in point, I'm spending my afternoon in a laundromat."

"I was actually going to ask you the same thing. I saw you in the window looking all lonely and decided you needed my company." I also knew that her building furnished washer and dryers because I've been called out there a time or two. And yeah, I may have also hooked up with a woman there as well, but I wasn't going to tell her that.

"Oh well, you know, I decided what better way to spend my day off than wasting it away in the laundromat. Tell you the truth, this place creeps me out. But the washer in my apartment is broken."

"Why didn't you go use Tillie's?" That would've been the most obvious choice rather than to come here.

"Because it would be an endless encounter of questions. Which then the real explanation would've came out that my washer has been unrepaired for almost three weeks. She would've marched over to my landlord and given him a big piece of her mind. I don't like getting my gran all riled up. She may only be four foot eleven, but they say that big things come in small packages. That woman can be mighty scary when provoked."

I remembered back to the time I got so drunk in Tillie's that she kicked me out. Quite literally. That little woman packed a mighty punch, enough for me to stay in her good graces from there on out. I could've swore that night that her eyes turned red and she had smoke streaming in ribbons from her ears. That was not a sight

I would forget anytime soon and one I didn't particularly want to experience again.

"I don't like the thought of you here by yourself, but I understand your reasoning." Great, now I sounded more along the lines of a big brother.

I saw her fiddling with her iPod in her hands, so by being the ornery person that I was, I snatched it away. The first thing I noticed when I glanced at the screen was that she had nearly ten thousand songs stored on this thing. I couldn't even begin to name ten thousand songs. I wasn't even entirely certain that I even knew one thousand let alone ten.

"Let's see what you've got going on here…"

She went to reach for it, but I quickly moved my hand back towards my torso, careful of the length of the cord. I wanted an insight into her musical library, not choke her out. Moving my thumb across the screen, I began scrolling through her playlist library and decided to have a bit of fun.

""If You Think I'm Sexy," well, we already know that you do."

She lunged for her device again, but her attempt was futile. She may be fast, but I was quicker. I continued to nose through her songs. Even though there were so many to choose from, I felt as if I was able to have a better insight to the person that Miri was. I stopped abruptly on an artist that made me cringe. She even had an entire folder dedicated to her.

"We can't be friends. You have Janis on your iPod, practically a shrine dedicated to the woman." I lowered my voice, "You know she rarely showered," then followed up by shivering in repulsion.

I finally let her snatch it away from me. "How often she showered doesn't depict away from the fact that she was a musical genius. She was considered the Queen of Rock & Roll."

"Yeah, yeah, you won't sell me on her." I plucked the iPod from her grasp again, this time she released a huff. "Let's see what else you should be embarrassed by listening to."

My brows raised at a singer in particular. "Roy Orbison? Who are you?"

""If You Want My Body," Classic! I should've used that one at the auction. I could've come up with some good moves for that one."

"I think the one you chose was just fine." she said in almost a whisper.

My head snapped up. She was there? I tried to recall if she bid on anyone, but I was drawing a blank. That entire night was a blur, I think I was half drunk and expected some hot piece of ass to win the bid, but it was one of Tillie's old biddy friends. I shook my head to clear the thought from my mind and looked back towards Miri. Seeing her with her headphones around her neck reminded me of the first time I met her. I handed over her iPod and I could see her visibly relax. I didn't know that I put her on edge so much.

"You know, the first day I met you, you had a pair of headphones around your neck." We had already talked about that day at the wedding, but I hadn't expanded on the details I had remembered.

"You remember that?"

"Of course, I remember a lot about that day. Especially that you were the only girl I knew who would kick the shit out of a locker. If it was another girl, she wouldn't have stood a chance." I knew I had adapted a faraway look of sorts. "There was greatness that occurred of epic proportion at that locker."

She frowned, "So you've mentioned before." Her voice changed to portray a bit of an annoyed tone.

But little did she know that she was one of the great things that resulted from locker 141, possibly even the greatest. When I first met that shy girl, I instantly knew she was lost. Perhaps as much as I was. When I met her eyes, the simplest of hues, I felt they saw through me deep into my soul. So innocent but stripped me entirely.

Today that feeling had intensified. Who knew it would take ten years for me to acknowledge and then achieve that greatness. I needed to take a breather, just a minute to gather my thoughts without her presence clouding my judgment.

I patted a hand on her knee as I stood from my seat on the bench. I took a moment to watch an elderly lady who was having trouble getting her full laundry basket on the counter, so I made my way over to help. "Here, let me get that for you." I bent at the waist and picked up the plastic basket with ease and set it on the metal surface counter.

Appreciation filled her eyes as she repeatedly thanked me. Just a small act of kindness could make anyone's day and the way she was acting, she didn't see polite behavior much anymore. I could feel Miri's heated stare on my back as I followed the tiled floor to the vending machine. I needed something to keep my hands busy and food was going to have to do it. I filled the machine with the exact change and made my selection, watching the coils circle around bringing my snack closer and closer to dropping into the bin below.

Miri's eyes were definitely on me as I walked back towards her. She almost looked surprised that I helped the older lady, or was that admiration shining in her depths? I was just going with the latter. I needed the ego boost today.

"Think fast," I muttered, giving her only a fraction of a second to register what I said before I underhandedly tossed a package of Ding Dongs in the direction of her lap. For saying that she was more or less accident prone, she caught the package with the utmost ease, careful not to damage the package or any of the cakes inside.

Her mouth immediately curved into a smile, one that reached all the way to her eyes, "You bought me a Ding Dong?"

The one thing I didn't want her to do was make a big deal of it or look into any hidden meaning behind my purchasing the confection. So I had to downplay the entire situation and fast.

"Yeah, well, I couldn't have you salivating after my chips." I grabbed ahold of the top edges of the bag I was holding and pulled it apart, opening my own snack. The nacho cheese smell instantly invaded my senses. These were my absolute favorite. "Doritos are *my* one weakness, and I may appear to be polite at times, but I don't share."

"Even though I'm your friend? You wouldn't even share with me?"

"Being my friend doesn't make you exempt from my no sharing rule on my Doritos. If anything, it's more prominent because you would know my love of the artificial chip."

"Touché. Duly noted, doesn't share his chips. Even if I'm starving beyond belief and to the point of withering away, I won't dare ask for a Dorito." Her smile turned into a pointed stare, she was going for all seriousness, "But the same goes for me, I will not share my Ding Dongs, so don't even ask."

I put my hands up in surrender, "You've got it. I've got my own Ding Dong to handle, definitely won't be asking for yours."

Her mouth gaped open before she threw her head back and busted out the biggest laugh that came straight from her belly.

*God, she was beautiful.*

It didn't take long for me to join in, her laughter was beyond infectious. We laughed so hard that my side hurt, and I couldn't for the life of me remember the last time I had laughed so much. It may have actually never happened. You would think you'd remember a time when that had actually happened, laughing so hard you can't breathe or even see straight. The more we tried to stop laughing, the harder she would get going. It was like a domino effect that neither of us could stop.

I didn't know it right then, but I actually lost a piece of my heart to Miri that day. I had never experienced that feeling before, so I chalked it up to nothing other than partaking in the best medicine to cure a bad day. I wouldn't have ever fathomed it would be the beginning feeling of love.

"Let's actually plan something instead of just *bumping* into each other, shall we?" I mentioned once we were finally able to catch our breaths. I knew I was treading in pretty shallow water with the choice of words I was using. You would think that I would learn since it was just pissing off my dick with each and every innuendo.

You could physically see the wheels turning in her head. She was skeptical of my suggestion.

"Friends hang out all the time. I could bring by some takeout tomorrow and watch movies. After the mediocre ending of tonight, spending it amongst piles of laundry, we need something to step up our entertainment." She was softening to the idea. "People will start to spread the word that I'm dull. Bentley Jenkins and dull don't belong in the same sentence."

# Chapter 7

## *Bentley*

Checking my watch, I noticed that I was actually five minutes early. I got through my work day extra quick, just knowing that I would get to see Miri tonight. To say that I was over-eager was an extreme understatement.

And now that I was here, in front of her door, I was nervous. I readjusted the collar of my polo shirt and made sure there were no wrinkles in the cotton material. I hadn't been on a date since I was in High School and even then, it was just a means to an end. Once the girls realized that it'd most likely be a no-brainer sure thing for me to sleep with them, they began flaunting about and throwing themselves at me and the need to wine and dine was thrown by the wayside.

Then there was the date with Tillie's pinochle friend, which really didn't count. She fell asleep during dinner, so conversation was pretty boring and not to mention futile to say the least.

*But this wasn't a date.*

This was just dinner and a movie between friends. At Miri's apartment.

So why was I disappointed that was all this was?

I poised my hand in the air, getting ready to knock on her door. My knuckles barely coming in contact with the wood surface when the door wretched open. Crowding the doorway with their height, was a tall blond man with black plastic framed glasses. My first instinct was to get defensive, I wanted to know who this man was and what the hell he was doing. My eyes narrowed and my anger spiked by being completely caught off-guard.

Next, my thoughts turned to that I could take this guy if necessary. I mean he was a virtual wimp. Tall, lanky frame, and a baby face to top it all off, he couldn't look menacing if he dressed up like it for Halloween.

And finally, above all else, Miri didn't mention anything about a guy being here. That's one particular piece of information that I would've distinctly remembered. Him being here pissed me off more than it should. I didn't have any claim to Miri, she could have anyone come and go as she pleased. But it didn't mean that it wouldn't make me madder than hell.

He readjusted the frames on his nose and squared his shoulders back, probably trying to steel himself from my lifted chin and flared nostrils, or it could even possibly be the icy glare I was throwing in his direction. He knew that I didn't like the thought of him being here, whoever the hell he was.

He was most likely scared, as he should be. I could be polite with the best of them, but catch me on a bad day or when I was severely pissed off and you'd be meeting what an asshole I could be.

"Who the hell are you?" I bit out between my clenched jaw as my back molars ground together.

He extended his arm and open palm towards me, which wavered just a bit. He tried to cover up his fear, but in the end, failed, "I'm Oliver Tildon."

*Tildon.*

The name sounded vastly familiar, but I couldn't place where I had heard it from. His hand lingered within my reach, but I had yet to make a move to reciprocate his action. "You've told me your name, but not *who* you are." I was getting impatient. I knew we were both men, but I didn't think I had to spell it out for him.

"I'm a veterinarian." So that's where I must've heard his name. I looked down at the t-shirt he was wearing, which read, "50% Veterinarian, 50% Superhero."

"And apparently part superhero as well if your shirt is any indication." That still didn't answer my question. I guessed we needed to break it down, for being a Vet, he sure wasn't too bright.

"Who the hell are you to Miri?"

You could tell by the realization in his eyes that my underlying question had finally clicked.

"Oh, I'm her friend of ten years and roommate."

I blanched by his response but quickly schooled my features as I took his clammy hand in mine.

"Bentley Jenkins, is Miri here?"

I was well on my way to making a fool of myself before, but in my defense I had no clue that Miri had a roommate, a male one at that. I didn't know exactly how to treat this new information, but I had no other choice but to take it.

I vaguely wondered if there had ever been anything between the two of them.

"Yeah, she's here. I was just on my way out actually to get more laundry detergent. Our washer just got fixed this morning, and I was so behind that I ran out."

He didn't need to explain to me about the washer being fixed, I knew all about it. Hell, I was the one who paid a visit to the landlord to finally get the fucking ball rolling. The pissant's carefree, cheery disposition was quickly replaced once I was done with my little chat. He definitely met the asshole side of Bentley

Jenkins. I may have come across as a bit forward, but I didn't want Miri to have to sit in that seedy laundromat again. And after three weeks of getting the runaround, nor should she have to.

"Hey Miri," he yelled back into the void of the apartment.

A moment later she came out in a pair of plaid pajama capris and a small tank top.

*Fuck me, is she trying to kill me?* This night was going to be harder than I thought. Take the double entendre as you will.

I could see the hot pink straps of her bra underneath and I had to silently thank the good lord that she had the decency to leave that particular undergarment on or *it* would be over right here.

It, meaning our friendship status, it would be out the window. It would take a running leap right out the nearest opening, didn't matter what floor we were standing on. I would bend her over and fuck her senseless, right here in the entryway if need be. Then once she finally came to, even though she'd be thoroughly sated, she would hate me. And it all would be because I couldn't control my urges and my desire for her if she was flaunting around braless in a tiny ass scrap of a tank top.

My dick needed to calm the fuck down and quit running the show.

"Hey, Bent…" her voice trailed off once she got a sight of what was in my hands and her whole face lit up. "You brought wine? You don't know how much I needed greasy Chinese food and wine today." She came up and grabbed the chilled glass bottle from my hand. "You are now my very best friend. He's thoughtful, isn't he Oliver?" She sneered, completely giving him the cold shoulder as she rounded the corner, and I couldn't help but revel in Oliver's hurt expression.

"But I thought I was your best friend?"

80

"You've been downgraded, deal with it!" she yelled, carrying her voice from across the apartment.

I finally stepped inside the apartment and before I could fully slip past Oliver, his arm shot out to grab ahold of my bicep.

*Oh, this dude had balls.*

I looked down at his hand as it was gripped around the flesh of my upper arm and he quickly removed it. "Don't hurt Miri. I know how to neuter, just keep that little nugget in the forefront of your mind."

If his intentions were to scare me, then he was way off base. Instead, it was creepy as hell, but my balls were definitely listening to his threats, they shriveled up the tiniest bit.

What a bizarre character.

I followed in Miri's footsteps, rounding the corner in her hallway, trying to find the kitchen. When I found her, she had two wine glasses on the counter, filling each with the red liquid I brought. I should mention that I wasn't the biggest of fans of wine, but I would suffer for tonight.

Lifting up the sack of hot Chinese food, I rested it on the counter next to the glasses and started removing the various sealed cartons. I heard Miri inhale through her nose, "That smells so divine. I haven't had Chinese in forever. Thank you so much." I got an odd thrill out of the fact that she was so excited over Chinese takeout before I thought better of my actions. What the hell was happening to me? Actually caring about a woman's feelings definitely was a new territory and I didn't know how to handle it.

She retrieved two plates from the cabinet and then two forks from the drawer.

As I started dishing out the some fried rice, I asked, "So did you have a bad day today?" I was genuinely concerned. Although,

I didn't know Miri all that well, she just looked as if she's had a rather stressful day. The way she handled Oliver, even though I wanted to applaud her on her copout, it just didn't seem like something she would normally do.

"Well, I didn't have a bad day *per say*. I'm just in dire need of reinforcements of the grease and alcohol variety." She snapped her fingers as she turned and stood on her tiptoes digging around in a cabinet. Her eyes lit up when she produced a package of her favorite snack cake, "And I can't forget chocolate."

And now it was my turn to appear dumbfounded. My first initial thought was that she was trying to cure a hangover, but she wouldn't want more alcohol feeding on top of that, so I was lost. I stared blankly ahead, not knowing where exactly she was going with this.

"I have a special visitor…" Her face became enflamed, the redness heating up her cheeks and neck, but I was still at a loss.

"Yeah, I got nothing," I muttered. I was the only visitor she had. Was she nervous because I was here?

She slammed her hand down on the counter, "I started my period today!" she hollered, taking me much by surprise. Casting her glance aside, she proceeded to pick up her wine glass and take a big, healthy gulp.

"Holy shit!" I coughed trying to clear my throat. "Yeah, definitely wasn't prepared for that answer." I don't think I ever would've been prepared for that answer. But that answer had my dick calming down a few notches, so for that I was thankful.

"Well, you asked! And then wouldn't relent. What was I supposed to do?!"

Ok, I needed to get her to calm down. She was going all She-Woman on me, and I was becoming more than a little bit terrified.

"I'm tenacious, what can I say?" Then I think I actually surprised her when I said, "I supposed I should've gotten you a box of Ding Dongs or something to go along with the grease and wine?"

I pondered for a moment and then snapped my fingers. "I know, next time send me a code word or an S.O.S. text and I'll come running with reinforcements."

Her eyes began welling up with tears and my immediate reaction was that I must've said something wrong. That was the last thing I ever wanted to do, was make Miri cry. I hated it when women cried.

She sat her glass down and just as I got ready to cower down, she threw herself at me and slung her arms around my neck. I stumbled back and blindly felt around to place my plate down, with her hair in my face and her body molded to mine, I couldn't be positive that I wouldn't drop my food all over the floor.

I was at a loss here, I had no idea what in the world was happening. She began crying but was now hugging me for dear life.

Believe me, I wasn't complaining, I was rather enjoying the hugging.

A bit too much in fact.

My dick had seemed to completely forget about her little comment from a moment ago about being on her period. He was standing at attention and ready for action. I tentatively patted her back, being weary of the fact that her mood could switch up at any time.

Women, they were impossible to understand.

She released her hold on me and took a step back, wiping the remaining tears away from under her eyes with her fingertips.

Placing my finger under her chin, I tilted it up so I could look into her eyes. I tenderly asked, "Are you alright now?"

She let out a small chuckle, "Yeah, sorry. You were being all sweet and kind to me, and I got tripped up on my hormones. I hate being a woman sometimes."

"None of that. Being a woman is one of your greatest attributes. And I don't really think you'd made a great man. You'd be too pretty." I shook my head in disgust, definitely glad she wasn't a man.

That earned me the small blush and smile that I was looking for. We finished loading up on different varieties of meats and vegetables because I seemed to bring the entire smorgasbord, and brought our overcrowded plates to the living room.

Well, my plate was overcrowded and Miri's was…Well, I hadn't a clue what it was.

None of her food was touching. She had strategically created little sections so that each separate item was in its own assigned place.

"What's up with your plate?"

She sat down on her bright red couch, propping her bare feet on the coffee table in front of her, her plate sat on her upper thighs as she stared down at her food.

"None of my food can touch." Yeah, I had gathered that much. "If it touches, I can't eat it. It weirds me out and makes me physically cringe." She glanced up and noticed my bemused expression and rolled her eyes at me. "Normally, I have paper plates with different sections separated by dividers." Her voice became low and almost resembling a grumble of sorts, if an innocent sweet woman such as Miri could grumble. "But Oliver used the last one without replacing them. He is now the highest contender for my internal hit list. And now you're looking at me as if I have four heads. Do you not have any crazy quirks?"

Yeah, my look definitely wasn't associated with her plate, although that was pretty weird, but the fact that she had an internal hit list.

She was staring intently at me, waiting for an answer, and I didn't know if I could actually give her one worthy of being a crazy quirk. Could men even have crazy quirks? Could they even have those words in their vocabulary?

I was officially stumped…

"I really enjoy sleeping alone. So much that I use up the entire capacity of my bed to stretch out on. If I were to ever have a woman in my bed overnight, she would most likely end up on the floor." I didn't know if that could be considered even remotely to what she was looking for, but it'd be the best she'd get.

"That's all you've got?" And now I've been called out. What was I supposed to say, that I scratched my balls for a solid two minutes before I got out of bed in the morning?

"Maybe I should hand off some of my unneeded quirks to you. I've got my no food can touch --" She started ticking items off on her fingers "Murphy's Law hates me --" she ticked off on another finger. "I hate cats."

I held up a hand, halting her words. "You hate cats, but you live with a Vet?"

Shrugging her shoulders, "It's true. Do you have any animals?"

"I do good to keep myself alive," I joked. "Are those the only quirks you have?" This was compiling to be one hell of a list. I couldn't even fully come up with a believable quirk and she had them in spades.

"Hm…I embarrass myself by falling or tripping at least once a week." Finally, one last tick, "Oh, and I don't curse."

"Wait a cotton-picking minute." Yeah, the damage had already been done as soon as the phrase came flying out of my mouth. No man should *ever* say those two words in a combination together for as long as they live. "You don't cuss? Like at all?"

"Nope," She shook her head, giving an extra added pop to the p on the end. "It's just a personal preference."

"Does anyone ever try to get you to cuss? Try to get under your skin or so angry that the words just slip out?"

"Oh, they've tried. And failed."

Hm. I tapped the tines of my fork against my lips, "I've just made it my mission to get you to cuss. Normal people would be satisfied with a simple *shit*, but not me, I'm going with gusto. I'm going to get you to say *fuck*."

"You can most certainly try, but I've gone twenty-five years not saying it. There is nothing you can say or do to make that word come out of my mouth."

I liked her defiance. Admired it even, but inside I was briskly rubbing my hands together, definitely looking forward to this challenge.

# Chapter 8

## *Miri*

Leaning forward, I placed my empty plate on my coffee table and tucked my legs underneath me as I snuggled back against the plush cushions of my couch.

Something was weighing on my mind, another insight into Bentley's intriguing mind. He mentioned that he had never slept with a woman before. Slept as in partaking in the act of closing one's eyes and falling into a peaceful slumber. We all knew that he's indulged in the other form of sleeping with a woman. An act that he would have absolutely no problem luxuriating in with me if I would only lower my giant red stop sign.

"Can I ask you a question?"

He tilted his head to the side and raised a brow. The thing with Bentley was that he was always eager and curious about everything. "Technically, you just did." And always a smarty pants.

My eyes rolled on their own accord, something that I have become accustomed to with him. Moving over to the side, I pulled one of my extra throw pillows from behind my back, settling it in my lap. "It's kind of a personal one…"

His raised brows now knitted together, I could tell that he was internally waging on whether or not he wanted to know what my question was.

"Ok, you've piqued my interest, but I'm not saying that I guarantee can an answer."

I took a deep breath and released it, gathering all of my courage. "Have you ever been in love?"

His posture visibly relaxed as he leaned back into the cushions. My intention wasn't to make him uncomfortable, I was just trying to learn more about why he jumped around from woman to woman.

Was it a tragic heartbreak? Something more?

"I can honestly say that I've never experienced the feeling of being in love," he answered bluntly as he turned his body so he could look at me better.

Well, there went my explanation. My lips pursed together to the side trying to figure this out. I was stumped.

"Are you analyzing me?" His voice came out as a terse whisper.

"What if I was?" I challenged. "What if I was trying to figure out what exactly makes Bentley Jenkins tick?" I closed only my left eye and bit my bottom lip awaiting his answer. His response could go either way. I just really hoped that my overbearing nosiness didn't get me yelled at.

His large hand covered and gripped my knee, which was barely visible underneath my throw pillow, and he shook it gently back and forth. "You can open your eyes, Miri. I get berated enough by my family for my lifestyle choices. At no point in time has anyone ever asked me why." His free hand scrubbed down his face and then back up through his hair, making it stand up in various wayward directions. "The answer is going to sound childish. I felt like growing up that I bonded mostly with my dad. Baylor was the good kid, everyone loved him, he literally could do no wrong. But my dad always found some way to not make me feel left out. So naturally when he passed, Bentley just kind of got thrown to the wayside and forgotten. Baylor was almost finished with college and instead of becoming an architect, he came back and started running our plumbing company. So I did what any ignored teenage boy would do, I lashed out for attention. At first it was cutting classes and ignoring curfew, which didn't have me high on the Sheriff and Principal's great citizens list. Next, I realized that I could satisfy my lack of attention at home by seeking the extra from women. I know there are so many different names floating around about me and my decisions."

"So you aren't against falling in love or marriage?"

He seemed to take a moment to ponder, "Not at all. I'm sure I'll know it when I meet "the one"." He raised his hands and used actual air quotes and shrugged. "Until then, I'm just enjoying not being tied down."

My first initial thought to run through my head was that he wouldn't ever find "the one" never sleeping with the same woman twice. Then my mood kind of depleted, instantly turning sour. I didn't know why I thought I'd have an honest, running chance of taming the playboy, but all hope has been diminished. Could I really go on being friends with the man that I was so quickly falling for? And doubting him of not being able to catch my heart, therefore leaving it a crumbled mess on the ground? Now that he had engrained himself so far into my life and my heart, I couldn't quite picture it without him.

"Now let's see how you like being in the hot seat," he boasted with a smirk. "Have you ever been in love?"

And there was the complete downside to sticking my nose where it didn't belong. I wasn't exactly intending on the tables being turned on me.

Forget my mood being sour, it was downright rotten.

I gave my empty wine glass a sideways glance and knew that I couldn't get through his reversal without a refill. Pushing myself off the couch, I retrieved our empty plates and allowed my bare feet to carry me along the hardwood floor into the kitchen. As I came back into the living room, holding the neck of the wine bottle, Bentley had moved into a standing position from his place on the couch. From the looks of how his body was turned he was on the verge of coming after me. "Listen, if it's a sore subject you don't have to talk about it."

"Oh it's a sore subject all right," I frowned. "But you appeased my curiosity by divulging about your past, so it's only fitting that I reciprocate." I lifted the bottle before tipping and refilling my bare glass to the rim. "This will help make my grueling tale easier to discuss."

Taking my seat once again, I slowly lifted the glass to my lips, careful not to spill a drop of the delicious liquid. Spilling even the tiniest of drops would be considered a heinous crime.

Bentley flopped back down on the couch, seeming a bit over eager to hear my tale of heartbreak. We were treading into some deep torrential waters with the direction our conversation was taking. Any other man would've hightailed it out the door, Oliver certainly wouldn't have stuck around.

Which reminded me that Oliver hadn't returned from his little shopping excursion. Maybe he would have the best timing and come in while I was talking about my ex, forcing me to stop.

That would be a pity.

I looked towards my white spackled ceiling, sending up a quick, silent prayer hoping that Oliver chose this exact moment to show his face, then I took another generous gulp of wine before settling myself back into the cushions with my pillow resting in my lap.

90

It had been four years since I dated the jerk, so naturally you would think talking about him wouldn't hurt so bad, right?

*Wrong!*

Releasing a huff, I finally said the name of the only man to ever fully capture my heart and then break it without so much of a blink. Voicing the two syllables was proving to be a daunting task and much harder than I'd anticipated.

My hands tightened around the throw pillow, squeezing it in my clutches. "His name was Travis and we dated for four years." I swallowed, "From the time we were seventeen until we turned twenty-one. Coincidentally he broke up with me on my mom's birthday, which just so happens to be here in a matter of days. He changed the entire path of his life and decided that I wasn't worth taking that path along with him."

Bentley's eyes widened, "Wow, the guy sounds like a real douche."

I began worrying the corner of the pillow as my voice took a defeated turn. "I wish I would've known how badly it would end, but that's the beauty of love, you just never know. I gave it my all in a relationship with him; including my virginity and all he did was take."

"Was he your only relationship?"

"Yup," I nodded my head in affirmation, letting go of the pillow. I retrieved my glass taking a sip and sitting it on my thigh, holding it by the stem. "He was my only sexual partner, too." I slapped my free hand over my mouth, it was definitely not my intention to spill all of my secrets. But the wine was flowing freely and Bentley was just a little too easy to talk to.

His eyes widened again, he certainly didn't intend on that little slip of my tongue.

"Interesting," he tapped his forefinger on his chin. "And how long ago did this relationship with Travis-the-dick end?"

I was almost too much of a chicken to answer. My voice squeaked as I muttered in the lowest tone I could manage without actually whispering. "Four years ago."

Bentley had his glass tipped to his lips and was in the middle of taking a drink and immediately ended up coughing. He jerked his hand back and set his glass down, covering his mouth with his hand until he was able to get control of his coughing and take a full breath.

"Holy shit! So it's been four years since you've had sex?"

I shrugged a shoulder, trying to not appear affected by his words when, in fact, I wanted to mimic the same response to myself. "So what?"

"I could never." He shook his head in disbelief. That was the main difference between the two of us, I could successfully keep it in my pants.

He chuckled, "My dick would fall off from nonuse."

I held up a hand. "I said that I hadn't had sex in four years, not that I was a prude." I countered with a smirk.

*Eat that.*

I was sure that he had heard of masturbation. But I was also pretty sure that with the number of women he ultimately had at his vast disposal, he never needed to resort to using his hand.

"Miri," he warned, the timber of his voice becoming low. It was almost predatory and made me shrink back in the cushions a bit further for added safety. "You need to change the topic of conversation." His threat held a promise of the one thing I so desperately wanted but wouldn't allow my values to slip in order to have. So I took heed of his warning and did just that.

"Are you ready to watch a movie?" I proceeded with caution and flashed an innocent smile.

"I'm afraid to ask if I'll have to suffer through a chick flick."

I scrunched my nose and shook my head. The idea of watching someone else fall in love in a movie wasn't exactly appealing to me at the moment. "No, I'd rather watch something action packed. The more gore, the better."

His brows raised as the corner of his lip twitched with a smirk.

"I've got it," I snapped my fingers as my face lit up. "Let's watch *Homefront*. It has Jason Statham in it and lots of action, I call that a win." I said matter-of-factly while wiggling my eyebrows.

Bentley chuckled and crossed his arms in front of the expanse of his chest. "And here I thought you were innocent."

"Oh, not when it comes to that man. You could spread him on a cracker and serve him as my last meal."

He eyed me wearily, but the amusement overpowering his voice, "I take it you like Jason Statham a bit?"

My hands were moving animatedly because I was so passionate about that man that I couldn't justify them solely based on words alone. "The man is a God. I would seriously rock his world. And add to him a baseball cap and a pair of tight Levi's totally has my ovaries crying out."

His body stiffened at my words and his mouth fell open. When he was able to speak, he began stumbling over his words. "So, uh, you'd have a one-night stand with him?"

I wanted to reiterate that this was Jason Statham we were talking about here. He wasn't just *anyone*. I think he would get a pass. But then I also wanted to snap my fingers in a diva-like fashion. "Please. Once he caught a British glimpse of all of this--" I swept a hand down my seated form. "He would never go back."

His eyes roved over the path my hands took and sweat broke out along his forehead. He looked as if he was suffering an agonizing struggle. He rubbed his hands up and down his jean-clad thighs before leaning forward utilizing them to support his elbows and braced his head in his hands.

Bentley was used to getting what he wanted and with the subtle glances and the inappropriate comments, there was no denying that he wanted me.

So maybe us being friends and spending time with me was killing him a little bit as well.

What if he was only hanging around me to try and wear me down? Thinking that I would renege my walls and let him have my body. And only for the one night? I so badly wanted to believe that he was better than that, but this was Bentley Jenkins we were talking about. The guy who attracted women like a bug zapper and had absolutely no remorse about sleeping with them and tossing them aside for fresh, unused meat.

If I needed any reminding or reassurance that I was worth more than a fling; then this realization one hundred percent confirmed it and couldn't have come at a better time.

I may be addicted to the man and his friendship, but I would do everything in my power to take all precautions to guarding my heart and my morals.

"There is no use denying that we are attracted to each other, but you only wanted to be friends, so I think we need to quickly change the topic of discussion to territory that doesn't involve you actively wanting to fuck famous actors who could and probably was a model for Levi's."

*Holy, wow.* I was so far out of my depth here.

# Chapter 9

## Miri

I folded myself into the driver's seat of my car, making sure my feet were in all the way before I yanked on the door with all of my might, slamming it closed.

The tears streaming down my face couldn't be kept at bay any longer. I sniffled and wiped my nose yet again with the back of my hand. It was completely unsanitary, but I was well past the point of even caring. Today was such an emotional day anyway, but adding to the mix that absolutely nothing went right.

My schedule was full, which in hindsight I thought would be best. Being too busy to sit and dwell on the fact that it was my mom's birthday. Paired with overbearing clients and a supervisor who obviously woke up on the wrong side of the bed, made for an overly sensitive and emotional Miri.

Flipping down my sun visor, I lifted up the cover for the mirror knowing all too well that I would be staring back at a big mess.

I really hated being right in this instance.

Puffy eyes and red, blotchy skin reflected back at me. I blindly reached over to retrieve my sunglasses from the console, slipping them over my eyes in an attempt to conceal the evidence of my sadness. I slammed the visor back up and rested my forehead against the steering wheel.

*I needed Bentley.*

Normally I would outright cringe at overt neediness, but I was in full-on desperation mode.

I lifted my head from my leather-wrapped steering wheel and dug around in my purse for my phone. After successfully grabbing it, I unlocked it by entering my password and scrolled through my contacts list, searching through the B's until I found the correct one.

The line only rang once before being sent to voicemail.

Once I hung up, I pulled up my text messaging app and started typing out my message. My fingers flew across the letters, and it seemed I had to sniffle every third word or so as I painstakingly kept trying to keep my tears at bay.

**Me: I had a terrible, horrible, the worst day ever. I need textual healing, Bentley. Cheer me up, please!**

I released a resigned sigh and placed my phone in the cup holder beside me and took off in the direction of my house. It wasn't until I pulled into my assigned parking space at my apartment that my phone chimed with an incoming text.

Pulling up the response from Bentley just made the tears well up in my eyes again as a frown formed on my lips.

Two words was all I got in return.

**Bentley: Busy. Sorry.**

He couldn't even send back a funny reply. Just blunt, cold, and not to mention, unfriendly. Entirely unlike the Bentley I knew.

Mentally sticking my tongue out at him, I threw my phone on top of my purse in the passenger seat. My life was beginning to resemble a big pile of steaming crap, and I had no one to wallow in my misery with or help revive me from my funk.

I turned my head to the right, intending to lay it back down on my steering wheel when something caught my eye. Oliver's SUV was in his parking space.

He wasn't at work!

There may be hope for this day after all.

"I still can't believe you talked me into coming here. Need I remind you that I'm on call?" Oliver looked around nervously and adjusted his glasses. He didn't particularly like coming to Tillie's Tavern.

"Yeah, yeah. So you keep telling me." My head was a fuzzy mess and I couldn't perpetually think straight. My blame was solely on all those tequila shots, they immediately went to my head, so much that my brain must've been floating around in the stuff.

Gran brought out a steaming basket full of mozzarella sticks and threatened me to eat them. She knew the mess I became on this particular day because she's always a bit off-kilter herself, being that my mom was her daughter. I'm never a sloppy drunk because I knew how horrid it made you act let alone feel, but this was one of the days when my blunder status was overlooked and Gran fed me even when I forget. The grease being the ticket to sop up some of the lingering alcohol in my stomach.

I raised a deep fried coated stick of cheese to my lips and took a much bigger bite than I anticipated.

The steaming, gooey mozzarella pulled off in strings and I had to quickly suck in some air into my mouth, thinking it would help cool off the bite in my mouth and ease my burning tongue simultaneously. Then came the waving hand in front of my mouth. I should just give up.

Oliver was just sitting there with his own cheese stick suspended in midair and an amused twinkle in his eyes. I sheepishly glanced away knowing I wouldn't have ever made such a spectacle sober. "I kind of forgot that it just came out of a scalding hot vat of oil."

"Obviously," he mused, taking the smart route and pulling his deep-fried goodness apart from either end, allowing the steam to rapidly escape and cool from the inside.

The fire from my mouth marginally eased, so I proceeded to dig into the delectable fried cheese musing on how great the grease was on my taste buds. I had no idea exactly how famished I was until I took my very first bite. Gran for the win.

Reaching my hand into the basket, my world became just a bit more dreary when I pulled it back empty.

It was then a dreadful voice boomed through the microphone, singing their obnoxious rendition of "Party Rock" by LMFAO and it took all of my willpower to not march over and pull the plug from the sound system. I groaned loudly and leaned my head on my crossed arms on the table.

"Is today Monday?" I lifted my face until my eyes were met with Oliver's apologetic ones.

He shook his head once and followed it up with a verbal confirmation, "Yup."

I avoided Tillie's like the plague on Monday's for this very reason; karaoke.

Why did this day have to fall on a Monday? There were six other days to choose from, the remaining being all days that I could tolerate attending the Tavern.

I was a lover of music, this was no secret, but having drunk patrons botch up perfectly good songs just for fun? And to give their friends the voluntary ammunition to blackmail them in the future with the humiliating videos they'd be too stupid not to record.

Not my idea of an entertaining evening.

The guy on stage took a bow after the song cut off and swayed a bit before stumbling over his feet trying to climb down the three short steps to the floor.

Seconds later another guy flew up the stairs and ripped the microphone from the stand, squeezing it in his grip. This guy stood with purpose and had an air of arrogance about him. At first glance, it looked like Bentley, matter of fact.

I had to do a double then a triple take just to make sure my eyes weren't deceiving me.

He came pretty dog darn close to being Bentley's twin. Same dark hair but his curled around his neck, whereas Bentley's was cut short. They both had that same strong jaw though with stubble growth covering it.

Even though Bentley was more handsome, this guy even had the same wicked glint in his eye that Bentley often had. He knew that he was about to have the women in the bar wrapped around his finger.

This just further confirmed how deep I already was with Bentley.

I rested my warm cheek against the cool wood surface of the tabletop. The contrast instantly helped tame my smoldering inferno. It was short-lived as the opening beats of the song the stunt double was about to sing, and my face inflamed hotter than it was before.

My body jerked upright, my back ramrod straight, as I looked over at Oliver with wide eyes and incredulously asked, "They have this song in the mix and Gran actually approved it to be there?"

He looked just as shell-shocked at the song choice as I was. His mouth kept opening and closing resembling a fish out of water. Darting my eyes around the room, I was searching for any sign of Gran but was coming up with nothing. My hand raised in the air as I snapped to get the waiter's attention ordering two fresh shots of tequila.

I gasped as he lifted the microphone to his lips and began singing, "Closer" by Nine Inch Nails verbatim.

Ladies rushed up flanking next to one another around the stage. The way they were waving their hands and screaming their heads off, you'd think they were at an honest to goodness NIN concert.

The two refreshed shots that I ordered appeared in front of me like magic and after spilling them down my throat, were gone just as fast.

The guy, who I heard being called Tyler from his group of friends seated at a table identical to ours cheered him on, was soaking this up like a sponge. Feeding off the other drunk's frenziness. As he repeated the chorus, so delicately stating that they would screw, for lack of a better term within my comfort of expressing, like energizer bunnies, my mind began to wander.

This wildly inappropriate song was right up Bentley's alley. Was that the way he enjoyed having sex, raw and feral? Some reason slow and tender weren't two words that I'd associate with the man offhand.

The last shots of tequila had hit me and now I was not only severely drunk, but I could now add horny to my list. And I had to pee something fierce. I braced my palms on the table, pushing myself out of my chair as I stood on wobbly legs. I was tipsier than I even realized.

Oliver was immediately out of his chair and at my side within the blink of an eye.

"Whoa! How'd you do that?" I stammered. "You must really be part ninja to be able to move that fast." Who would've thought that his dorky shirts actually held some semblance of truth in that 100% cotton?

"Where are you trying to go, Miri?" Oliver asked with concern as he braced my elbow within his hands.

My feet shuffled along the floor towards my destination, I had this walking thing in the bag. "I'm going to the bathroom," I paused, "even though I can't feel my legs and all these tables are suddenly blurring together, I know the way like the back of my hand."

He removed his hand from my elbow and quickly moved them to my shoulders, where I felt the gentle pressure as he proceeded to spin me around in the opposite direction. "I don't think you'll find what you're looking for in the kitchen, so how about we go in this direction."

I raised my forefinger in the air, "You're so smart Oliver. What would I do without you?"

His warm breath spread across my back as I felt him release a sigh, "Most likely violate some sort of health code by urinating in the kitchen."

A wave of nausea overcame me as bile rose in the back of my throat. "Ollie, time to kick it up a notch. I'm about 83% sure that I'm going to be sick."

He pushed me from behind a bit faster, then shoved me directly through the ladies room door. If I thought he was going to help me, the opposite was confirmed as I heard his voice fade as the door closed behind me. "You'll have to handle it from here. I don't deal with puke."

The man was a Veterinarian for crying out loud. He could deal with the guts and gore of any animal, but you say one measly word about vomit and his pansy butt headed for the hills quicker than you can say, "Hold my hair."

I felt the urgent wave of nausea hit me again, and I wasted no time diving into an available stall and hovering over the porcelain throne while on my knees. After resting in the same imminent position for several minutes, the nausea seemed to fade for a moment, but I wasn't going to take any chances. I would ride things out here for a few more minutes.

"Oh, I think I'm going to throw up," I whispered with my head partially shoved into the bowl, my voice echoing off of the ceramic interior. My thought logic was that if I actually acknowledged the feeling of sickness aloud, then perhaps it would hurry along and happen, so I could start feeling like a human again.

I wasn't actually anticipating on getting an actual verbal response. "Oh please don't," a small voice pleaded.

My eyes darted around, but naturally since I was on the floor of a bathroom stall there was no one within my sight. "Who said that?" I eyed the toilet warily. Several seconds later after no one responded, I chalked it up to the tequila ransacking my imagination.

An hour must've officially passed since I've been in the bathroom and Oliver hadn't even came to check on me. Some friend he was.

I hurried up and finished my business and rushed out into the hallway and directly into Oliver. "What gives?!" I pointed back towards the door to the bathroom. "I was in there for an hour and you didn't bother to check on me? I could've fallen face first into the toilet and drown!"

Oliver made it a point to lift his left wrist up towards his face to check his watch and gave me a raised brow, confirming that I may have exaggerated a bit. "Miri, you were only in there for six minutes. And I was getting ready to check on you. I got called in," his face fell. "A dog was hit by a car and needs emergency surgery."

Tears welled up my eyes because Oliver did incredibly noble things every day such as saving the lives of innocent dogs. But I also teared up because I didn't know how on earth I was going to get home. There were stairs at my apartment building and I didn't seeing my almost eighty-year-old Gran helping me climb up them.

Oliver was my official adult for the evening.

"Damn, even when you're plastered your mind never quits. I called Bentley and he's on his way over."

My heart fluttered, but now it seemed as if I was being pawned off on the one man I couldn't seem to get out of my head and couldn't even be bothered to answer my calls.

I held out my arm, struggling to hold it upright, "Guide me to the bar until my chariot arrives."

Oliver profusely apologized, but I told him not to worry and be the best he can be in the operating room.

And I was now left to my own drunkard devices.

My hair had partially fallen out of its braid, so I pulled my holder out and ruffled my fingers through each strand of hair until several waves framed my face.

Gran was nowhere to be found and karaoke was still in full swing, tone deaf posers singing amazing songs at high decibels. I grunted and thought that karaoke should be a highly punishable crime. Then a sudden feeling of déjà vu overcame me. Had I already mentioned that earlier?

There was literally nothing for me to do that wouldn't land me in some kind of trouble. My boredom was overtaking me and I suddenly felt extremely tired. I would just rest my arms on this incredibly sticky bar counter and lay my head down for a nice little nap.

# Chapter 10

## Bentley

"Take me just a bit deeper," I coaxed as I pushed the ditzy blonde's head down, giving her no other choice but to take in more of my dick.

All day my mind had been invaded by thoughts of Miri, so this was my solution to try and replace those unwarranted images. Find someone else to fill up the space. I didn't want to continuously run through all the ways I wanted to fuck Miri, there was no possibility of it ever happening.

The problem with having someone's mouth on me who wasn't Miri's, was that I couldn't physically get it up without picturing Miri's lips wrapped around my purple engorged head and her braided chestnut hair bobbing up and down on my lap.

So really my place to not think of her was pointless.

Finally, Fallon surged forward, swallowing the tip until I hit the back of her throat. "So fucking good," I praised her. Tingles were beginning to form at the base of my spine and I knew that any moment I could blow my load.

"Move your hand faster, baby." My head fell back into the top cushion of my chair and my fingers dug into the arms, ready to let my orgasm take over, giving me the release I was craving.

"That's it, Fallon," she hummed around my dick in her mouth and used her other hand to cup my balls instantly making them seize within her fingers.

"Babe, I'm about to come. This is your warning if you don't want me to blow my load in your mouth." My voice only made her more eager. My legs began to tremble despite them being firmly planted on the floor.

In my mind Fallon's hot, wet mouth was actually Miri's soaked, tight pussy. I was pounding into her hard and with wild abandon, our eyes never wavering from one another.

My vision went hazy then completely black as my orgasm ripped through me and into Miri, who was begging me for more.

But reality finally kicked in and I had released into Fallon's anxious mouth.

*I was a bastard.*

When I was quickly doused from my high with a proverbial bucket of ice cold water, I opened my eyes to see Fallon's ice blue eyes glimmering with need. Normally, I would be salivating over her perky breasts which were thrust upon display, but even with her offering herself to me I felt nothing for her. Absolutely nothing.

*What in the hell was wrong with me?*

Tucking myself into my jeans and sitting up from my slouched position, I was trying to come up with a viable excuse, anything to get rid of her. Give her the boot.

The shrill sound of my cell phone ringing had me mentally doing a fist bump in the air.

I glanced at Fallon apologetically as I reached to retrieve my ringing savior from the end table. At first glance, I saw Miri's number and instantly wanted to ignore it, but she could very well be my ticket out of this situation. Her calling wasn't helping me forget about her in the slightest.

That and the underlying guilt of partially blowing her off earlier when she texted that she needed me to cheer her up. She needed me and I showed her viable proof of what an asshole I could be.

I pressed the green button to accept her call and hoped like hell that Fallon kept her lips closed for the duration of the time I was on the phone. She had already sat back on her haunches with her arms crossed in front of her forcing her tits to be even further on display. I looked my fill as I raised my phone to my ear, and yet, *nothing.*

"Hello?"

"Bentley?" Hearing a male voice coming through on Miri's phone instantly had me scooting up to the edge of my seat, my anger spiking. "It's Oliver." The dumbass could've said that immediately. It definitely would've saved my blood pressure from going through the roof.

Clearing my throat, I responded with a simple, "Yeah?"

It was certainly odd that Oliver was calling me, and being that he used Miri's phone had me a bit uneasy still.

"Miri's at Tillie's Tavern drunk off of her ass and I just got called in for an emergency surgery so she needs a ride home."

"Shit," I cursed. "Why is she hammered?" It just didn't seem like the Miri I knew.

"You don't know what today is do you?"

I tried recalling any memory as to why today would be challenging for her and it finally hit me at the same time Oliver confirmed, "Her mom's birthday."

I roughly ran my fingers through my hair, scratching my scalp. How could I try and ignore her today of all days? "Fuck! And the day that dickweed dumped her."

"Right," Oliver sighed through the phone. He sounded exhausted, I could just picture drunk Miri being a little hellion.

"Is she alright?" Such a stupid question to ask. Of course she wasn't alright, she was drunk.

"In the physical or emotional sense?"

I found myself yelling, "Just answer the question," barking it through the line causing a yelp to come from Fallon. I shot her a warning glare, pretty much demanding that she not mess with me.

His voice lowered and it was hard to hear with all the loud music and people in the background. "She's in the bathroom getting sick. I left her at the door. I don't do vomit."

"Christ man! You're a fucking Vet! I'm on my way."

I disconnected the call and slid my phone into the front pocket of my jeans. Releasing a resigned sigh, I turned to Fallon whose brows were furrowed, making her face seem as if it was pinched. I didn't know how much of a fight she was going to put up, but with that expression it didn't look like it was going to be easy.

"Fallon, I gotta go." As if I owed her an explanation, I said, "My friend needs my help."

She raised up to her feet from her knees, her face puckering even more so in anger and she grabbed hold of my shirt, twisting it in her fist. "I was under the impression that you were going to fuck me. Not this, me sucking you off and me being sent on my merry way."

Obviously she didn't hear me correctly the first time, so I was going to be a gentleman and break it down for her into terms that she could relatively understand. "There was no precursor for you coming here. This wasn't your automatic ticket to fuck Bentley Jenkins. You are just one woman in a sea of millions, meaning replaceable." I gritted my teeth, "I'm needed to help my best fucking friend who *is* irreplaceable. She comes before any cheap fuck. So let go of my shirt and get the hell out of my house!" She immediately scrambled to her feet and grabbed her purse before running out the door.

I've never in my life had to be so terse and all around scary with a woman before. I had no other choice though, it had to be done, but I sure as hell wasn't left with a warm and fuzzy feeling right now.

But all that didn't matter because it got rid of her and now I could get to Miri.

The change of terrain caused me to jerk in the cab of my truck, going from the asphalt of the main road to the gravel lot of Tillie's. The rocks crunched under the weight of my heavy boots as I bounded down from my seat and closed the driver's side door.

Taking long strides to reach the building quicker, I yanked the heavy oak door towards me and went in in search of *my* girl. The sentiment that slipped wasn't all lost on me. I just pushed it to the back of my mind as I started on my search for Miri.

Once I didn't see her usual pulled back hair right away, I began to panic.

What if some guy picked her up or even worse, drugged her and then took her home.

My movements became even faster as I picked up my frantic pace, being forced to look at each individual table. I didn't care how long it would take me or how much I would piss off the customers, I was going to find her.

It was then I saw Tillie fussing over a bent over body at the bar, rubbing her back obviously trying to soothe her.

I felt my heart rate returning to normal as I let out a sigh of relief. All of my tension suddenly dissipated and I allowed my lips to slowly tip up in a smile. Weaving around the scattered tables, I took in Tillie coddling Miri and I couldn't help thinking how grateful I was that they had each other.

My smile lingered on my face as I continued approaching the bar, until Tillie dropped her hand from Miri's back and turned around with a scowl on her face, then it slid right off and my steps faltered.

A blonde female sidestepped in front of me, immediately making me halt in place. A bright smile lit up her face and under any other normal circumstances I wouldn't have hesitated to chat her up.

"Hey, Bentley," she stepped forward and put her hand in the center of my chest. "How about buying me a drink?" Her hand lingered on my chest and proceeded to begin to travel south. Grabbing hold of her wrist, I briskly removed her from my person.

"Not interested tonight, sorry," I shrugged, walking around her and back towards Miri.

At this point, an even deeper scowl was set on Tillie's face. Was that resting bitch face for me? If it wasn't for the distinct fact that Miri needed me, I would've turned my ass around and hightailed it out of there.

*Don't let her smell your fear or it'll be all over with.*

Straightening up my posture to appear that I was standing a bit taller, I fiddled with the collar of my shirt smelling the sweet smell of Fallon's perfume and wondered if I should've changed before coming. It was a bit too late to be thinking about semantics.

Maybe her senses have dulled with her old age.

"Hey, Tillie," I waved awkwardly, then shoved my hands into the pockets of my jeans. "I'm here to bring Miri home."

Her nose curled up in disgust as she shook her head back and forth, clearly sizing me up and muttering something unintelligible under her breath. Narrowing her eyes into slits, she grumbled, "My granddaughter is a rare gem you know…" She posed this as a statement because we both knew it to be true.

Tillie's apparent displeasure was getting us nowhere. I didn't think my charm would win with her, so I turned to the next best thing; humor.

"Who Maisie?"

With a huff and a roll of her eyes, Tillie crooked her finger so I would lean down closer to being on her level, height wise. I bent at the waist and Tillie's arm swung around until her hand smacked me on the back of the head.

Ole girl may not have age on her side, but there seemed to be nothing wrong with her agility.

My hand came up to rub the spot where she struck, trying to soothe out some of the sting.

"Maisie was dubbed a lost cause a long time ago." Her face contorted as if she was hit with a putrid smell, and once she began waving a hand in front of her nose, it was confirmed. "Boy, you smell like a cheap two dollar whore. You didn't even have the common courtesy to change before you came to get my granddaughter?"

Shit! I knew I should've taken the extra precautions to cover up Fallon's smell, but my priority was only on Miri.

She took a shaky step in my direction and I automatically took one back. I wasn't too much of a man to admit that the old bird scared the shit out of me.

Since I wasn't allowing her to come any closer without a fight, she raised her hand and pointed her slender finger at me, "If you think that you and Miri will be anything but friends, you'd better get that shit out of your skull right now." She pointed that same forefinger at Miri's slumped over back and said, "That girl has been through enough hell in her lifetime that she doesn't need an overused prick ruining anything else. You'll break her to the point she'd be a shell of her former self." Her finger was back to being pointed at me again and she extended her arm to dig her overgrown nail into the middle of my chest, "Bottom line, my Miri is way too good for the likes of you."

A thick lump formed at the base of my throat, not because I was being judged and berated by someone new, but because she was one hundred percent correct.

Miri was too good for me and the more I learned about her, the more this statement became abundantly clear. There was just no telling exactly why she wanted to be friends with me, but that was just the good-hearted person that she was.

One thing was certain though, I would be in Miri's life for however long she needed me to be. Tomorrow morning if she woke up and never wanted to see me again, I would adhere to her request even though it would violently tear me up inside.

Thoughts and emotions that I tried to drown out about Miri with Fallon earlier, have not only returned but have intensified. I was addicted to her.

With her I could exponentially be myself, no added show.

"With Miri things are different. There are no looming expectations being held over my head with her. Therefore, I won't be fucking something up because I'm such a monumental screw-up. I can without a doubt call her my best friend and there is nothing I wouldn't do for her. All she has to do is say the word."

I could see Tillie's emotions swimming in her eyes as she quickly looked away.

Taking two steps forward, I was now at Miri's side. I placed my open hand in the middle of her back and felt her deep even breaths, letting me know that she was indeed sleeping. I glanced back at Tillie, who was eyeing Miri so cautiously, I could see every single ounce of love she had for her granddaughter right there on the surface of her face. "I think it's about time I took this lush home." One last attempt at humor, which thankfully garnered me a slight smile. I would consider that half attempt, a full win.

Bringing my other arm under the back of her knees and with a little effort I cradled her passed out form to my chest. It was hard work carrying someone who was pretty much dead weight. I hitched her body up a bit allowing for her head to rest on my shoulder and her arms instinctively wrapped around me.

I pivoted my boot so I could start for the door, but the hand that was placed on my forearm had me halting and casting my eyes downward.

"Please take care of her." The hidden connotation behind Tillie's words didn't go unnoticed. She wasn't just referring to tonight.

"Promise," I spoke past that lump that had made a repeat appearance.

Walking out of the tavern and through the gravel towards my truck, I was careful not to lose my footing and internally hoped like hell that I never broke my promise, not only to Tillie but especially Miri. Failure when it came to this fragile woman in my arms wasn't an option.

Not only was carrying someone who was unconscious a difficult task, but situating them up in a truck by far took the cake. Even though I frequented the gym several times a week, it still took me a moment just to garner the strength to make the first attempt. By try number three I finally got her in the seat, then came the daunting task of fastening her seatbelt.

114

Miri must've decided that tonight of all nights she would allow for her tits to be so abundantly on display. The scoop neck t-shirt she had on housed her breasts with perfection and at the same time revealed ample cleavage. It was all I could do to avert my gaze as I stretched the belt across her body securing it in place.

Then I had to send up a silent prayer that she would remain in the upright position until I was able to close the door.

As I pulled out onto the main road, I was able to finally take my first full breath in almost an hour. I didn't know if this breath was more of relief for the fact that I had Miri secured in my truck safe and sound under my watch, or that I was out of the crossfire from Tillie.

There was no one to blame but myself for receiving the third degree from various individuals, but I had never wanted things to be more different than the eye opening experience from Miri's gran.

Out of habit, when I realized I was too far gone into my own head, I extended my right arm reaching to turn on the radio, then instantly jerked it back to the wheel. I would just have to suffer in silence, there was no way I'd chance waking Miri up.

Although the silence was deafening, I took this opportunity to take random peeks at the stunning woman passed out against my door panel. Her dark chocolate hair was fanned across most of her face, her nose, and just a glimpse of her left eye was peeking through.

Every time I've seen Miri, she's worn her hair up in some form, whether it was in a simple ponytail or in some sort of braid. But tonight, her hair was down completely. I could just imagine her in her drunken state un-securing the holder allowing it to tumble free from being bound.

Approaching a red light, I slowly applied pressure to the brake pedal allowing the truck to come to a complete stop. Then and only then did I allow myself the ability to feel vulnerable. I reached across my center console, which I was cursing its existence, if it weren't for the damn hindrance she could be curled up into my side.

Inching my hand closer towards Miri, I gently tucked a strand of her thick hair behind her ear. Since she was sleeping so soundly, I allowed my fingers to linger on her exposed cheek, casting just the briefest of caresses. Her nose twitched and I instinctively pulled my hand back so I wouldn't get caught if she decided now was the time to open her eyes. My heart accelerated when I was so bold to touch her in a way that felt foreign to me and dare I say even a bit intimate.

I refocused my attention on the road before me and the now green light. Within a few minutes I'd have Miri safe and sound in her apartment and I'd be well on my way away from this uncomfortable yet eye opening evening.

"Do you think you'll have a magnum opus?"

I craned my head towards the right, I wasn't expecting Miri to be awake let alone talking. She hadn't slept long enough for the alcohol to have worn off and the question she was inquiring about confirmed that.

My brows knitted together, I didn't know if she would end up asleep again if I ignored her, but the way she was looking at me, so expectantly and almost as if I didn't answer she would burst out in tears.

"A what?"

She shifted in her seat, her left leg partially underneath her so she could look at me a bit easier. As we passed under the fluorescent street lights, it illuminated inside of the truck, especially her eyes which were heavily glassed over. Although her speech had her almost appearing sober, there may be a distinct possibility that she wouldn't remember having this conversation, so I would appease her for the time being.

"A magnum opus mostly pertains to writers or artists, but it's basically your greatest achievement. My mother was an incredible artist, but she always said that I was the best thing she could've ever created. I was her magnum opus."

I wasn't entirely certain on how I should respond, I couldn't even chance a glance looking in her direction.

There was no great accomplishment for me, nor did I think that I would ever deserve one. My options for my future weren't anything but bleak. I saw myself living a life of solitude for how I chose to live my life early on. The way things were going, I would only receive everlasting damnation.

A few minutes had elapsed and neither of us broke the silence again. For a second I thought that she had passed out again, but she finally spoke, this time with a tremor in her voice. She was crying. My heart instantly ached to hear the sadness laced in her tone. "Bentley can you promise me one thing?"

*Aw, hell. Two promises in one night.*

I felt myself grip the steering wheel a little tighter, wishing this drive would hurry the hell up. "Miri," I began. "I'm no good with promises. But for you, I'll do my best to try and keep it."

"You can't ever leave me." Her voice was dejected, nothing like the Miri I knew.

Her request was like a punch to the gut, because wasn't that exactly what I was trying to do mere hours earlier? Leave Miri alone and forget about her.

What was I supposed to do? Lie through my teeth as if I hadn't already tried beginning the process of withdrawing from her?

There was no other choice. I wished like hell that I could be the friend that she needed. The man that she deserved.

I took my eyes off the road for a split second to glance her way. "I won't."

She released a staggered breath, "Everyone leaves me." I saw her look down and fiddle with her nails, she truly believed in what she was saying. "My parents left me, Travis, and now Oliver. I can't have you leave me too."

Confused, I uttered, "Oliver didn't leave you, Miri, he had an emergency surgery."

"Oh."

I pulled into an empty parking spot at Miri's apartment complex and killed the engine. It seemed that she had already fallen back asleep and I was thankful for small miracles and the fact that I wouldn't be bombarded with any more questions.

Before pulling her out of her seat and into my arms, I had to go where no man ever wanted to go without the woman's knowledge for fear of being bludgeoned or worse, castrated with a dull object. I had to go digging in her purse for her keys. We wouldn't be getting in the apartment without them. So I sucked up my unease and went for it.

After blindly stumbling up step after grueling step until I reached the third floor, I was cursing the sheer existence of multi-floor apartments, especially ones without elevators.

As I continued down the hallway towards Miri's door, I heard random clicks of the locks coming from her neighbors. I could just imagine the things that were going through their minds. A stranger carrying sweet, innocent Miri, passed out at that. Even worse if they actually had a clue as to who I was.

This entire situation just proved to others as well as myself that I could be every bit of the doting gentleman, it's just that most didn't expect it or would even believe it. My mother and brother being two of those people.

After a few failed attempts, I was finally successfully able to finagle the key into Miri's front door lock and granted us access to the apartment. And literally not a moment too soon. I felt my arms begin to shake as they threatened to give out. Quickly shuffling my boots along the hardwood flooring as fast as my feet would carry me, I was able to lay her gently back onto the cushions of her bright red vibrant couch.

She instantly curled up onto her side with both of her hands shoved underneath her head. Resting so peacefully, her eyelashes fanned across her cheeks and her lips parted just a fraction of an inch to breathe out any air she was taking in through her nose. It was weird because I never really cared to watch a woman sleep before, but something warmed within me at Miri being the first.

I shoved my hands into the front pockets of my jeans and began walking aimlessly around the living room. I had no clue on what to do now that I brought her home and she was sleeping off her drunkenness soundly. With Oliver not being home and not having the slightest idea what time he would be coming through the door, there was no chance in hell that I would leave her alone.

I stopped pacing when the gigantic painting situated behind the couch caught my eye. I had taken notice of the beautiful artwork when I first came to her apartment the other night, but never really had the chance to look at it uninterrupted.

It was of a breathtaking skyline, the sun setting in the clouds. The vast colors of pinks and oranges settling into the sky. The signature on the bottom right hand corner caught my eye next. The black wispy strokes of their penmanship.

*A. Armstrong*

If Miri hadn't mentioned to me that her mother was an artist, I'd have assumed that it was a mere relative, the painting possibly passed down the generations.

Random thoughts were now running through my head, did Miri favor her mother? Did they have the same dark brown hair and captivating eyes? Did they share their love of music? I peered back down at Miri in time to see her twitch her nose again right before her eyes immediately snapped open. Her face literally turned a putrid shade of green as she scrambled off the couch and ran into the bathroom with her hand covering her mouth.

The retching began as soon as I saw the light flicker on. "Don't come in here, Bentley!" her voice echoed with her plea.

So, naturally, I didn't listen and carefully walked towards the bathroom. I had no idea if Miri had actually made it the entire way, so I had to be prepared for anything. If I had any sort of heads up warning, I could have run into the kitchen and picked up some pot holders or something equally as absorbent for protection.

At first glance, the coast was clear, but seeing Miri bent over the toilet had my heart aching in my chest. "Don't jump!" I hollered trying to crack a joke in an uncomfortable situation but not garnering any type of reaction other than a grunt. But even more than finding myself vulnerable, I hated that she had to go through the stages of being drunk.

Mindless chitchat.

Inadvertent confessions.

Pukefest, which was *not* my favorite.

Splitting headache and raging hangover.

But thus, was the consequences.

Her unsecured hair was dangling in her face, so I made myself useful. Can't say this was anything I've ever done before either. Miri was making me experience the unknown. I sat down on the edge of her bathtub and pulled the strands of her hair back and secured them in my hand at the nape of her neck.

She abruptly began coughing and I instinctively found myself rubbing the entire length of her back with my free hand.

"Bentley," she raised up a hand and thrust it blindly near my face. "I told you not to come in here!" she whined before spitting into the water. Her other hand raised up to flush the toilet. I took this as my cue to give her a hand getting things ready for her. First, I rummaged through her bathroom cabinets for a washcloth, ran it under cool water, wrung it out and pressed it against her forehead. Her skin was flushed and clammy, and with the way she was squinting her eyes, she was on the verge of passing out again.

Her eyes looked directly into mine as she frowned and whispered, "What are you doing?"

I removed my hand as well as the rag from her face, "I'm washing the dishes," I deadpanned. "What does it look like I'm doing? I'm cleaning you up and putting your drunk ass to bed."

Miri's shoulders slumped forward, the exhaustion of the entire evening was taking over. I took her hand in mine and placed the cool washcloth in the center of her palm and clamped her hand around it.

Giving her strict instructions, "Finish cleaning up and then come into your bedroom for the next set of instructions."

I smiled as a pout began to form on her lips, and I could sense an argument brewing in that clouded head of hers. Before I could allow a rebuttal to fly from her lips, I turned on my heel in search of her bedroom.

This whole night was unchartered territory for me, but this took the cake. There were only two bedrooms to choose from and I was secretly hoping that I would get it right the first time. Oliver seemed like the kind of person who would have *Save the 'insert animal here'* posters splattered all over his walls.

Stopping at the end of the hall, I came upon a juncture. Left or right.

Go right, choose right, please be right. I flicked on the light switch, which illuminated a rather simple room. Miri's full-sized bed was pushed flush up against the wall, the black vanity dresser on the opposite wall, and a black desk and floor-length mirror rested against the adjacent wall. Another one of her mother's paintings was hung over her desk, rounding out the entire room.

Now standing in front of her dresser, I was utterly afraid of going through her drawers for something for her to sleep in. If picking the wrong room unnerved me, this task was daunting and terrifying as hell. Shit like this wasn't supposed to get to me, I was Bentley fucking Jenkins. I should be eating this shit up, rummaging through a woman's panty drawer.

The sound of feet shuffling as they made their way into the room startled me as I snapped around to face Miri. I felt as if I was just caught doing something that I shouldn't be doing. Once her pitiful face came into view I pointed at the dresser behind me and cleared my throat before saying, "Which one has your pajamas in it?"

She lazily lifted a finger, indicating the second drawer up from the bottom on the left and took a seat on the edge of her bed. I slowly pulled the drawer towards me and pulled out a t-shirt and pair of pants and threw them down on the bed beside her.

"Get dressed and I'll be right back." She stood on shaky legs and with a jerk of her wrist gave me a brief smartass salute. I all but raced out of the room, I hoped like hell that she could manage to undress herself and put on the clothes I picked out. I didn't think that I could withstand watching her creamy pale skin come into view and refrain from doing anything to it.

I had waited a few minutes before I returned with a bottle of cold water from the fridge, praying that she was currently under the covers of her bed. Breathing a sigh of relief at the sight of her curled up under the blanket, I held out the water showing that I was placing it on her bedside table.

I wasn't expecting her to scoot over and flip her covers back and patting on the empty space next to her on the bed. "Lay with me, Bentley," her nervousness was making her voice shake. The effects of the alcohol must be wearing off if her nerves were making an appearance.

I looked down at the ground and the heap of her clothes on the floor, her discarded pale pink lace bra sitting next to the pants I pulled from her drawer. So she was in bed with only a t-shirt and lord almighty, please tell me I'm not overlooking her panties on the floor.

*Dear God, she was killing me.*

"Please," she pleaded. She had to go and add that in. I looked up at the ceiling this time, figuring it was safer, willing God to just strike me dead right where I stood.

Did I want to break my spell of never actually sleeping in the same bed with another woman?

This wasn't just *some* woman, though, this was Miri. My best friend. And this would be purely platonic…for her.

No sleep would be had by me because I would be trying my hardest to focus and make sure that the last fragment of my resolve didn't snap and keeping my dick in check. He wasn't entirely getting the message right now though, an invitation to bed by a beautiful woman, he was up and ready to party.

Rolling my eyes, I toed off my boots and left every other scrap of clothing intact. I loathed sleeping in jeans, but they weren't going anywhere. Being that I was a back sleeper, I made sure that I was as close to the edge of the bed I could get without falling onto the floor, thinking that I would be safe from all contact. Call it being overly tired or wishful thinking because there wasn't a chance in hell that we wouldn't touch one another in a full-sized bed. That entire thought was obliterated when she rolled over and curled into my side.

For the first time in my entire life I was being cuddled and let me tell you, the snuggle was fucking real.

Her leg hooked over my jeans and her head somehow burrowed into the crook of my arm. I so badly wanted to relax and enjoy having Miri in my arms, but I couldn't allow that for myself. I didn't deserve it. This was going to be one long, sleepless night. It would end up being the ultimate miracle if I actually survived.

# *Chapter 11*

## *Miri*

God awful pounding woke me from my once drunken slumber. I couldn't believe that I let down my defenses and allowed myself to consume so much alcohol. That was so unlike me, I knew my limits and rarely ever surpassed them without caring.

Trying to open my eyes was proving to be no easy task, I felt as if I needed to physically pry my eyelids apart. I cannot believe that I was stupid enough to leave my contacts in overnight. Now my eyes were as dry as the Sahara desert and no doubt puffy and irritated.

I couldn't even tell what time it was on my bedside clock. I hoped that I would be lucky enough to catch Oliver home before his shift.

"Oliver!" I shouted, immediately grabbing ahold of my head with both hands, applying the smallest bit of pressure hoping it would alleviate some of the pain radiating throughout my skull.

Several minutes had to have passed even though it seemed time was standing still. I was getting ready to yell again, despite the ten man band rehearsing in my head, when Oliver came into my room.

"What Miri?" he said in his normal tone but sounded like he was shouting down to me from the top of the tallest mountain. I could already tell how this day was going to pan out. And it wasn't pretty.

"Can you please go grab my contact case and glasses from the bathroom?"

Once I was able to peel my contacts from my eyeballs, apply eye drops and put on my glasses I was officially a quarter of the way to feeling human.

Bunching my covers up around me, I sat up in the middle of my bed and finally glanced up at Oliver. His arms were crossed in front of his chest and he had a bemused expression on his face. I could only take his amusement to signify my behavior for last night.

Releasing a heavy sigh, "All right, Ollie, lay it on me. How embarrassing was I last night?"

His eyes gleamed behind his frames as he leisurely strolled over to lean up against my desk. I was already internally cringing. "Actually," he started, scratching the nape of his neck as he looked at me with his tender eyes, allowing my tension eased the slightest bit. "You weren't too bad…with me."

One of my brows rose and I gasped, "Who else was I with?" And pieces of last night's puzzle slowly began forming together.

"Oh no!" My entire body froze in place including my beating heart in my chest.

"Oh yes," he began confirming my worst nightmare. "I got called in and had to get ahold of Bentley to come take you home." Oliver immediately threw up his hands in a surrendering manner. "Now I don't know all of the specifics, but if the horrified expression on your face is any indication, bits and pieces are coming back to you. But I do know this, Bentley slipped out of your room about three hours ago and looked rather uncomfortable." I threw my hands on top of my head, feeling the matted strands of my nappy, unwashed hair. I didn't necessarily want Oliver to proceed, but I needed to be one hundred percent positive that nothing transpired between the two of us.

"He said you got sick once you got home and then you begged him to sleep with you." My eyes went wide and then bugged out of my head. Oliver thrust his hand towards me again in a calming manner. "Calm your tits, woman!" My eyes bulged even more with his choice phrase. "All that took place was actual sleep. Although, with the bags under his eyes and his strained features, I don't know how much sleep he actually got."

I released a long, dramatic groan as I flopped back against my mattress. I was *sure* I *just* begged him to sleep, but that didn't mean I wasn't thinking the complete opposite. I was such a hussy.

Grasping the edge of my blanket, I pulled it up and over my head covering my entire body. "I'm going back to bed." Hopefully, sleep would be just the ticket to get rid of my embarrassment and the throbbing of my temples.

The sound of Oliver's laughter lasted until he was out of my room. Before closing my bedroom door, he muttered, "I'll see you in the morning."

"Three cups of buttermilk," I muttered to myself as I measured out the last ingredient for my light and fluffy pancakes. Pouring the buttermilk into my dry ingredients, I took my wire whisk and began whisking everything together vigorously, being careful not to overmix the batter.

"What're you doing?" Oliver came up behind me, startling and making me jump in the process.

"Geez Louise, Oliver. Make some kind of noise before sneaking up on someone." I brought my mixing bowl full of batter over to the heated pan on the stove, then flipped over the bacon that was sizzling on the other burner. "I'm making breakfast for you and Bentley as a thank you for taking care of me the other night." I looked over my shoulder as Oliver paused in rubbing his eyes underneath his glasses and eyed me appreciatively.

"I'll help you whenever if it'll get you to cook for me." I was the only one of the two of us who could cook, hence the real reason Oliver was stuck on ramen noodles still because that was all he had up his sleeve. But I just didn't cook all that often. With our schedules that didn't exactly coincide, it just didn't make much sense.

"Yeah, but I have to hurry and bring this by before Bentley goes to work," I said as I poured the batter in the pan and waited for the edges to bubble indicating they were ready to flip.

Oliver came up and leaned against the cabinets on the other side of the stove opposite me. He glanced down at his watch, "Miri, it isn't even seven yet."

Mocking him, I swatted in his direction with the spatula before I flipped over the perfect pancake. "I know what time is." Proving my point by pointing at the clock on the stove that illuminated the numbers 6:46 in green. "I want to run by Gran's also before I head into work."

Thirty minutes later, I was standing outside of Bentley's house on his front porch holding Tupperware that was filled with breakfast items. My heart was beating a mile a minute because I was nervous about what Bentley would say. Taking a deep breath, I guessed it was now or never.

I quietly rapped on the door three times and dropped my hand so I could wrap it around the container.

Almost two minutes had passed and I was almost to the point of giving up, when I heard the deadbolt click. The white wooden door opened and my mouth went slack, but only after it completely went dry.

Bentley leaned against the open door frame in nothing but pajama pants. His chest was bare, meaning no shirt and no hair. It looked as smooth as a baby's bottom. If I wasn't careful, I would end up dropping the Tupperware, leaving my hands completely free to wander. Explore the contours and ridges of all one, two, three…yeah, six of his abs.

*Holy cannoli.* It was only April, but it was really rather humid this time of the morning.

"I'm so…I'm sorry." I snapped out of whatever fantasy-filled haze I was in. Clearing my throat, "Did I wake you?"

He pushed himself off of the doorjamb and brought his hand up towards my face. Bentley's thumb swiped across my bottom lip and I raised a brow. "You had a bit of drool there," he smirked and winked as he took his thumb and wiped it on his pajama pants for added effect, because I knew good and well there was no drool on my mouth.

He wasn't *all* that great to look at. I would just have to evade looking at his chest, which was perfectly on display, *and* his face, that strong chiseled jaw, and deep brown eyes.

Pants. His pajama pants were safe, but wait a minute…I shoved the Tupperware container into Bentley's hands and bent down to get closer to see what was on his pants.

"Careful there, Miri. I've tried to tell him that we're just friends, but the closer you get he won't see it that way," he said referring to his nether region. But I wasn't paying attention to his words.

"Are those? Are those pickles on your pants? Little green cartoon pickles, what are we five?" Then I noticed the wording and busted out laughing. "I'm kind of a big dill?"

"Laugh it up, but my niece got me these for Christmas. And besides --" he shrugged a shoulder and proudly said, "it houses my much larger pickle."

My eyes went wide as I snapped up to my full height and busted out laughing again. "Yeah, I'll just bet that makes him want to come out and party when you refer to your penis as a pickle. I really didn't know that I was here for comedy hour."

He rolled his eyes, clearly not amused. I strike my earlier comment about him being a morning person. "What *are* you here for?"

"Oh right!" I yanked the container back out of his hands, thankful for the ice breaker to hide my embarrassment over my extreme inebriation the other night. I lifted the corner of the lid, allowing any remaining steam to escape and showed him the food.

His eyes flared, "I wanted to thank you for coming to my rescue the other night and to apologize for any discomfort I caused." I looked down at the dish and muttered, "Buttermilk pancakes made from scratch and bacon."

He yanked the container out of my hands and into his once more, "I love it when you talk bacon to me." Lifting the dish up to his face he inhaled deeply allowing his eyes to roll back into his head. "I appreciate this and really it was no trouble." He took a piece of the bacon and bit off more than half of what was in his hand with one bite. "You want to come in?" He shifted to the side leaving enough room for me to get through.

I thought my laughter was completely out of my system, but a fleeting giggle bubbled up my throat. Those pants were super distracting. Placing my hand on my chest, I said, "Thanks for the offer, but I need to run and get gas then stop by Gran's."

Bentley's eyes shifted away from me at the mention of Gran. It had me wondering if anything transpired between the two of them. I knew that she didn't have the best picture of him painted in her mind, but she needed to lay off.

Between the combination of the line at the gas station and the unusual traffic backup due to a three vehicle collision, I was officially running behind.

Gran wasn't expecting me, so she wouldn't think anything of it if I didn't stop by, but something, a feeling in my gut had me wanting to at least check on her.

Pulling into her driveway of her two bedroom bungalow, I saw that her old compact car was still sitting there. I felt relieved that I caught her before she left for the Tavern, it seemed all she ever did was work. I put my car into park and reached across the console to grab my purse and the remaining Tupperware container I brought with me. After locking my car with the fob, I took the stairs one by one until I reached Gran's front porch.

I knocked on the door and after a minute of waiting, I tried knocking again but this time a little louder. This wasn't like her to not answer the door. She may have been climbing through the ages, but it wouldn't even take her this long even if she was in the far back of the house.

Cupping my free hand over my eyes, I peered in through the small window next to the door. Nothing looked amiss, but I had a bad feeling in the pit of my stomach, so I dug around in my purse for Gran's spare house key. Once I felt the metal ridges in the small interior pocket, I clutched it in my palm and proceeded to unlock the door.

My heart rate accelerated for the second time that day, but for two extremely different reasons. I had no clue what awaited me on the other side of the door. Slowly turning the handle, I finally pushed open the door letting myself slip inside. The house was quiet, almost eerily so.

"Gran?" I stammered, raising my voice enough to be heard throughout the thousand square foot home. My hand adjusted the strap of my purse higher on my shoulder and I clutched it a bit tighter to my side with my elbow. I tiptoed across the plush living room carpet, noticing that her morning coffee cup was still resting on its coaster on the end table next to her recliner.

"Gran, are you home?" My steps picked up as well as my heart frantically beating against my ribs. *Where was she?*

A barely audible sound had me halting in place. It almost sounded like a whimper. Then I heard it again, this time marginally louder. Tears pricked the corners of my eyes as I rushed into her bedroom.

I gasped as my heart sunk in my chest. I didn't want to assume the worst, but that's where my mind immediately went. The bathroom light was on and cascading down on her limp form as my gran laid on the floor in between her bathroom and bedroom entry.

Her frail body was completely still. The container of food slipped from my hand and bounced off the ground as I rushed to her side, dropping to my knees beside her. Gran's eyes were closed and her brows furrowed, she was in extreme distress that much was obvious. I went to touch her but tentatively pulled away, I didn't know where she was hurt.

"Gran?" I shuddered. The only response I received was another moan and more worrying along her brow line. With her being unconscious, there was no way to find out where she was hurting. After just a visual inspection, I didn't see any bumps or scrapes, but that didn't mean it wasn't internal.

What if she had a heart attack?

The slow rise and fall of her chest let me know that she was at least breathing, so I finally snapped into action grabbing my phone and pressing buttons before holding it to my ear. I called 9-1-1 and gave them as much information as I had.

Immediately after hanging up, I shakily pressed even more buttons and held the phone to my ear again hoping that he would answer his phone.

"Hello?" His deep voice rumbled through the line.

"Bentley, I need you!"

# Chapter 12

## Bentley

Driving the fastest I think I ever have across town, I made it to Tillie's house in mere minutes after hanging up with Miri. She was incredibly vague on the phone, but the frantic tremor in her voice didn't have me questioning it. Seeing the ambulance in the driveway, I threw my gear shift into park after just barely coming to a complete stop.

Bounding down out of my truck, I was halfway to the porch when Miri appeared in the doorway, puffy red-rimmed eyes, evidence of the tears I knew were threatening to erupt the brief time we were on the phone.

Once her eyes connected with mine, her bottom lip trembled making my steps falter. No matter what happened I needed to be strong for Miri, be the shoulder to cry on if and when she needed it.

She walked directly into my chest, curling her arms around my body, clinging on for dear life. "Shh," I whispered into her hair, trying my best to comfort her even though I was so far out of my depth. Seemed to happen a lot when I was around Miri. My fingers weaved their way into a few strands of her ponytail as I tilted her head back so she would look up at me.

"Have the paramedics said anything?" As soon as the words left my mouth, two paramedics walked past the threshold outside of Tillie's house, one in front of the other behind the stretcher carrying Miri's gran. They had secured an IV line to begin fluids and an oxygen mask was settled over her nose and mouth.

By now a group of people began gathering around in Tillie's front yard, so it wouldn't be long until the entire town caught wind of what was going on.

Miri finally shook her head, "With Gran being unconscious they don't really have much to go on. They think she may have fallen and possibly fractured something and the searing pain is what caused her to black out."

After the gurney was down the steps and they were rolling her to the back of the ambulance, Miri broke free from her hold on me. "I'm going with her," she announced as she bounded down the steps.

After lifting up the back end of the stretcher into the ambulance, Miri started up after them when one of the men held up their hand and stated, "I'm sorry, but since we don't know what exactly we are dealing with you'll need to follow us to the hospital." The sorrow had lined his face before he shut the doors. The ambulance took off down the road, their sirens blaring, Miri staying rooted to the spot watching it until it disappeared into the distance.

"I can drive you," I muttered into her ear as I came up behind her.

"Huh?" She looked back at me over her shoulder, pulling herself out of her thoughts. "No, I'm going to drive." She marched towards her four-door Mazda, adamant about getting in the driver's side door.

"Miri, I don't think that's such a good idea." The idea of her distraught and placing herself behind the wheel didn't sit well with me.

She released a huff and placed her hand on her hip, "And why not?" Her tears were being replaced with anger, her face turning red for an entirely different reason.

It was a good thing that I was safely on the opposite side from her, leaning against the passenger door. "Your gran was just taken away in the back of an ambulance, clearly your head isn't where it should be." I knew I was being harsh, but I needed her to know that the choice she was trying to make wasn't the right one.

She blinked once, then twice not saying a word, but I could tell by the fire in her eyes that she was getting worked up. Calling her out was getting to her.

Her hands moved to rest on the top of her car and she balled them into tight fists.

If it were me, I'd be calling myself every evil name I could conjure up, but this wasn't me. Miri was on the verge of a major tongue lashing and my narrowed eyes were challenging her to just burst out with an explicit word.

We were in a standoff, and although this was wasting time we could be spending getting to the hospital, it was taking her mind off of it.

"Do it," I dared, "let me have it!" I spread my arms wide open allowing for the verbal jabs to commence.

Finally, she slammed her fist onto the top surface of her car and growled. Oh yes, I couldn't believe the low grumble that erupted deep from within her belly.

"Bentley Jenkins, if you do not get in this car right now, sit down and shut up, I will spread around to every woman in town that you…" Thankfully she didn't even finished that statement as some of the passerby's looked in our direction, but she wasn't done yet. "Don't even test me right now. I need to drive to keep my mind focused and off the fact that my gran could possibly be dying. So I suggest you sit down and be a good little pretty boy before I find something to use to rearrange that flawless face of yours!" She deeply inhaled air into her lungs having ground that threat out all in one breath.

There was that feisty side that rarely made an appearance but was cute as hell. I should be concerned that she just threatened mutilation on my face, but that was the farthest thing from my mind.

With my hand paused on the door handle, I took my free hand a rubbed along the stubble on my cheek. "You really think my face is flawless?" I joked, hoping it would lighten the mood and defuse the situation, but, by the way, she pursed her lips I knew I had struck out.

"Bentley!!!" she screamed.

Translation: that was my cue to cut the shit and get in the damn car.

Heavy silence filled the air of the car, the tension just pouring off of Miri. She said that just by driving it would keep her mind void of plaguing thoughts of Tillie, but by the looks of her white knuckles on the steering wheel I'd say she was doing a *swell* job.

I contemplated what to do to help get her out of her own head and to get us to the hospital in one piece. Idle chitchat was out, I could already see her quick backhand now.

I came up with an idea and reaching for the knob to the radio, I stopped midway shooting her a glance, "You mind?" A shoulder shrug was all I got, but at least it wasn't a grunt, so I called that winning.

Pressing the power button, watching the neon green numbers come to life, a familiar rock song surged through the speakers filling the dead air. "I haven't heard this song in forever,"

I said before performing my own little head bang while singing the lyrics.

Miri's face stayed blank but her grip started to loosen up its clutch on the wheel. My mission to make her smile started out as a rocky one. After belting out the chorus, I was seriously feeling this song down in my veins. "I think this song could be my anthem," I admitted.

She stared deadpanned at me, "Seriously? You want to claim "Nookie" by Limp Bizkit as your "anthem"?" She briefly took her hands off the wheel to use actual air quotes before returning them to their position.

I rested my arm on the door frame and listened to the lyrics for a second. "Well, not the part about my girl taking my money and leaving me heartbroken 'cause that shit doesn't happen to me. But doing it all for pussy, that's me in a nutshell."

"That's a small and lonely nutshell," she responded before reaching to push the number two preset.

I ignored her obvious jab, even though it felt like a blow to my gut and put out my feelers for the next song. Ahhh, "Super Bass" by Nikki Minaj. Wonderful song. Without hesitation, I began thumping my hand on my chest during the chorus and started rapping "Somebody, please tell them who the fuck I is, I am Bentley Jenkins..."

"Ugh!" she grumbled punching the next preset button.

It was a country station and she flashed a smirk knowing that I wasn't really into the country music scene. I was getting the impression that she wasn't fond of my form of distraction. She thought she won.

Luckily for her, I was a fan of Carrie Underwood, because let's face it, she was smokin' hot. I began making little jerky motions left and right with my head each and every word as "Undo It" flowed from my lips.

I wasn't vain enough to brag that my voice was spectacular because it wasn't even close, some would even go as far to claim that I was tone deaf, but none of that mattered. What did matter was the small smile that was trying so hard to lift the corners of Miri's mouth, but she was using all of her might to appear annoyed.

"Are you flipping serious?" She huffed again. "Don't tell me that you're one of those friends who think you have to out sing the singer on Every. Blasted. Song!"

I slapped my palm on my jean clad thigh and asked, "Was I that obvious?"

This time she released an exasperated sigh and pushed on the last preset. Now it was a game to see if she could find a song that I didn't know. I admit that I didn't know as many as Miri, but I had a few tricks up my sleeve.

Holding in my smile was one of the hardest things to do, especially with her self-satisfied smirk on her face when I didn't start immediately singing the song, or in this case, rapping.

I waited for the female singer to finish off the beginning of the song, sucked in a breath seeing Miri shift her head and bug her eyes as I sang about those "Good Vibrations" by Marky Mark and the Funky Bunch.

"NO! NO!" she wagged her finger at me before punching the power button. "You cannot ruin Mark Wahlberg like that for me."

"Don't tell me." I feigned a pout, or at least that's what I was telling myself. "You'd rock *his* world too."

*Evidently she rocks everyone's world but Bentley's.*

*And now I was talking about myself in the third person.*

This was bad.

Her brows raised as if silently conveying why I was even asking.

"So, uh --" I turned my head to look out the window. "Did you try calling anyone before you called me?"

"What do you mean? I called 9-1-1." Her brows wrinkled, she was confused by my question, hell I was confused by my question.

"So, you didn't call Oliver?" My own voice came out as pathetic.

"No, I called you, Bentley."

My heart thumped wildly in my chest. No one voluntarily relied on me for anything and here Miri did it and strictly without hesitation. It made leaving a job all that much easier.

I'll most likely hear it from Baylor about how unprofessional it was to show up at a client's just to leave merely five minutes later. None of that mattered, though, Miri needed me and there was no way that I was going to let her down.

She pulled into the emergency room parking lot and whipped into a spot without barely slowing down. After throwing the car into park, she sat unmoving for a moment and I could physically see her nerves and fear creeping up to overtake her. Her hands began to visibly tremble and without much thought behind my actions, I reached over grabbing ahold of her hand, taking it in mine. They were clammy as a result of gripping the steering wheel so hard and quite possibly because of the unknown once we entered through the front automatic doors.

"It's going to be alright, Miri," I said softly, trying to comfort her but not really knowing what else to say.

A single tear welled up in the corner of her eye threatening to spill over, and it took only seconds before she blinked and it toppled down her cheek. "I can't lose her too, Bentley."

Her words brought me back to the night of her drunken escapades and her begging me never to leave her. As of now, I was so invested in this woman before me there would be no way that I ever could voluntarily leave. My calloused, overworked fingers caressed her soft, gentle hand letting her know that I was there for her. "Let's go see what the doctor can tell us."

Walking into the emergency room, it was a whirlwind of activity. The receptionist's desk had a line backed up seven people deep, and I could sense the panic in Miri's eyes at the fact that the longer we had to wait here, the longer it would be to know exactly what the situation was.

A nurse finally came through the double doors that separated the waiting room from the emergency area and I wasted no time nonchalantly walking up to her and grabbing her attention. "Well, hello there," I said with just the briefest hint of flirtation in my tone. I didn't want to come out of the gates guns blazing if I didn't have to.

She glanced at her chart, not even bothering to give me the time of day. "If you'll excuse me, I have to call my next patient." Nurse Chelsea, by her nametag, tried to sidestep around me, still not even giving me any minimal eye contact.

I darted back in her path to will her to just look up. All it would take was just a small glance.

I didn't want to have to resort to desperate measures, but this was for Miri.

I'll give her until the count of five.

One…

Two…

*Bingo…*

Her beautiful green eyes snapped to mine and flared once she took in my mega-watt smile.

She definitely liked what she saw. The girl was gorgeous, but the kicker was I actually felt nothing towards her. No degree of attraction, even my dick was staying neutral. This almost never happened where there was no movement down south whatsoever.

*What in the hell was happening to me?*

I cleared my throat because she was still standing there struck dumb over my 'flawless' face. "Perhaps you can help us?" I looked over my shoulder at Miri and waved her over. "I'm looking for my friend's grandmother who was just transported in. Her name is Tillie…" My mind went completely blank. I didn't know Tillie's last name. To everyone she was just that, Tillie.

"Shilling," Miri filled in for me as she stepped up to my side.

"Wait," I held up a hand in disbelief, "Your gran's name is Tillie Shilling? That's almost as ridiculous as Eden's dad, Richard Richardt."

"Do you know where she is?" Miri pleaded with Nurse Chelsea, completely ignoring me.

She eyed Miri suspiciously, then myself where I released another grin and a quick wink.

"Come on back," she said, motioning with her paperwork before scanning her ID to allow entrance into the back.

"Easy tiger," Miri admonished a bit sarcastically as we followed Chelsea through the double doors. From the average person, it would've seemed like I was flirting with the nurse and normally that would've been the case. But this wasn't a normal situation and things were changing, I was changing and menial hookups just weren't all that appealing to me any longer. Could I actually be reaching the point of growing out of all my old ways and reaching the maturity level I was supposed to be on?

Sweat beaded on my brow and I reached up to pull at my collar because it was reaching sauna-like temperatures in this Hospital. "Does it seem hot in here to you?" I now knew what it felt like to have a hot flash, the only problem was that I wasn't supposed to actually be fucking having them.

"We can see that she's pretty, but please try and keep it in your pants."

"What? No, I wasn't…" I tried to correct her but was cut off when we stopped abruptly.

"She's in this room, but I can only allow one person to go in."

Miri rushed forward and covered Chelsea's arm with her hand, "Thank you so much!" She proceeded to push on the door handle and turned her body to face mine, but then came up to me, stood on her tiptoes and planted a small kiss on my cheek. "And thank you, Bentley, for everything." Before I even had a moment to react she had disappeared behind the door to her gran's room without another backward glance.

I couldn't help but just stand there looking at the closed door, the warmth from Miri's lips still lingering on my skin.

To my immediate right, movement caught my attention and before I knew it Chelsea's body was flush with my side. My eyes closed of their own volition, and I sighed. I walked myself right into this. My reputation coming back to haunt me.

"I get off of work soon," she whispered into my ear. "If you'll still be around, maybe we can…"

Before allowing her to go any further and continue to embarrass herself, I took a step out of her reach and turned to face her and explained as apologetically as I could muster. "I'm sorry if I gave you the wrong idea earlier, but I'm not interested."

She laughed, "But you're Bentley Jenkins…"

So, she was well aware of who I was. "And your point being?" My voice took on a grave rasp, a bit of harshness to it. "Just because you know who the hell I am and you dredge up the courage to come and proposition me, doesn't mean that I'm automatically going to drop everything and fuck you right here."

The clipboard she was carrying was now braced against her chest and she looked genuinely surprised by my response. But no one was more surprised than me. "It's because of her isn't it?"

It was so blatantly obvious to me that she was referring to Miri. Did it have to be because of someone else? Couldn't it be because I was tired of the same goddamn lifestyle that wasn't getting me anywhere? Instead of delving deeper into meanings and allowing myself to continue to get worked up, I took the easy way out.

"Partially. We are in a hospital and my best friend is worried about her grandmother. I'm here to offer any amount of support and be the person that she leans on if and when she needs it." Turning on my heel, I went straight towards the small waiting area that was around the corner from the room Tillie was currently in.

Once I got to the waiting area, I halted. Of course there would only be two open seats, one by an attractive female who instantly straightened her posture once she spotted me, causing me to inwardly groan. The other open seat was next to an older woman who was crying her eyes out and had already repeatedly blown her nose into her tissue within the thirty seconds I had been standing here.

The attractive woman was making not so subtle sideways glances at the empty chair directly to her left using her super powers to force me into it. Was there a sign in the bathroom with my picture stating that I was easy? Had women always been this crazy and I just always let my dick do the steering? And why in the hell was I seeing everything differently now?

Walking towards the woman, she made a display out of uncrossing her legs and the recrossing them. When I walked past her, I heard a small huff which made me grin before I threw myself into the chair next to Mrs. Blubberfest and slumped down in my seat. I decided to go ahead and make myself useful, so I picked up the box of tissues that was planted on the table next to me and handed them towards the elderly lady. "Here you go, ma'am."

"Thank you, darling. You're mighty sweet," she crowed. I could hear another huff come from the floozy down the way.

Folding my fingers over my stomach, I rested my head against the wall trying to make myself as comfortable as possible in these unforgiving chairs. Now that I pissed off the nurse there was no telling how long we would be here. My eyes had just drifted shut when I felt my phone vibrate in my pocket. After fishing it out, my brother's name was what I found staring back at me. I knew this phone call wouldn't be good but decided to go ahead and get it over with.

I could just imagine it now, Baylor in his older brother condescending tone, "I was just waiting for you to fail, for you to prove me right once again that you aren't suitable to run the business."

Connecting the call and holding the phone to my ear, I answered with a clipped, "Yeah?"

"Bentley can you please explain to me why I just got a personal phone call at the firm from Mrs. Stewart informing me that you showed up this morning to fix her toilet, only to leave five minutes later saying you needed to reschedule?"

Great, now he had our clients tattling on me like this was first grade and I just took Sally Myers eraser. And if I hadn't actually known it to be my brother, I would've sworn it was my dad. Difference was, my dad wouldn't ever talk to me like that and act like I was some kind of insolent nimrod.

Baylor thought he was so high and mighty, especially now that he was following *his* dream of working at the architecture firm.

"I had an emergency that couldn't wait. Her toilet will still be there tomorrow and besides, she has two bathrooms." I knew that I was only adding fuel to the fire, but I was well past the point of giving a shit. I ran Jenkins Plumbing and I shouldn't have to constantly report to my older brother regarding my whereabouts.

"What was so important that you had to run off at the beginning of the workday? Did one of your little tarts get knocked up?"

With my anger now flaring, I surged forward in my chair, bracing my elbows on my knees, "You know what Baylor, screw you. I for one don't sleep with girls like Kristina, who trick you into thinking they're knocked up." I knew that I was now bracing a fine line bringing up Baylor's ex-wife, but he had it coming.

"No, Bentley, screw you! That's a low blow even for you. When the hell are you going to grow up and accept responsibility?"

"When you stop trying to be my fucking dad!" If he said anything further I didn't know because I hit the button disconnecting the call and followed that by powering down my entire phone. I knew my mother's phone call would be next, and I didn't feel like dealing with her lashing out as well. Forget positive reinforcement and everything I continued to do right, he could only focus on my past misgivings and wrongdoings.

What had started out as a small pounding in my skull had now turned into a full-blown headache with the potential to soar into a migraine of epic proportions. I tried pinching the bridge of my nose to alleviate some of the pressure building behind my eyes, but I could only concentrate on replaying Baylor's words.

I didn't know what happened between the two of us. Weren't brothers supposed to have each other's backs? I couldn't ever recall a day that we fully got along willingly. More often than not we would save face and play nice just to appease our mother, but now even those days were few and far between.

Luckily, just a bit later Miri came out but not without looking any less worried. Pushing my hands off of the arms of the chair, I raised and within two long strides met her halfway.

"You're still here?" She looked stunned to see me still sitting in the waiting room after a few hours.

"Of course, I was here in case you needed me. Well, and because you drove. Did they find out what was wrong?"

Her frown led me to believe that the news was worse than what she anticipated. "She suffered a fall and fractured her hip." Her grip became tighter around the stack of papers and pamphlets she had in her hands. "They need to operate, but her blood pressure has skyrocketed due to the pain, so they are putting her in a room to try and get her comfortable so her blood pressure will decrease enough to be safe to operate."

"Don't they only have a certain window of time to be able to operate?"

"Yeah, seventy-two hours is the maximum they would want to wait. The doctor thinks the surgery will happen in the morning. I need to call my work, then I think I will go to the Tavern for a bit and make sure things are all right. Gran needs to get her rest."

She began walking towards the designated exit sign and I had to make quick strides just to keep up with her. "She kicked you out, huh?"

Her response came in the form of a curt nod and a dejected, "Yeah. She told me to go home."

Leave it to Tillie to be a stubborn old woman and still worrying about her granddaughter even when she was laid up and in pain in the hospital. And leave it to Miri to be the exact same way, stubborn and strong-willed trying to save the world by doing all that she could even if it meant running herself ragged in the process.

# Chapter 13

## *Miri*

I couldn't tell you exactly how long it had been since I've slung drinks at the Tavern, but bartending was the exact thing I was doing this evening.

As I was driving Bentley back to his truck and I was explaining things further, the realization of the enormity of the entire situation hit me head on.

Gran didn't have medical insurance.

It didn't make sense to me because she busted her tail to make sure she could offer her full-time employees the benefits they needed and deserved, but didn't take advantage of it for herself.

Was she convinced that she was so invincible that she'd never need it? Or was she just that stubborn? Both are more than likely true. Once I got over the initial shock of her informing the patient care tech, I tried asking her about it and her way of avoiding the question was to kick me out of her room.

Luckily, she would qualify for some financial assistance, but with her having a major surgery and then physical therapy, the bills would just continue to add up. Bentley suggested that we come up with a way to help out, but between his headache and my stress level, neither of us could think of anything off of the top of our heads.

When I called Maisie, she didn't help much with my surging stress level either. She wasn't the least affected by the fact that Gran was in the hospital and would be undergoing hip replacement surgery in the morning, she was more concerned with the fact that I was hanging out with Bentley on a regular basis. Maisie's mom, my Aunt Karen, on the other hand, was beyond thankful for the notification. She informed me that her and my Uncle Kent would be coming into town and Kent would take over Tillie's duties at the Tavern, so that portion was all taken care of.

To tell you the truth, they may be able to care of some of Tillie's expenses, but the way Gran took care of the community, this could be a way to give back to her. Show her just how much Cottage Grove loved and appreciated her.

I got back to wiping the counter clean of any spills and signs of condensation when Baylor came to the counter and practically threw himself into a barstool, then proceeded to yank at his tie, loosening it from around his neck. His apparent stress level greatly resembled my own.

"Rough day?"

He glanced up, seeing me for the first time, "Oh hey, Miri." He finished pulling the silken material free from the confines of his dress shirt and tossed it down on the countertop.

"I'll take that as a yes, what can I get ya?"

"Vodka, straight up and a Heineken…please." He looked remorseful for his actions and his rudeness, but it was all completely understandable.

I filled his glass with the clear liquid and retrieved his beer of choice from the cooler and sat them each in front of him with a small smile. My inner fixer wanted to know what was wrong, but I didn't want to pry into something that clearly wasn't my business.

Maybe his marital bliss had already fizzled out.

He was Bentley's brother and seeing him frazzled bothered me deeply. Just looking at his dark hair, he and Bentley really did have quite a bit of similar characteristics. There definitely was no denying that they were family.

His large hand curled around the glass and he threw back the entire contents with one large gulp.

"You know that's not water, right?"

I started to turn around, deciding to restock the clean glasses and leave him be because he obviously didn't feel like talking when he slammed the glass on the counter and spoke up. By some miracle, the glass didn't even manage to crack. That was some extreme force.

"Do you have someone in your life, such as a family member who only lets you down? No matter how many times you want to give them the benefit of the doubt, they continue to screw everything up like it's the only thing that they're good at?"

I took the wet bar towel in my hands and wad it up before throwing it on the wooden countertop. I leaned down on my elbows and quirked a brow. "You *do* know my cousin Maisie, right? Everything you just said describes her to a T."

He took a swig from his beer, leaving the bottle dangling in his hand, "Yeah, well, it perfectly describes my brother, too."

I blanched, "Bentley?" I managed to choke out, a bit surprised at this admission because it sounded nothing like the Bentley I knew.

"That'd be him, the guy is an absolute joke."

I scoffed, earning a shocked look of my own from Baylor. My blood was beginning to boil at his negative words. "I'm sorry, but I'm going to have to disagree with you there. Bentley is a dependable and all around caring guy."

"Yeah, if you're servicing his dick." I slammed my hand down on the counter, seriously appalled by Baylor's crass behavior. I'd never known him to exude such rudeness. He perked up his head, "Wait a minute, are you sleeping with him?"

If I was any closer to the guy and not working, I would've slapped the smugness right off of his face. The audacity. I was actually on the verge of cussing, if only Bentley could see me now. "I certainly am not," I ground out with conviction.

"Then why are you defending my brother?" He eyed me warily, as if he hadn't been well aware of my lingering crush on him from many moons ago. But it was more than that now. What was I supposed to say? Tell him that I was hopelessly and unabashedly in love with my best friend with absolutely no chance of him returning those feelings? No chance, so I took option number two and remained silent.

Taking the chicken way out. But one thing was abundantly clear, if I had ever had any doubt that I was in love with Bentley, my surge in anger just solidified it. It couldn't have been any more apparent than if I had wrapped that little tidbit and presented it with a bow.

"He won't ever grow up." I had no idea why he was pushing this further when it was perfectly clear that this conversation had fizzled out. "Just this morning he showed up at a job only to claim an emergency merely five minutes later just to get out of work. When I called him out on it, he just said he was busy like it was no big deal." My stomach sank, he got chewed out because of me? Why didn't he defend himself to Baylor?

I threw my hand up in front of me. "Stop right there!" I screeched, my agitation rising. "This morning *was* an emergency."

"How do you know this?" His interest was piqued.

"Because it was me that called him. I found Tillie unconscious on the floor this morning, and I called Bentley to come and help me down from a major freak out. He was with me at the hospital until I took him back to his truck. He had an awful headache, which I'm guessing was from your argument that I knew nothing about. Even though he felt awful, he told me that he had to go by and finish up the job from this morning!"

Baylor blinked a few times, clearly trying to process everything I had just finished saying. "My brother—"he pointed to himself. "Was with *you* at the hospital?"

"Why is that so hard for you to comprehend? Bentley has been with me a lot lately. He's my best friend. Maybe you need to take in the bigger picture here before you start casting stones. Bentley, yes his reputation is always looming over his head, but he's an amazing guy. The best ever actually." I looked off into the distance, just thinking to myself how true those words really were. I glanced back over to Baylor and smiled a small smile before I walked down towards the other end of the bar to take care of a customer who had just approached.

Several minutes had passed and when I went back down to where Baylor was seated, he still had the same stunned expression on his face. It was a pretty sad and eye opening thing to behold and witness firsthand that I knew and had more faith in Bentley than his own brother did.

"So what happened with Tillie? Is that why you're here working?"

Shaking my head in the affirmative, "It is. My Uncle and Aunt are on their way to relieve me for tomorrow. Gran goes in tomorrow morning for a hip replacement and then physical therapy after that. She doesn't have medical insurance, and it was actually Bentley who suggested that we should come up with some way to help her since she is so loved and helps out so many others."

Baylor's brows knitted together as a lady came up next to him, "Hey, can I get a bottle of Bud Light?"

"Coming up," I replied as I went to retrieve her order from the cooler. I walked back to the counter and grabbed my towel to wipe off the excess condensation. "That'll be $3." I said as I placed the bottle in front of her.

She passes a five dollar bill to me and says, "Keep the change."

"Hey, thanks!"

Baylor snapped his fingers. "I've got it. Why don't we set up an account for donations and a jar here as well as Richardt's Grocery, I'm sure Eden's dad wouldn't mind. Eden works in Eugene, but she would even say something on the air."

My spirits were already beginning to lift. I took my pad of paper out of my apron and grabbed a pen from off of the counter and began writing down his ideas. "These are fantastic!"

"Wait!" He shouted as if he had conjured up the biggest and best idea. His finger dug into the countertop repeatedly as he tapped it along with each word, "What does Tillie hold every year in this very bar?" He paused for a moment. "An auction!" He spread his arms wide as if he was the king of all ideas.

"Yeah, but she normally only holds them in December, it's April." I tapped my pen on my notepad and chewed on my bottom lip while I tried to think of a way to change up and expand on his idea. "What if we did the auction, but instead of auctioning off dates with men, like usual, we did dates with the most eligible bachelorettes of Cottage Grove instead?"

Baylor began turning the bottle of beer around with his fingertips, mulling over my further suggestion. "That could work, and you know Maisie would be chomping at the bit for it."

A tried and true laugh bubbled from my stomach, "Isn't that the truth. Maybe I need to further think on this and place a stipulation that disqualifies Maisie from participating."

"Good luck with that," he chuckled. "You would have to auction yourself off too of course,"

My smile faded, any lingering signs of laughter long gone. "Oh, I don't know about that."

"Nonsense!" He waved me off. "Any single man in his right mind would be stupid to not bid on you."

Yeah, but it wouldn't be the one man that I actually wanted, was what I wanted to really say, but again said nothing on the matter instead.

"We'll see," I replied in order to appease him. Dropping my pen to the counter, I picked up my notepad and stuffed it in my apron. "Thanks for your help," I said starting to back away.

Baylor stood from his seat and began to grab for his wallet from his back pocket, but I stopped him before he dug it out. "It's on the house."

He dropped his hand, smiled and said, "Thank you for the insight."

I couldn't help the smile that tugged at the edges of my lips and think that I could've quite possibly helped things between the Jenkins brothers, but I also could've hindered things further as well. Perhaps things between them were beyond repair.

My cell phone vibrated in my back pocket and my smile deepened once I saw Bentley's name flash across my screen.

**Bentley: What time is Tillie's surgery in the morning? I want to know what time I should be there.**

My heart skipped an actual beat after reading his words.

**Me: You have work tomorrow, you don't have to come to the hospital.**

**Bentley: You'll be at the hospital, so I'll be there. Now, what time?**

Bentley Jenkins held my whole heart in his over-worked, calloused hands. I was such a fool to give it to someone who wouldn't give me his in return. But I couldn't help it, my blissful future be damned, because I loved him.

**Me: I'll be there at 8.**

**Bentley: I'll bring coffee. See you in the morning. I know you're worried, but try and get some rest.**

I held my phone pressed against my chest and sighed at his thoughtfulness.

I wasn't any better than Baylor. My first initial assumption of Bentley was that he wasn't worthy of me. I was so wrong, despite his choices in life he was worthy of anything and everything.

I could only hope that one day he would open his eyes and see what we could be together. I only pray he would deem me worthy enough to take care of his heart. I would treat it with the utmost care and precision.

# *Chapter 14*

## *Bentley*

True to my word, I was at the hospital promptly at 8am. Baylor seemed to take my news of taking the morning off better than I ever imagined. It was almost as if something had gotten into him, such as a bit of decency against his only brother. Or maybe he had been infiltrated by those illustrious pod people. Either way, I wasn't going to push it, so I quickly got off the phone before he had a chance to change his mind and yell at me.

Along with the coffee, I brought enough donuts for Miri and myself as well as her Aunt and Uncle, whom I got to meet. Tillie was pissed at me for flaunting around deep fried pastry when she wasn't allowed to eat before surgery, but promised to issue a truce if I brought some back especially for her once she was out of recovery. I called this a win and a possibility to get in Tillie's good graces. She called it payback for us standing around her and stuffing our faces, she thought we'd be jealous of only her eating an excess amount of doughy goodness in front of us. And I might have been if I hadn't snuck one in on the way.

All these extra carbs, such as donuts and pancakes were wreaking havoc on my daily food regimen. Can't keep up this slim and trim figure by eating my weight in breakfast food on a daily basis.

Meeting Miri's Aunt and Uncle was different and it shocked the shit out of me to learn that they were Maisie's parents, they seemed so…normal. Kent was cool, a retired Chef who was chomping at the bit to get into the bars kitchen to check everything out. He didn't know much about bartending, but didn't hesitate lending a helping hand. Karen was a school teacher who went ahead and took the last month of school off so she could be here for her mom.

I learned that Miri was a stress eater. Forget about the overload of Chinese food she inhaled the night we had dinner, the girl knew how to put away some food. When I opened the box full of donuts I immediately saw her frown before I produced a bag from around my back that contained a fresh chocolate cream-filled long john that hadn't touched another assorted donut in its short life.

"Thank you," she mouthed, and the appreciation in her eyes and the smile that graced her face that was all for me made me feel invincible for the first time in my life. I couldn't exactly explain it. It was unlike anything I'd ever experienced before. It was as if I were a superhero coming through for her when no one else did.

Okay, okay. I know I was getting an over-inflated ego boost over donuts, but you didn't see that gleam in her eyes and smile. It just felt nice doing something right for a change.

"Bentley, where were you just now?" My mother's voice pulled me back to the present where I was gathered around her desk in her office with all my work orders for the week resting in front of me.

Mom took care of the billing for Jenkins Plumbing, and every Friday afternoon we had a standing meeting to go over all the jobs I handled throughout the week and the supplies I used.

"Oh, sorry, I was just thinking," I answered as I shuffled all my invoices together in a nice, neat stack. She eyed the papers curiously, even my demeanor at work was changing, I couldn't recall a time that I had actually tried to make all the papers presentable. Normally they were folded individually every which way and presented to her completely out of order.

"Well, what about, darling? Baylor said that you also took off earlier in the week for an emergency."

Leave it to my mother to try and pry and understand my life now. I stood up and moved to look out the window at her overgrown lawn that I needed to find the time to cut. "It's nothing to worry about, ma."

My phone vibrated in the holster on my hip that I wore during work hours because it's easier to reach if I'm stuck under a sink and looked at the screen. Oliver's name lit up and my brows knitted together as I looked at my mom apologetically.

"Hey, Oliver," I said smoothly into the phone.

"Bentley, it's Miri…" He sounded out of breath, but didn't actually proceed with any other information, I had to actually glance at my screen to make sure he hadn't hung up.

"What about her?" My heart rate spiked at his failure to explain further.

Dead silence.

"Oliver, what's wrong with Miri?" I raised my voice a bit more, trying to get him to snap out of whatever trance he was in.

"Oh, sorry. She's at the hospital."

"Uh huh. She's probably just visiting Tillie." This was turning into one bazaar conversation.

"No, damn I'm not explaining this well." I could just imagine him fidgeting and adjusting his glasses on his face. "She's in the hospital, as a patient. In the emergency room, actually." After hearing that Miri was hurt I checked out of anything else that was said.

"Oliver, I'm on my way." I hung up and looked back at my mom and the stunned expression on her face on my way out. "I gotta go, Ma. I'll call you later."

Oliver texted the room number to me so I didn't even stop at the overcrowded reception desk before catching the double doors before they fully closed behind a nurse.

The closer I got to her room the faster I walked and the more I started to worry about what could've been wrong. I saw Oliver slip out of the room and turn in the other direction, so I knew I was nearing closer.

Bursting through the door and then the curtain of the room, Miri was sitting upright in the bed with her hand wrapped in an ace bandage resting on her lap. My heart plummeted in my chest seeing her hurt, but I was also able to finally inhale a breath of fresh air, filling my lungs of what had been depleted on the way here.

I've never been privy to Miri's acute clumsiness, but I had a feeling by her reddened cheeks that this was number one out of many.

"Miri!" I rushed to her side of the bed and slid down into the seat closest to her. "What happened?" I went to reach for her face but refrained at the last moment optioning to rest my hand in my lap.

Her face inflamed even more so into a bright shade of red, her fingers on her uninjured hand began worrying the edge of the blanket that was wrapped around her legs. She wouldn't even look at me.

"Miri?" I asked once more.

She began turning her wrist, I guess to test out her complete range of motion, but soon after winced and sat it back in the same position it was before on her lap.

"This is nothing." She tried casting the injury aside.

"Is it broken?" The worrying in my tone couldn't be overlooked.

"No, just badly sprained. They are going to be fitting me for a brace to use instead of this, and I'll be new in no time at all." She tried appeasing me with a smile, but it was incredibly forced. She wasn't fooling anyone. "I was lucky that it was just a sprain."

"Yeah, you dodged a real bullet." I quipped, still looking at her bandaged hand. It didn't settle well with me that she hurt herself and dismissed it so easily, even more so that she wouldn't tell me how.

"Why won't you tell me what happened?" I tried once more to coax it out of her, and I could tell by the way she opened and closed her mouth repeatedly that I was closer to her finally spilling.

"It's embarrassing…"

"Embarrassing should really be your middle name." I hated to break it to her, but by what she's told me, this is only a fact.

"Bentley," she chastised and reached around trying to smack my shoulder. She must've had some pain medication, because my reflexes were like lightening compared to hers. It was as if she was moving in slow motion.

"You know I'm only kidding…or am I?"

She rolled her eyes at me which let me know that she wasn't taking it to heart. You never really knew if a woman was going to go berzerk over a snide comment, joking or not. Miri took a deep breath and focused on the blanket that was covering her legs. I could just make out the tremble in her hands, she was really scared to tell me. What in the world happened?

"I was practicing walking in high heels around my apartment." I had to lean in closer to hear her as it was barely coming out above a whisper.

I jerked back, not expecting that to be what she told me. "Why in the hell were you doing that?" I couldn't fathom why she would do something against her better judgement. She knew that she was a walking accident disaster, she told me so herself at Baylor and Eden's wedding.

"I was trying to appear more desirable so men would bid on me." She hurried out all in one breath.

"Why the fuck would you want to do that for?" I was well aware that my voice was escalating almost resembling a yell and the fact that I was more or less repeating my words.

Miri cowered herself back into the flimsy mattress on the bed, and I felt like an asshole for snapping at her.

"You said yourself that you preferred women in heels." Shit, I had said that, but that was before...

"Never mind what I said, let's get back to what you said, so men would bid on you...for what?" My hands wrapped around the arms of the chair I was occupying and tightened as my anger continued to grow.

Her posture stiffened until her back was ramrod straight. She was frightened as hell, but still willing to stand up to me. "Because we are going to hold a bachelorette auction to raise money for Gran. I was just worried that no one will bid on me, so I'll have to pick out a great song since heels are obviously out. You'll have to help me." She was talking so animatedly with her hands, even with her sprained wrist. I couldn't believe how excited she was when I was barely holding myself together.

It hit me like a tidal wave, nearly taking me down with it. My first ever experience with jealousy surged through me as I shot up out of my seat. "No!" was all I said, was all I could say.

"No...you won't help me pick out a song?"

"No, you aren't doing it." The thought of any other man putting his dirty paws on her made me want to go on a rampage just to try and curb my all-consuming rage that was furiously building within me.

"Excuse me?" She threw her legs over the side of the bed, preparing herself to stand. "I most certainly am. I was leery about it at first, but my grandmother took me in when I had no one…Now, it's my turn to be the one to stand up and help her out."

I crossed my arms in front of my chest standing rooted to the spot in front of her, not budging in the slightest. "I stand by my decision, you're not doing it."

Surging to her feet, she stood just centimeters from me, her finger poking into my chest. I had never seen Miri so worked up, but with the fire flaring in her eyes it was one helluva turn on.

"I don't know who you think you are, but you aren't my dad and you sure as hell aren't my boyfriend! You don't do the boyfriend thing, remember? So stop acting like it!" She abruptly stopped her words as if she said too much, but then something dawned on her. "That's it!" Her voice raised even louder, "Your ego is still bruised because I wouldn't sleep with you!" That's what she thought? I blanched as if I'd been slapped. To tell you the truth, I'd almost prefer the slapping to the alternative; my heart felt like it was literally breaking open in my chest. "News Flash Bentley, it's for a date and to help my gran. Doesn't mean I'm going to go spread my legs for the highest bidder." Tears welled up in her eyes and her finger prodding in my chest might as well have been a knife. "I'm not Maisie and I'm not you. And I'm sure as hell not a whore!"

She fell to the bed and buried her face in her hands.

And that was my cue.

I was breaking my promise to Miri and walking away, it was all I could do.

Forget my pride and forget my dignity, if that's what Miri thought of me, then there really was no reason for me to be here.

"Leaving so soon?" Oliver surprised me, but I was so crestfallen that it didn't faze me in the slightest. I glanced up for the first time in the middle of the hallway, seeing him head my way carefully carrying three cups of coffee. "The coffee here sucks, so gas station coffee will have to do." He handed me the cup that was perched strategically on top of another.

I raised it to him, "Thanks, man." My voice sounded dejected and so unlike my own. "I gotta go, but Miri probably needs you."

"Wow, you sound like you just lost your childhood dog." Leave it to Oliver to say it straight and put a veterinary spin on it.

"Yeah, something like that."

I sidestepped past him and continued on down the never ending hallway replaying the last ten minutes, adding it to everything that's gone wrong in my life.

Going back over what was said I realized that I made Miri so angry that she cursed, twice. Instead of being able to revel in my accomplishment, I wanted to punch myself for pushing her to that level. So instead, I threw my full cup of coffee against the side of my truck.

# Chapter 15

## *Bentley*

Sometime throughout the day I ran out of beer, so I had the brilliant idea to head to Tillie's. I didn't know if I was hoping for a glimpse of Miri or what it was. Apparently I was a glutton for punishment.

Once I paid the cab and threw open the front doors, I immediately saw my brother and sister-in-law as well as their friends Dean and Julia, laughing around a large round table. I hadn't seen Julia since the wedding and had done my best to steer clear of Dean, but the two seemed to be pretty cozy with one another, which wasn't really a surprise to me.

Fine and fucking dandy for them.

Weaving around each of the tables, I stopped short once I saw Miri's Uncle Kent at the bar. I didn't know if they'd caught wind of mine and Miri's fight, but I sure as shit didn't anticipate finding out. I turned around in my spot and began moving towards my brother's table. The only two spots open were between Baylor and Dean and this could ultimately end badly, but at this point, what did I have to lose?

"I would be thrilled," Julia exclaimed as she looked lovingly at Dean. There was so much lovey doviness soaring around this table that there was a good possibility of it making me sick.

"What are we thrilled about?" I asked as I placed myself in between my brother and my biggest enemy. I could literally hear Dean sneer as I walked up and made my presence known.

Baylor looked at me with disgust, which was pretty much his normal glance of endearment towards me. "Jesus, Bentley, do you ever keep it in your pants?" he admonished while looking at my rumpled clothing.

I peered down at myself and my wrinkled jeans and polo that I pulled from the top of my laundry pile before coming here. Wearing just plain boxer briefs went against the dress code of this establishment and finding clean clothes took too much time and effort when I could be getting my drink on.

I shrugged a shoulder and replied, "Actually, I have." Glancing around and taking in each of their stunned expressions, it was clear that they didn't believe me. "Yeah, I can't believe it either," I muttered while rolling my eyes.

The table remained silent until Dean began chuckling to my left. "Well, color me surprised, Bentley Jenkins is wrecked over a woman. Never thought I'd see the day." He kept chuckling as he lifted his glass of what appeared to be bourbon only for me to intercept it in midair.

"What the…" Dean growled. I must either be drunker than I was aware of or I had a death wish. You know the old saying about never poking a sleeping bear, well I just fucking poked Dean Parker.

I lifted the glass to my lips and took a small drink. Hm… Wild Turkey wouldn't have been my first choice of bourbon. "I'm not wrecked over a fucking woman." I was totally wrecked over *the* woman. Miri.

Raising my hand in the air, I signaled for the bartender in our section. Once he approached us I raised Dean's mostly empty glass in the air towards him and jingled the ice around, "Can we get two more of these?" I asked and once he nodded in confirmation I quickly tossed back the remainder that was in the glass.

"Yeah, for some reason I don't believe you," Baylor goaded. He almost looked as if he knew something that I didn't, but how would he? Unless Ma mentioned something about the phone call yesterday.

I finally pulled out the chair I was standing behind and plopped down into it. "Believe what you want, brother of mine," I responded gruffly.

At last, everyone resumed their conversations around me and I was invisible once again, I almost preferred it that way. My how the times had changed, before I would stop at literally nothing to focus on being the center of attention and now I was content being out of it.

My fresh bourbon on the rocks appeared in front of me, and I chose that exact moment to look up at all the other patrons. My eyes widened in shock and my body flinched as I silently cursed, "Fuck," under my breath.

My stare was transfixed on Miri and I couldn't look away. She seemed to be put together better than I was and was obviously fairing better as well. Now my jealousy extended to the fact that she was taking our entire fight better. But her eyes were equally as focused on mine.

It'd only been a full day, but I was miserable that we'd had a fight. Oliver was standing next to her and he guided her by the elbow to the back office.

My eyes flashed to Julia and I had to quickly try to mask the pain from their depths. She smiled a small smile and I could see the wheels turning in her mind. With a curt shake of my head no, I was conveying that I didn't want her to pry and thankfully she left it at that.

Raising my glass to my lips, I took another long gulp of the mediocre bourbon allowing the fire to travel straight to my stomach.

Eden finally spoke up and I focused my attention on her, but then wished I hadn't. "You know what I just realized, Jules? You and I finally got our happy ever after."

I coughed in my glass, nearly choking on its contents. "Happy ever afters are for fucking losers." I downed the remainder of my drink, stood slamming the chair underneath the table and stormed off in the direction of the bathroom.

Looking at my reflection in the mirror that was placed over the sink, what I saw staring back at me, I didn't like. My hair was a disheveled mess and I didn't think I got more than an hour of sleep last night. How was Miri looking just as gorgeous as ever when I looked as if I've been drug through the ringer?

*How did I get here?* Not physically here in this bathroom of course, but here in this situation. I didn't know what the hell to do. I needed guidance, and the first person that came to mind to ask was the person who the problem was about.

# Chapter 16

## Miri

I reluctantly drug myself into Tillie's, or I should say Oliver did. He forced me to get out of bed and take a shower since I looked like death and go on about my day. He wasn't one for doling out good advice, but in this circumstance he was right, I had things to do for Gran and I couldn't get them done from underneath my covers being mopey.

Gran pulled through her surgery with flying colors as well as colorful language. She's going to have to learn to take things easier, which will be a feat in itself for her. She was already arguing with the doctor's about not wanting to stay at the rehabilitation center for her physical therapy, which refers to the colorful language, I had never heard such words come from my Gran's mouth. So now Aunt Karen or myself would be transporting her back and forth for PT on a daily basis. Not the most ideal solution, but it was the one that made her the most comfortable, therefore we'll pull together and do what we have to do, for her.

That brings me to why I was at Tillie's on a Saturday night. I wished that it was to partake in a few drinks, but that wouldn't bode well with the meds I was taking due to my wrist injury. My very stupid injury that I wish I could just erase, then the fight with Bentley would've never happened.

So tonight, Oliver and I would be taking care of all the ordering and bills for the month ahead so no one else had to worry about it. One less thing to check off of our always growing to do list.

I took a glimpse around the room and stopped short when my eyes locked on Bentley's. I didn't expect to see him here, but leave it to me that he'd be the first person I'd subconsciously seek out.

He looked awful, his hair an atrocious mess; he almost looked as if he'd just been privy to a bathroom romp. Knowing Bentley, that's exactly what he'd done and already thrown her away. But then his eyes were sad and sullen like he didn't get a wink of sleep last night.

Oliver grasped my arm, guiding me to the backroom and thankfully pulling my eyes off of Bentley's. I was having a harder time with this than I thought. Sure. It was a fight and many friends had them, but I said some horrible, awful things to him that I could never take back, and things just felt so final. As if our friendship always had a looming expiration date and our time had already elapsed.

Oliver reached over and flipped on the light switch, illuminating Tillie's office under the fluorescent lights and released my arm. I walked over and flung myself into her chair causing it to roll back several inches on the linoleum floor.

"Why couldn't we come before the bar opened and any customers were here?"

"And miss all that tension and awkwardness?" I shot Oliver a look, one that translated to that he didn't need to mess with me right now. "We could've, but someone decided to wallow herself in pity and misery."

I rolled up to Tillie's computer that needed replaced and fired back as I turned the decrepit machine on, "It's a wonder that I keep you around."

"Please--" he scoffed, "we've been friends so long you wouldn't know how to function without me."

I fired back, "And vice versa." Bentley and I had only been friends a fraction of the amount of time that Oliver and I had, and I'm finding it hard to function without him. He's ingrained himself into my heart so deeply, that it's really going to be hard to let him go.

"Absolutely," he pulled up the extra chair next to mine and allowed me to lay my head on his shoulder as soon as he sat down.

"I love you, Ollie." His arm came up around my back and he began rubbing along my shoulder trying to comfort me.

I wanted nothing more than to talk to Bentley, but I wasn't going to be the one to crack. We each owed one another an apology, in a big way, but I didn't even know if he thought there was anything left to fight for.

The computer finally finished booting up, and over the next hour Oliver and I did all the paperwork for the upcoming month. Purchasing was done, bills were paid, and employees were scheduled.

"I'm ready to go home and indulge in a giant tub of ice cream. The most fattening kind we can find," I whimpered as I flicked off the lights.

We walked out of Gran's office and immediately I saw that their table was still fully occupied, including Bentley. That he lasted this long in the presence of his brother had to account for something, right?

"Hey," I stopped and looked at Oliver, "I need to go over and ask Julia and Eden about the auction, I'll be right back. Will you turn the light back on in the office?"

"Sure --" he seemed rather reluctant, "are you going to be all right?"

"Thanks, I'll be fine." He faltered, acting a bit hesitant for me to go over there. "Go!"

I turned back and resumed walking, but this time towards Bentley. He meticulously watched my every movement, especially when I straightened my posture and readjusted my shirt. His eyes flared when I approached him between Julia and Eden, his eyes almost seemed a bit hazy. Was he that drunk?

Everyone ceased their conversation and looked up at me and I almost felt ridiculous for coming over and interrupting, especially when a phone call would've been a little more convenient and a little less awkward.

"Hey, guys…" I tried to say cheerfully, "Bentley." My eyes looked to his purely on their own accord as if it was programmed into my brain to constantly seek out Bentley. The best I got out of him was a grunt in acknowledgment. At least it was almost a word and not just a stare down. I didn't know if this meant he was talking to me or not.

"Julia, Eden, can I talk to you for a moment?" I asked as I began to pick at my nails exposing the brace on my wrist that I meant to keep hidden.

# *Chapter 17*

## *Bentley*

My fist slammed down on the tabletop, "They have nothing to say to you!"

"Bentley!" Eden chastised as if that was supposed to bother me.

Then Julia grabbed Miri by the hand inspecting her brace and I wanted to rip her hand off. I had officially lost it. *It* being my goddamn mind.

"What happened to your hand?" Julia asked, concern in her eyes as she stood from the table, Eden following suite.

I took the liberty of answering for Miri, "Fucking stupidity," I bit out and instantly regretted my choice of words when I saw tears well up in Miri's eyes. The girls followed Miri in a huff, and I just slunk down in my seat just a bit further.

"What the hell is your problem, man?" Baylor asked, his tone furious. "You're even more of a dick than you normally are." That was the thing, I wasn't normally a dick to anyone but Baylor and Dean, so this was stooping to a new low.

I said nothing because once again, he was right. Baylor was *always* right. And I will always be a downright moron who can't seem to do *anything* right.

The girls came back without Miri and remorse set in on just how badly I acted. I wanted to go off and look for her, the need was consuming me. Julia took her seat all while shooting me her death glare. Eden, on the other hand, didn't sit right away. Instead, she meandered over to my side of the table and smacked the back of my head before wandering back to her seat.

Rubbing over the place she hit me, I asked, "What was that for?"

"For being an ass!" She leaned against the table and hollered at me. Baylor looked positively pleased with his wife, Dean was back to chuckling. Laugh it up you schmuck. I'd like to shove my foot so far up his ass that...

Baylor pulled me from my plotting when he asked the million dollar question, "What did Miri want?"

Eden laid both of her hands on the table, "As most everyone knows, Tillie had a hip replacement the other day. Apparently, she took a pretty nasty fall and doesn't have medical insurance for herself." She was just repeating things that I already knew, and I was almost positive I knew what Miri needed them for. "Miri is having an auction for bachelorettes and wanted our help." She exuded excitement, Eden loved it when people needed her help on things, me on the other hand, my hands proceeded to curl into fists under the table. "She wants me to emcee and Julia..."

"She's not participating!" Dean boasted loud and clear. Maybe he would be on my side, for once.

Julia placed her hand over his, "Not to be in it, sweetheart. I told her that I was happily taken."

"Damn right you are," he curled his arm around her neck and pulled her to his side.

"You said you'd help, right?" Baylor looked at Eden.

"You know I did."

"Good, because the auction was my idea. I came in the other night after Bentley pissed me off and after Tillie's fall." My brother looked at me. "Miri told me that you were at the hospital with her all day, why didn't you just tell me the truth?"

"Doesn't matter," I snapped. "Get back to it being your idea." My nostrils were flaring, I was well past the point of being pissed.

"She was trying to find ways to help raise money and I suggested an auction. She came up with the idea of it being women and I told her that she should be in it, too." He looked at the rest of the table and said, "Could you imagine the bids she would get?"

My head went hazy and there was a ringing in my ears. I stood up, knocking my chair back and grabbed my brother by the collar of his shirt and jerked him out of his chair, pulling him to my face.

"You put the idea into Miri's head about being auctioned off for a date? That was the main reason behind her getting injured." Baylor's eyes were wide, I wouldn't call them scared, just well aware. "I outta kick your ass!"

Once I came back down to earth, I heard Eden gasp, felt Dean's hand on my arm, and then looked over at Julia as she eyed me cautiously. I slowly released my hold around Baylor's shirt, picked up my chair and silently took my seat.

I'd never felt more on display. My emotions were fucking with my carefree vibe.

Julia asked in a calming tone, "It happened, didn't it?"

I exasperatedly ran my hands through my hair, too ashamed to look at anyone but Julia. "What happened?"

"She knocked you on your ass, just as I explained it would happen to you someday. Happened sooner than I expected." She seemed pretty satisfied with herself.

"Would anyone care to explain to the rest of us what the hell is going on?" Dean asked, almost as perplexed as I was.

"Bent's in love," Baylor chimed in with the biggest smile on his face, making me sit straight up in my chair.

I look to him incredulously, "I am?" I quirked a brow just as the realization hit me and completely blindsided me. "Jesus fuck, I am."

Everything was perfectly clear now. The reasoning behind the jealousy and anger, why I constantly wanted to be only around her. And not to mention the extreme lack of wanting to partake in meaningless sexual exploitations, that alone should've been a big fucking red sign. I was completely in love with Miriam Armstrong. And there was a good chance that now she wanted absolutely nothing to do with me.

# Chapter 18

## Miri

I was succumbing to all-encompassing nervous jitters. As I stood under the spray in the shower, I allowed the hot water to scald my skin. I kept going back and forth toying with the idea of either passing out, or going for the extreme gusto and throwing up.

The auction was tonight and I didn't know how it would be received. Oliver helped me print out and pass around flyers, letting Cottage Grove know about the event. But ultimately there was no guarantee that I wouldn't make an idiot of myself, and in the back of my mind I was sure it would all be for nothing.

Gran was doing much better and at two weeks post-op was excelling in physical therapy. It still wore her out to move a whole lot, but at least she was following the doctor's orders and taking things easier.

A sudden pounding on the bathroom door startled me almost making me lose my footing on the slippery ceramic of the bathtub. My knee jerk reaction was to place my hands on the wall to try and help stabilize myself. I instantly winced, then cried out as searing pain radiated up my forearm and extending to my elbow. My sprained wrist was on the mend and beginning to feel a bit better, but I was afraid this little incident just placed me back at square one.

I cradled my arm against my body as the water continued to pelt my bare skin and a few seconds later Oliver stuck his head in through a small opening in the doorway. A yelp escaped my mouth and I immediately moved to cover myself, even though the shower curtain was still firmly in place blocking out our view of one another. You'd almost think for as long as we've lived together this wouldn't be as awkward, but it was.

"Oliver, what are you doing?" I screeched, the echo inside of the shower making my voice come out much louder than I anticipated.

"I came to tell you to get a move on, but then I heard you cry out in pain. Are you all right?" he asked, concerned.

I jerked back the edge of the shower curtain, leaving me just enough room to fit my soaked head through. Squinting in his general direction, I could only make out the shape of his body. "I was good until you scared the bejesus out of me by banging on the door. Scaring me into injuring myself won't get me to move any faster, hate to break it to you."

I could just imagine the amusement that danced in his pale blue depths, "Well, I 'hate to break it ya'," he said mocking me, even went as far as air quoting it. "But, Eden called and they will be on their way soon. So this time I won't scare you, but I am going to put emphasis on the fact that you need to get a move on!"

"Crud!" I jumped, blocking out the pain in my wrist as I turned the shower faucet off and blindly stuck my hand out trying to feel around for my towel on the hook. At least now I didn't have time to feel anxious about tonight, I was in too big of a rush.

It's been said before on more than one occasion that I could be a world class procrastinator. Everyone had to have a downfall, or several in my case, but right now I wished that statement didn't hold any weight of truth.

Finding something to wear hadn't even crossed my fashion deprived brain, and I literally was grasping at straws while standing in front of my closet. What I wore needed to be dressy, but the first dress that came to mind was unfortunately wrinkled.

I hardly ever wore dresses because I felt out of place in them and the only ones I owned were ones that I've worn around most of the people attending tonight.

The only distinct possibility was buried, way…way back in the far depths of my closet. One of those out of sight out of mind instances. I wasn't even one hundred percent certain that it was still back there and intact.

I stretched my arm back shoving away all my other clothes and felt the silky material as I grabbed ahold of the hanger. Maisie made me buy this dress when I was feeling sorry for myself. The irony was that I think I'll feel sorry for myself by wearing it. Dropping my wet towel onto the floor of my bedroom, I stepped into what little scrap of material there was to the 'dress.'

As I braced my arm in front of my chest to hold my girls up as well as the dress, I called to Oliver to come zip up the back. He came into my room in a pair of blue jeans, chucks on his feet, one of his corny t-shirts that made the man, and I guess his idea of making it dressy was to wear a black suit jacket, completing the ensemble.

His eyes grew wide once he caught sight of either the short dress or all of the exposure my poor white legs were getting.

"That's it, I'm just going to wear a wrinkled dress," I exclaimed, second guessing myself.

"You will not," he scoffed, taking off his glasses and wiping them clean with the bottom hem of his shirt before replacing them and continuing to stare. "If Bentley doesn't bid on you, maybe I should."

I stomped my foot, "Oh hush and zip me so we can go. Besides Bentley won't be there, and he would never bid on a date with me." Sadness swept over my tone at the mere mentioning of his name. I hadn't been in contact with Bentley since the night he lashed out at me in front of his brother and God at Tillie's. I didn't know how to feel about the entire situation anymore, but I did know that I missed him with every fiber of my soul.

I felt the material encase around me as Oliver drew the zipper up my back. I walked in front of my floor-length mirror to take a look at myself. Adjusting the top of the dress and making sure that the girls were ok, this would be the most uncomfortable I've ever been and since it was strapless, there was no way I could wear a bra.

I shook my head with the slightest amount of disgust when Oliver stepped up behind me and held my head still so I had no other choice but to look at myself. He brought his head forward and rested his chin on my shoulder and said, "You look stunning, Miri. If I didn't consider you as my sister, I might have developed a little crush. Just be yourself tonight, the person everyone knows and loves."

Breathing a deep sigh of relief, I squared back my shoulders trying to channel as much confidence that I could muster. If anything, I could focus on the positive aspects of the outfit. I slipped my feet into my hot pink ballet flats, put a silver dangle bracelet on my uninjured wrist to try and stray focus from the eyesore brace on my other. I even realized that the dress had pockets, which was an added bonus.

"Can I get Cinderella to her ball now?" Oliver asked, exasperated as he held out his elbow for me to take hold of.

"Oh all right. I'll just braid my hair on the way." There wasn't time for anything else so it would have to make do.

Several vehicles were already parked at Tillie's including a Jenkins Plumbing work truck that had me careening up in my seat until I realized it was Baylor's.

"You should just reach out to him," Oliver interjected.

"When did you become the voice of reason?" I joked, but ultimately knowing that he was right.

I rushed in through the door ready to scramble to get things done when I halted in place noticing that everything was set and ready to go down to the last smallest detail. Crisp black linens were covering the otherwise simple wooden tables and each was all topped off with a little lit votive candle that was nestled in a beautiful frosted glass mason jar.

Eden was standing on the stage holding the microphone up to her lips, "Check one, two. Hey, Miri!" she shrieked and began waving her arm once she saw me standing there with my jaw slacked open.

"I am so sorry everyone! I promise that I didn't intend on being so late."

Baylor came up beside me. "It's no problem, we were here and your aunt Karen here," he used his thumb to indicate over his shoulder to my aunt who I smiled and waved at, "started letting us know what to do." He cupped his hand around the side of his mouth and whispered, "You can tell she's Tillie's daughter, she's bossy just like her."

I couldn't help but giggle at his comparison between the two of them. "You're absolutely right, they definitely do know how to bark out orders," I said slyly.

I walked out further on the floor just trying to take everything in. My vision of this evening coming to life. "You guys, this all looks incredible. How can I ever thank you?"

"Holy wow!" Julia exclaimed, coming out of Gran's office teetering on four-inch heels that just had me envisioning and then cringing at the spill I would take in those. "That dress is fabulous." She walked closer towards me and pointed at my normal braided hair, "but the way you can thank me is by getting your hot piece of ass into Tillie's office and letting me have free reign to work my magic on that mess of hair."

"How can I argue with that?"

"Oh, you don't want to argue with Julia, it won't end well," Dean muttered before leaning down and planting a kiss on Julia's cheek. They were adorable together, and seeing them made me a bit jealous as well as made me realize that I wanted what they had.

I wanted it so badly, and I wanted it with Bentley.

Julia snapped her fingers, "Let's go, we don't have much time."

I hesitated in front of Baylor. "Don't worry, we have everything handled and if not, we've got Karen to whip us into shape." He smiled and I heard Julia's clacking heels slow down so I knew I didn't have much time. I looked down at my cell phone in my hands. "How's Bentley doing?"

Although they weren't close for being brothers, I knew he would've talked to him sometime in the last few weeks.

"Uh, you know." He scratched the back of his head. "Bentley is Bentley." I got the feeling that he was beating around the bush. Translation could very well mean that he didn't even miss me being around. He could be going through so many women that he's completely forgotten about me.

"That's what I was afraid of." I tried my best to keep my head held high as I made my way around the tables towards the awaiting Julia. Even more so, I was trying my hardest to not shed a tear. I needed to do one thing and then put any and all thoughts of Bentley to bed for the remainder of the evening.

Opening my text app and scrolling to Bentley's name, I typed in three small, simple words, hit send and placed my phone in Gran's desk drawer so I wouldn't have any further distractions.

"Sit, chickadee," Julia pointed to a chair and I complied not saying a word. I felt her untangle my braid before she began brushing through my long locks. Perhaps sitting here with virtually nothing to do wasn't the brightest idea; now my mind was free to wander. It also allowed my nerves to return.

All I could do was pray that this evening was a success and nothing disastrous occurred.

The metaphor that popped in my head was like asking a shark not to attack; virtually inevitable.

# *Chapter 19*

## *Bentley*

I paced back and forth along the floor between my kitchen and living room, likely to wear a hole in my rug. I made the final decision to attend the auction only an hour ago. Afterwards, I received the first text from Miri in almost two weeks, letting me know that I was making the right decision.

**Miri: I miss you!**

Reading those words put a smile on my face for the first time in just as long.

After coming to the realization that I was in love with Miri, I didn't reach out to her because I knew she deserved better than me. I have a despicable past that could come back to haunt me at any given time, allowing the possibility to hinder our relationship.

It hurt to think that I couldn't actually be with the first and only person I've ever exposed those feelings to because of how I chose to live my life.

It was only after the extreme revelation that I've been changing my ways the entire time I've known Miri did I realize that she wasn't beating me up about my sluttiness, so why should I?

Then I recalled the last time I had sex and I almost fainted from disbelief. The beginning of January. It was now May, that's a new record even for myself. But it told me that my heart has always been Miri's, without me consciously knowing it.

So now I paced in my monkey suit hoping like hell I could win the girl for once and that there would be a small chance that she felt the same way.

The rational thing to do would've been to smooth things over beforehand, then she wouldn't have to be in the auction at all, but I was under the assumption that she was mad at me, so if I won her in the bidding she'd have to go on a date with me and then she'd ultimately have to hear me out as well.

I've wasted enough time twiddling my fucking thumbs, I was ready to get this thing over and done with so I could confess my love for the first time ever.

Mark this day down in the fucking history books.

As I pulled into Tillie's, the lot was already packed, hardly any parking to spare. I hoped Oliver didn't hate me and read my message asking to save me a seat. The Sheriff was stationed at the door, as he generally was at these events, making sure it didn't go over capacity allowed by the Fire Marshall. I was lucky that I got here when I did because I heard him cut off entrance three people back.

It wasn't very often that I got nervous, but I had butterflies batting around in my stomach like some pussy. I needed a drink to tamp that shit down because it was quickly becoming a nuisance.

Finally, I spotted Oliver sitting at a table with my brother and Dean. Since calling me out, things between us hadn't been as strained, but I wouldn't go as far as to call us best buds either. No, that title would always be reserved for Miri, whether she chose to accept it or not being entirely up to her. I could think of a few more titles I'd like to give her as well.

I spotted a drink in front of the only empty chair at the table and wondered if it was meant for someone else.

"Is this seat taken?" I asked and then glanced at the three seated men.

"It's for you, I just took the liberty of ordering it for you so you wouldn't have to think of touching mine," Dean answered, hovering over his own drink tenaciously trying to guard it. The thought of taking his drink anyways briefly crossed my mind, but I'd rather have my face intact for tonight, but it didn't stop me from having a bit of fun.

I pulled the free chair next to Oliver out from underneath the table, situating it to where I could see the stage clearly and said before picking my drink up off of the black tablecloth, "Sweetheart, you didn't have to. You really are so thoughtful." I took my seat and glanced at Dean before flashing a half-hearted smile and batting my naturally long lashes in his direction.

The entire exchange earned me an eye roll before he picked up his glass and took a drink. "You're a dumbass."

I placed my hand under my chin, and replied dreamily, "Oh Deano, that's the nicest thing you've ever said to me."

"Bent, I wouldn't press your luck, I think Dean is feeling mighty generous at the moment, you don't want that to expire," Baylor warned. Always being the voice of reason.

Once again, he was right, it only took one match for me to go up in flames and in this instance, Dean was a fire starter ready to burn.

I threw my hands up in front of me, "All right, I'm done, besides Eden just took the stage." We all turned and focused on her. My sister-in-law really was in her element basking in the limelight. Give her a microphone and a stage or DJ booth and she would shine brighter than any star in the sky.

"Good evening! How is everyone tonight?" She took a moment to look at each every person with a smile on her face. I saw Julia sneak around to sit behind the table used for karaoke. I knew that she was helping tonight and being in charge of the music must be her assignment.

"I know this is a little out of the norm, but we thought we'd give the guys a chance for a date this time as well as raise money for our dear Tillie."

A spotlight flashed in the middle of the room illuminating Tillie's seated form. Typical to Tillie fashion, she was sporting an extremely loud shade of pink lipstick with her hair piled high on top of her head. Her choice of lip color screamed 1980 while her bouffant was the 1950s. Homegirl was stuck in past decades.

"Let's not delay things any further, I give you our bachelorettes." Eden drew out her arm as five women took the stage. I automatically recognized Maisie and Briar, the girl from Miri's work. But no Miri.

Did she decide against participating?

I turned to look at the table, then Tillie's closed office door. I knew this wasn't Miri's thing, but she was dead set on doing it for her gran.

Dean leaned in on his elbow towards me and whispered, "Julia just texted me saying Miri got sick from her nerves, but she's getting cleaned up and will be out in a bit."

My stomach sank hearing that her nerves were getting the better of her, but ultimately she placed herself in this predicament.

Meanwhile, Eden had started the bidding on bachelorette number one. I missed her name, but she looked like the hygienist from Dr. Holmes', our local Dentist's office.

"Sold! For two hundred and fifty dollars!"

"I'd like to see someone try and bid higher than Julia did on me," Dean said smugly. "That had to have set some kind of record," he added, gloating while we all clapped the highest bidder.

I wasn't aware of the fact that we were all going to sit around and reminisce about who raised the most money on a single bid. I bet if we were to add up all the times Baylor and I had participated, my overall amount would trump both Dean's one time and all of Baylor's combined.

"Ok, next up is Maisie Vickers," Eden's voice was monotone and flat, she was clearly less than enthused. No one dug Maisie around here. Although, she was compared often to being the female equivalent of myself, she was a downright gold digger. Low and behold that very song began blaring through the speakers and aptly so. "Maisie, is our very own Tillie's granddaughter," I heard a scoff come from the crowd that closely resembled Tillie's voice. "As well as an employee at the Tavern. Shall we start the bidding at fifty dollars?" Maisie seemed pissed, which if I had to guess would be because of the choice of song. Julia was blaringly enjoying herself and found it amusing as her head was tipped back laughing her ass off.

Eden's lips were set in a thin line as she glanced around the room, giving everyone ample time to bid if they chose to do so. "Come on people, this is for a good cause! No one?" She placed a hand on her hip while Maisie continued to huff and cross her arms in front of her chest. "How about thirty dollars?"

Maisie had surely made her rounds around this room several times before but evidently hadn't made a lasting impression on anyone in particular. Her mouth flew open and at any moment she looked as if she could bust out throwing a major bitch fit. Oh, she was pissed all right, and I had to give it my all to suppress down my laughter that threatened to erupt.

Eden narrowed her eyes at the crowd, but I could just make out the self-satisfied amusement playing at her lips. She was enjoying this. You see, out of all the guys at this table, Baylor was the closest to hooking up with her and that fact alone irked Eden royally.

She thrust her hip out even more, resting her hand where it protruded, "Twenty dollars? Somebody has to deem Maisie worthy of a twenty. Come on, it's almost a guaranteed home run with her."

Baylor began coughing uncontrollably and I had officially reached my peak, I couldn't contain my laughter any longer.

"Twenty dollars!" Was yelled from the patrons, and simultaneously every head turned trying to spot the one person amongst two hundred or so who spoke up for a date with Maisie.

The spotlight landed on Dr. Holmes, the town dentist as he shielded his eyes from the bright light with his arm.

"Twenty dollars going once!" She pointed out towards the awaiting doctor. "Twice, SOLD!" Eden announced his winning prize producing a solid grin on his face. But from the stage you heard a stomp of a heel at the same time Maisie groaned and stomped down the stairs.

The sound of only one person clapping was heard and with one glance I learned it was Tillie. She cupped her hands around her mouth and hollered at Maisie, "Must be true love, Mais! He's your big spender seeing as how he spent eighteen dollars too much!"

Gasps and snickers were heard from all around the room.

Eden looked at Julia stunned, then spoke into the mic, "Now, I'm not sure, but I think her own grandma called her a two dollar whore."

"Miss Independent" by Destiny's Child began playing and I knew right away that Briar was up next. She just gave off the whole 'take no shit' vibe. It really surprised the hell out of me that she was up there being put on display in the first place.

"Moving on to Briar Prescott. She's a newer resident of our wonderful town but has made quite an impact. When she isn't throwing around her 'cheery' disposition at Cottage Grove Massage Specialists, you'll find her pursuing her true passion of art. She recently dedicated her time to paint the fabulous mural you'll find in the new children's section of the library. I'll start the bidding at fifty dollars."

The things you learn at these functions. She was quiet, and you probably wouldn't have known about her artistic side. Although, the half-sleeved tattoo she had on her left arm was on display with her sleeveless dress.

The first initial bid was called right out of the gate and she was up to two hundred dollars within a matter of seconds.

"Two-fifty!" Oliver yelled as he threw his arm in the air.

Briar's eyes widened, obviously she was just as surprised as all of us.

"Two hundred and fifty going once, twice, sold to Dr. Oliver Tildon!"

Baylor grabbed ahold of Oliver's shoulder in congratulations. Oliver turned towards the table, straightening out the lapels on his jacket, "That's how it's done boys. Miri may not have wanted a date that she had to pay for, but I certainly have no qualms about it."

"I'm sorry, what?" I had to make sure I was hearing him correctly.

"People kept pressuring Miri to bid on you at the last auction since she's been in love with you for like ever. She didn't want to con you into a date that she had to pay for."

I was completely confused. "Wait, Miri loves me?"

"Seriously? Are you really that obtuse? For the longest time she always thought she wasn't good enough for you. Don't you see why she stuck you in the friend zone? She couldn't bear to sleep with you once and have you toss her aside like all of the rest. Of course she didn't see you two really becoming friends, but she's never expressed her feelings to you because she'd rather have you as a friend than not at all. And…I've said too much."

"No," I shook my head, still trying to process everything he just said. "No, you said just enough." I knew she had a childhood crush and there was a definite degree of attraction, but to actually hear that she felt the exact same way as I did gave me a burst of another feeling new to me; hope.

Rubbing my hands together, I sat back in my seat and took a good long look around the room at all the chumps. I was going to bring it when it was Miri's turn because she was mine.

Eden announced the winner of the other woman in which I missed the entire exchange. But it was just as well because she didn't matter in the least bit anyways.

I was literally on the edge of my seat waiting for Eden to call Miri's name. I also hoped that she was feeling better.

"Ok, now we have one last bachelorette for this evening, she's feeling a bit nervous so can we show some love for Cottage Grove's own sweetheart, Miri Armstrong!"

My heart thumped wildly in my chest knowing that at any moment I would get a glimpse of Miri, I had missed her over these past few days. Everyone promptly began cheering and clapping, Oliver even joined in when he stuck two fingers in his mouth and released a loud whistle.

The spotlight followed Miri as she made her way towards the stage, her cheeks inflamed from being the center of attention. Catcalls were made from several of the guys in attendance, but not from me. No, I couldn't speak because I had just about swallowed my tongue whole.

She was a fucking vision in a short black strapless dress that flared out a bit at her waist. This girl had legs for fucking days, and I wanted them wrapped around me for just as long. Days and days.

I craned my neck just to try and get a glimpse of her chosen footwear for the evening. I knew she had decided to forgo the heels because she wasn't wobbling in the slightest. The corners of my mouth lifted when I saw her signature bright pink ballet flats.

*There's my Miri.*

I was going to have to officially recant my former statement regarding women in heels being sexy because this woman in pink ballet flats was sexier than anyone I've ever seen.

Julia produced a microphone of her own just as Miri hit the bottom of the stairs. "Miri wanted a *Janis* song, but I decided on something a bit more *my* style." When "Naughty Girl" by Beyonce came through the speakers, Miri's steps faltered, pausing as she stared open-mouthed at Julia.

She wanted a Janis song. If that wasn't a blatant clue, the only more obvious sign would've been to hit me in the face with a stop sign. But the song Julia picked was provocative and so unlike Miri it wasn't even funny.

"Come on Miri, don't be shy." Eden coaxed her by holding out her hand for her to grab ahold of.

Miri awkwardly put her hands in her pockets and stood in the middle of the stage with a half-hearted smile on her face, glancing out at everyone in the crowd, until she spotted Oliver, then it turned into a full-fledged one. Once her eyes locked on mine, that genuine smile slid off of her face and was replaced with shock.

I smiled my own genuine smile and graced her with a small wave. Her look could've been taken one of two ways. She was shocked in an excited manner because she didn't think I'd show up to show my support for her and her gran, or she thought I was going to mess shit up.

Once Eden began talking again, Miri's attention snapped away from me to her.

"Now, we have Tillie's other granddaughter. Miri came to live with her gran ten years ago and has weaved her way into the hearts of Cottage Grove and rightfully so. It's been said that Miri's good with her hands, especially by my husband." My brows instantly rose. "Get your minds out of the gutter, she's a massage therapist."

Eden walked behind Miri laughing at her own little joke and put her arm around her shoulders, "Who wants to start the bidding at fifty dollars?"

My plan was to sit back and bide my time as the low ballers were all weeded out. And it was a good, solid plan until a frenzy of sorts broke out as the bids kept getting higher and higher. And why wouldn't they? She was a complete sweetheart to everyone, this just created a problem of stiff competition for myself and I began to panic. What if I didn't win the date with her?

The bidding was up to five hundred dollars when a gentleman stood up and casually raised the bid to one thousand dollars. Everyone's head turned and I just barely heard Oliver mutter, "Of all the dog shit in the world…"

Trying to get a better inspection of the guy, he didn't look at all familiar to me. I couldn't place seeing him in town before.

"Who in the hell is that?" Baylor questioned, literally taking the words from right out of my mouth.

"That -- " Oliver pointed to the smug looking asshole who had his hands buried deep in his pockets and acted as if he was daring someone to bid him up and had all the time in the world. "Would be Travis."

"Fuck," I grunted, pounding my fist against the table. Of course the game changer would make his presence known *now*...

"What am I missing?" Baylor asked with genuine concern.

"Her ex," I relented, exasperated.

"Shit," he muttered.

Miri's gaze was set due north, directly on Travis.

This wasn't happening. I slammed my hand down on the table once more before shooting to my feet and declaring war in the form of, "Fifteen hundred dollars!"

Miri's eyes snapped back and forth between to two of us men after each and every bid was cast until Travis topped me out at four thousand.

"I'm out," I said, dejected to the table. "Four thousand is all I have in savings."

Oliver piped up, leaning over to his side towards me, "Make it another grand. I'll cover ya. The guy is a prick."

"Five thousand!" Gasps were thrown around left and right as if they couldn't believe that I was the one making all of these backs. Miri continued standing rooted in her spot with absolute disbelief painted all over her face. I composed my cockiness towards pretty boy Travis and willed him not to outbid me.

He turned his head a fraction of an inch and raised a brow exuding his own cocky tendencies.

"Ten. Thousand. Dollars."

"Shit on a fucking stick," Julia gasped into the microphone as her eyes were transfixed on Travis and the mic lazily dangling from her fingertips.

My shoulders slumped forward, I had never felt as disappointed in myself as I did right this moment. There was no way I could compete with a ghost of her past. The guy she shared four years of her life with.

Once Eden declared Travis the winner, I slumped down further in my chair.

"I believe that I failed to mention that he was a prick with money…"

*Now he tells me.*

Miri's face was one of pure elation and surprise as she quietly mouthed the one name that I now hated down to my bones, "Travis."

There was no way that I could stay here and watch them be reunited like the happy couple.

I withdrew my checkbook from the inner pocket of my jacket and quickly wrote out a check to Tillie for one thousand dollars. I tore the check away at the perforation and excused myself from the table without another word.

It was hard as hell to do, but I managed to veer my eyes away from the stage and their little reunion as I approached Tillie. Her gaze was sympathetic towards me as I bent down and kissed her cheek and placed the check down in front of her. "I'm glad to see that you're doing well."

Turning towards the door, I shoved my hands in my pockets allowing my hand to squeeze around my keys. I needed something to focus and concentrate on so I didn't make even more of a fool of myself.

As I walked out the door, I wondered if this was going to be the last time I saw Miri.

# *Chapter 20*

## *Miri*

My sights were zeroed in on the last person I expected to see tonight. If I thought that person was Bentley, it was blown out of the water once I saw the two men bidding against me.

Past and present colliding.

My feet were glued to the stage, not allowing me to move the smallest of centimeters.

There was a ruckus of chatter and I could faintly hear Eden utter the words, "Sold! To this gentleman for ten thousand dollars."

*Ten thousand freaking dollars.*

My breath rushed out of me and I'm quite certain that my face had turned completely white. But Travis, he had the same youthful appearance as if he hadn't aged a day in four years. It was as if time stood still for him.

He eyed me graciously before allowing a smile to appear on his face, and as if on cue my knees wobbled a bit just like old times. Once my initial shock wore off, I came unglued from my spot and instead of reciprocating his smile or running and jumping into his awaiting arms as he would expect for putting up such a hefty amount, I hastily ran off the stage in search of the other bidder.

My nerves and shock were replaced by anger, first Bentley forbid me to participate then he showed up himself and tried to outbid everyone like it was some kind of pissing match. The only thing I couldn't figure out was *why*. He had no desire to be with me, but no one else could have me either?

I stopped and put one hand on my hip and the other on my forehead, this entire evening was now giving me a headache. "Hey, Miri." I whipped around when I heard Baylor's voice.

"Where's your brother?" I cut to the chase without any preemptive salutations.

"My brother?" No, Dean's brother, was what I sarcastically wanted to say knowing that the other man had no siblings. He scratched his face along his jawline, "Uh, Bent had to go."

The way Baylor was trying to evade my question led me to believe the worst. "I get it. He had to go to someone, I mean somewhere else." That's what it always boiled down to. In the back of my mind, I was never going to be good enough for the likes of Bentley Jenkins.

"Miri --" he dropped his hand and moved a step closer. "That's not fair."

I crossed my arms in front of my chest, aware of my injured wrist, putting up my defenses for myself or Bentley I wasn't sure. "Isn't it, though? How would you know what was fair or otherwise when it comes to Bentley? When was the last time you said something positive to him? You always cut him down, I've seen it. He may not let it show, but your words affect him. Deep inside, he wants to be accepted by his big brother above all else." My thoughts become a jumbled mess just thinking about how extremely protective I was of Bentley.

"Even when I'm pissed at him I continue to defend him." I looked down at the ground wondering where I've gone wrong.

"It's because you love him," Baylor retorted, hitting the nail right on the flipping head.

My eyes instantly snapped to Baylor's, if it was that obvious to him then why couldn't his brother figure it out. "Yeah," I spoke around the sudden lump in my throat. "I do." I continued on by shrugging my shoulders and allowing a tear to well up in the corner of my eye. "I'm in love with Bentley with little to no chance of him ever loving me back."

Baylor broke out in a small, sad smile that one could construe as pity. "You need to talk to him."

Truer words have never been spoken, but I hadn't the slightest idea what to say.

Baylor walked away leaving me completely alone with my thoughts, forgetting about Travis until he appeared in front of me.

"Miri," he stated before leaning down towards my lips. At the last possible second, I turned my head making his bombardment of a kiss land on my cheek instead. His kiss used to warm me fully inside but now left me feeling hollow and cold. As his baby blue eyes bore into mine, they twinkled when he smiled, just like old times. But my how times have changed, for me at least.

"Travis, what are you doing here?"

He had the audacity to appear sheepish. "I was home visiting my parents when I heard about Tillie and the 'benefit.' I'm so sorry."

"You can say what it was Travis, an auction. One where you paid…" my jaw clenched together. "Ten thousand dollars for a date with me."

"That was nothing." He waved off as if money grew on trees, but in his case it just magically appeared in his bank account month after month courtesy of mommy and daddy. "I wanted to talk to you and this guaranteed me that opportunity."

He tried reaching for my uninjured hand in which I hastily pulled it away. His gaze roved over my entire body and it made me physically ill. "You look good, Miri, real good." I didn't know whether he was expecting me to reply, but he was going to be disappointed if so. He waited a moment before he continued, "So, I'll pick you up tomorrow at seven. You still live with Oliver?"

And now Oliver appeared at my back, loved his always impeccable timing. "Yeah, she does."

Travis pursed his lips. "Figures. Well, until tomorrow, Oliver, Miri." He bid farewell before retreating out the doors.

"Congratulations, you and Travis just made Cottage Grove auction history." Oliver sarcastically commented as soon as Travis was out of earshot.

"I would've rather won a fake sweepstakes from Publisher's Clearing House." He was lucky that I took a vow to never physically harm another person because I really wanted to elbow him in the stomach. Knowing my high track record, I would only end up injuring myself some way or another.

"He just did the same thing he always did, didn't he?" I pointed at the blank space my ex-boyfriend occupied seconds ago.

"You mean tell you when he's coming rather than allowing for your input? Or do you mean his look of disgust or pity because we're still roommates because that totally happened too."

I turned to look at Oliver, then looked up at the ceiling and let out an audible, completely unladylike groan.

"I'm guessing that little surge of annoyance meant you felt nothing from seeing him again after all these years?"

I furrowed my brows and just focused on how I did feel. I always thought if we were to come face to face again I would feel a sense of longing and further heartbreak because we were no longer together. But the only thing I felt besides nothing at all was free.

To see the real Travis without the hindrance of love involved and how uppity and pompous he truly was, I felt free because I was no longer tied down to him. It was a relief and a breath of fresh air.

"Disgust maybe? Was he always like that, throwing around ten thousand dollars as if it was literally chump change?"

"While Bentley bid his entire life savings for a date with you…"

"Pssh…" I tried to wave off, wondering suddenly where my anger went. "That was purely out of jealousy or God knows what on his part."

All because he had some misguided misconception because I wouldn't sleep with him, right? Even though that was several months ago.

He wouldn't actually bid on me *because* in reality he truly cared for me?

That much was already true, he was my best friend. Could Bentley possibly have deeper feelings for me?

*Could he love me?*

The realization must've appeared on my face because Oliver pulled me in a side hug and teased, "Ah, ladies and gentleman, I think she finally gets it. Ding ding ding, Bob, tell her what she's won!"

I completely ignored Oliver and his over the top sense of self and thought to myself that I just had to get through this date with Travis and then I would be free to talk to Bentley. Really talk to Bentley, heartfelt words and feelings being brought to light.

Hopefully Travis didn't plan on a lengthy evening, I had more important engagements to attend to right afterwards.

# *Chapter 21*

## *Bentley*

I had never in my life been so thankful for such a full schedule on the books. Figuring that by keeping myself busy wouldn't leave much room for my mind to wander into dangerous territory.

*Boy was I wrong.*

The image of Miri's shocked face when Travis won the date and then her mouthing his name as if they were long lost lovers reunited after his stint at war, was on constant agonizing replay all damn day.

There was absolutely no way that I could compete with her first love. It's painfully obvious that he wanted her back, I could name a number of not so subtle hints he's dropped her, about ten thousand of them to be exact.

He wasn't the better man though, sure he may have a shit ton of money, but the main difference between the two of us, if I ever had the luxury of calling Miri mine, there was nothing and I repeat nothing that would make me give her up.

I could never let her go.

Putting the finishing touches on the new sink system I was installing at Richardt's Grocery, my phone vibrated on my hip.

Drying my hands the quickest as humanly possible, I was anticipating to finally see Miri's name flash across my screen.

After several failed attempts to unclip my phone from my belt holder I had to take a deep breaths releasing it slowly. I had gotten myself all worked up and my heart was beating against my ribs like a sledgehammer. Finally able to glance at the screen, I was sorely disappointed.

"Hey, Baylor," I answered, my tone and mood coming out so resigned that I couldn't even be bothered to answer in my usual snide way.

"Think you can swing by mom's here in a bit, there are some things I want to talk to you about."

And then it would come, the finishing touches to this shitstorm of a life I lived.

"Sure, it isn't like I have anything else planned anyways." Further reminding me of my lonely and pathetic life.

It took me about an hour to finish up the job at Richardt's and make it to my mom's house. As I pulled into her driveway and let myself in through her front door, I was immediately accosted by my mother's orange tabby cat, aptly named Garfield.

As he wove himself in between my legs, it made me think back to Miri confessing that she hated cats. She was a complete conundrum and even had me chuckling without her being near.

I was hopelessly in love for the first time in my life and not able to do a damn thing about it. Hell, if this wasn't karma knocking on my door and laughing in my face.

"Hey, Ma!" I hollered into the emptiness of the living room, announcing my arrival before bending down to scratch her lazy cat behind his ears.

Mom rounded the corner from the kitchen, wiping her hands on the edge of her apron. She was always cooking or baking, it was something she was great at and found solace in it especially after my dad passed. "Hi, Bentley," she spoke while coaxing me to bend down so she could plant a kiss on my cheek.

Cooking for my mom was kind of like plumbing for me. Sure people instantly turned their noses at the mere mention, but it's a needed trade and what's more was that I was damn good at it. It's therapeutic to see a broken or busted sink and to know with a little manual labor I could get it fixed and working like new again. It's pretty lame that I looked at objects for gratification, but no one ever truly made me feel like I belonged, until Miri came into my life.

She allowed me the pleasure of learning what it felt like to actually be wholeheartedly depended on.

"Baylor isn't here yet, but why don't you come in the kitchen and get something to eat."

Normally, I'd be jumping at the chance to dive in first into one of my mother's recipes, but right now just the thought of indulging had my stomach revolting in protest.

Was this what being lovesick felt like? I was under the impression that it was just a phrase, but this feeling was incredibly real and I for one wasn't a fan. I wanted to learn the inside secret to making it stop because I felt mopey and miserable.

I followed my mother into the kitchen and flopped down into one of her dining room chairs before I answered, "I'm not feeling too much like eating, Ma."

All I heard was the thump of her spoon as it clattered against the hood of the stove before she was right beside me in an instant with her hand pressed against my forehead. "You don't seem to have a temperature, do you feel sick?"

Of course I felt sick, the worst kind of sick it seemed.

I couldn't suppress my grin, even at twenty-eight years old she was still in mom mode in a split second. "I'm not sick, Ma! At least that kind of sick." I didn't really feel like unfolding all the wrongdoings in my life to my mother.

She smacked my shoulder with her dish towel, "Bentley Aaron, don't you laugh at me. I will always be your mother and you will always be my baby boy." She pulled out the middle name, that's when you really knew she meant business.

The closing of the front door and the voice of my brother ceased any further conversation. "Hey, mom," he grinned as he allowed his backpack to slide down his shoulders into his firm grasp. You heard him audibly sniff the air like a bloodhound before darting towards the stove, "Oh what's cooking, I'm starving."

"Pork steaks and green beans," my mother beamed.

Baylor lifted the lid on the pot of green beans, "But it doesn't look like any has been eaten and Bentley is here."

My eyes rolled at his dig, but if I were up to eating a good portion would've been gone. But then again, I probably would've taken too much just out of spite.

"He's not hungry," Mom replied, disbelief dripping from her words.

He peeked around the glass lid and asked, "He sick?"

"*He* is right here, and no I'm not sick. It isn't a crime that I'm not hungry," I defended, always having to explain myself and have my guard firmly in place.

Replacing the lid, he walked over and sat in the seat directly to my right. "Yeah, but it isn't exactly normal either. Hey Ma, do you mind fixing me a plate while I talk to Bent?"

"Sure thing, dear," she walked past the two of us, squeezing Baylor on the shoulder before looking back at me, "You sure you're not hungry?"

I waved her off, "Naw, Ma, I'm good. Promise."

I really just wanted to get this so-called meeting over with so I could go home and bask in my self-pity in peace. "So what's this about?" I leaned forward resting my elbows on the table.

Baylor leaned back in his chair and released a large breath, "I'm sorry…"

Immediately, I dropped my arms and leaned forward even more to make sure I was hearing him correctly. "Repeat that for me, please. Just so I can be clear." What was the apology for?

"You and I never exactly saw eye to eye," he admitted.

"Isn't that the fucking truth."

"Bentley --" my mom scolded. "Watch your language!"

"Sorry, Ma," I grumbled.

"But I've always been extremely hard on you," Baylor continued. I opened my mouth to retort when he shot me a dirty look, so I closed my mouth and tried to relax. "See when Dad died, I was the oldest and felt obligated to keep things afloat with the business. I'm in a constant state of fear that I'm going to fail, so I hold things to a higher standard and harp on you for your menial mistakes."

Now there was no stopping my interruption. "Do you not think I'm afraid of failing? This business is just as much my dream as it was Dad's. I sat back and watched him for hours perfecting his craft, but I learned everything from him. I may not do things your way, but I do complete them in Dad's way." Just talking about my dad made me realize just how much I missed him, and my voice reflected that by growing thick with emotion.

"Without the business mom will have nothing," Baylor stated.

My mom sat down Baylor's plate in front of him and took a seat across the table from me. "Baylor, I know you thought you had to look out for me, but you're wrong. Your dear old momma doesn't need the business to stay afloat. Someone else could've taken over until Bentley was finished with school and was ready to step up in the only place he's wanted to be. I'll always have my two boys."

"Guess I really screwed things up, huh?" Baylor ran a hand through his hair, his fork forgotten on the edge of his plate. This entire conversation was a big deal. In all my years, I've never heard my brother assume responsibility for anything he ever remotely did wrong because he lived this perfect life in which he never screwed up. But him manning up for his own indiscretions made me look up to him and respect him even more.

"Just let me prove to you that I'm not the same immature guy who'd rather party until dawn rather than keep our father's business afloat. Let me run things without your close watchful eye. You're a newlywed with your own full-time job at the Architect firm, live your life and let mom and I handle things from here on out."

Baylor lifted his fork and began scooting around the green beans on his plate, really trying to contemplate over my words. They were true, honest words. Sure when I was younger I made mistakes, it happened, but now I was truly one hundred percent on board with getting my life together. "Ok," he said, but then gave me a pointed stare and surged his green bean laden fork in my direction. "But you majorly screw things up, I'm back with no arguments."

Ma reached out her hand and covered Baylor's with her own. "The business will be fine, I think Bentley is ready for his time to shine." It felt good that for once my mother was on my side, cheering me on. She brought her attention to me. "Now, it's been no secret that I don't approve of your lifestyle, but it was because I always knew you had so much more potential than what you chose to convey." Wait a minute, how did this conversation turn from Baylor apologizing to talking about the way I lived my life? And just as I grew warm and fuzzy inside from her knowing just how much the plumbing business meant to me. I would never get away from this, it would always be looming on my doorstep waiting to be thrown up in my face. "I knew some special woman would come along and you would want to change your ways just for her. You remind me so much of your father," she ended by dabbing her kitchen towel to each of her eyes to wipe away her sudden tears.

"Dad had a way with the ladies, is what you're saying?" Baylor relayed exactly what I was thinking.

"Your father was ever the charmer." Surprise hit her face and she pointed at me from across the table. "You're not hungry, and I think you've tamed a bit…Bentley, are you in love?"

I buried my face in my hands and groaned because this wasn't a particular conversation I wanted to be having with my mother.

"He totally is." You could make out the humor in Baylor's tone.

Removing my hands, I deadpanned at my older brother, "Totally?" In a subtle way, I was criticizing his choice of words. Like he was trying to channel his inner valley girl.

I received a look from my brother so lethal that if actual looks could kill he'd be rotting in a cell for murder. I threw my hands up in surrender, not wanting to keep anyone on the edge of their seats regarding my life. "Ok, all right. Yes, Ma, I'm in love. Her name is Miri."

"Tillie's granddaughter?"

I couldn't wrap my head around the fact that we were sitting here discussing this so casually as if it was an everyday occurrence.

"The very same. But it doesn't matter, I tried to win a date with her for Tillie's benefit auction and was outbid by her ex-boyfriend."

"Have you told her how you feel?" she asked.

"Didn't you hear what I just told you?"

"What I heard was that you were being a typical man trying to 'claim your territory.' What I asked was if you've actually told her, with words, how you feel about her?"

"Well, no." Would doing that really be all that simple?

"I think you should." She reached across the table to cover my hand with her own. "You owe it to yourself to see if she feels the same." If what Oliver said was true, then I knew she felt the same way. But that doesn't hold any weight if she doesn't know that I do.

"I was under some impression that I needed to make some sort of grand gesture." I waved my hand.

My mother's brows knitted together in confusion, "Now honey, why would you need to do that?"

At the same time, my mother's and my eyes slowly moved until we were staring at Baylor.

His eyes widened and he asked, "What? I didn't tell him that."

"But you can see where he got the idea from. You did go the distance to get my girl." She boasted.

"Your girl?" Baylor scoffed.

"Yeah, I always wanted a daughter and Kristina didn't even fair close to earning that title," she said matter of fact.

Devoting her attention to me, she rolled her eyes. "You should know that your brother is somewhat of an overachiever."

"Ma!" Baylor whined, recreating my teenage years all over again.

"Baylor," she quipped. "You know it's true, so don't even try to deny it." Boom, she just put him in his place. Mom for the win.

He huffed, crossed his arms, and drove his back against his chair, making it creak with the force of his movements.

This entire conversation was so out of the norm for us, but oddly enough it was comforting. Even though I was under scrutiny, as always, I found solace in her words. For once I didn't feel as if I was a complete fuck-up.

"Bentley, you don't have to make a huge spectacle of confessing your love but make it memorable, some girls will just eat that up. In other words, don't do what your father did."

"Which was?" She couldn't just leave me hanging, she dangled the bait in front of my face now she needed to elaborate.

"He came up to me and said," she changed her tone to as deep as she could before continuing, "You and me, how 'bout it?"

I busted out laughing because that sounded just like something he would say. He was a man of very few words. "Duly noted." I rubbed my hands up and down the thighs of my dirty work jeans. "What time is it?"

Baylor looked at his watch on his wrist and answered, "It's twenty till six. Why?"

An idea sparked in my head and I was going to carry it out this minute. Give or a take a few so I could go home and get cleaned up. I raised out of my seat. "I gotta run."

"Let me know how it goes," Baylor surprised me by saying. Who was this man? First apologizing to me and now actually wanting to know things that are going on in my life.

"Oh, you'll know how it goes. If I'm not at work tomorrow, that means it went well," I winked.

"Call me if you won't be in and I'll reschedule all of your appointments." Being as how this came from my mother my steps faltered as I gained on the front door. It wasn't normal for her to be on board with irresponsibility. She came around to face me and reached up placing her hands on my cheeks, lowering my face to where our eyes were aligned.

I raised a brow. "Don't look at me like I've lost my mind. It isn't everyday my baby pronounces his love for someone." I bent down to give her a kiss on her cheek. "Just don't make a habit of playing hooky. Now, go bring me another daughter."

"Ma, please don't get your hopes up, I'll be doing that enough for the both of us. She may choose the ex."

"Don't be silly, she would have to be stupid or blind not to pick my son."

I hopped down out of my truck onto the asphalt of Miri's parking lot and released a staggered breath. I've never been nervous around women, especially Miri, but my anxiety has formed a ball of nerves in my stomach the size of a Clydesdale.

I wiped my clammy hands on my jeans and turned to retrieve the box that could make all the difference and push me to the top. A simple gesture, but could hold the most meaning? I don't know, this was all new to me and I could be making a colossal mistake.

Next thing I knew, I was standing in front of her apartment door, not even able to remember climbing the three grueling flights of stairs to get here.

I poised my shaky hand against the door and knocked three consecutive times, dropping my hand as I held my breath and pray that she's actually home. The sound of her deadbolt unlocking from the inside had my heart rate spiking to speeds unlike ever before and my mouth running completely dry. As the knob slowly turned, I had one last fleeting notion to turn around and hightail it out of the building as if the damn thing was on fire.

Once the door finally opened, it wasn't Miri or even Oliver who answered. The wind urgently deflated from my lungs, and I now wished I had listened to my head when it told me to get the fuck out of dodge.

I hastily cleared my throat, "Travass." He was dressed casually, suit jacket removed with his shirt sleeves rolled up as if he'd been here awhile. When the name I gave the asshole *accidentally* slipped, so did his smug smile. Right off his face into a puddle of fake on the floor.

"Is there something I can help you with?"

"Yeah, is Miri here?" I don't know why I was choosing to stick around. It was almost abundantly clear on where I stood in the thick of things.

"She's here, but she's currently indisposed," he said snootily, sporting a knowing grin.

Never in my life did I want to hit someone more than I did at this moment. My hatred for Dean paled in comparison to the rage I felt against this man.

"Bentley, is that you?" I heard Miri from the vicinity of her bedroom.

I narrowed my eyes as I sidestepped the man who rivaled me in height, but that was the only similarity. He exuded pansy right down to the leather tassels on his overpriced loafers. Following in the direction of her voice, I sat the box that I brought down on the edge of her coffee table and continued until I was standing outside her bedroom door.

The door flew open and what I saw made me want to simultaneously ravage her as well as double over from the pain. It was a conundrum of feelings, how one moment I could feel insane lust and love to pure hatred.

Her fresh-faced beauty and gentle smile drew me in, but the lack of a shirt had me seething. A black pencil skirt was wrapped around her hips and a pale pink lace bra was wrapped around her breasts. Breasts that had me salivating for a taste, but it seemed as if I was already too late. Waiting in a line that would never end with my turn. I averted my gaze up to the ceiling where things were safe and lifted the ball cap that was perched on my head and ran a hand through my hair before replacing it.

"What's wrong, Bentley?" she asked with genuine concern lacing her voice.

"Could you please put a shirt on, I only have so much restraint," I begged.

"I'm so sorry," she shrieked before I heard her rummaging through her dresser. "Ok, all better."

I took in her face and nonchalantly pointed to her nose. "You have…"

## *Chapter 22*

### *Miri*

I couldn't believe that Bentley was here. I went back and forth with the thought of calling him all day but in the end chickened out. I wanted to ask what last night was about, the result of their little pissing match was standing in the living room. Travis was early picking me up for our date, and I was entirely unprepared to be alone with him, which was why I was currently stalling in my room.

Bentley subtly rubbed a finger down his nose, "You have a little…"

Oh, fiddlesticks. I jumped and scurried to my full-length mirror and pulled the dry pore strip off of my nose wincing as it pried free from my skin. I was always embarrassing myself around him. First, answering the door in only my bra, then my pore strip.

"Sorry, not everyone is as perfect as you."

He shoved his hands deep into the pockets of his jeans, "I happen to think you're pretty perfect," he said softly.

The endearment caught me completely off-guard. I tried to cover up my sharp intake of breath and my increasing pulse by joking. "Are you trying to get into my pants again?" I asked lightheartedly with a chuckle. "I really didn't mean to open the door without a shirt on."

"No, Miri." His eyes bore into mine with such intensity. "I'm trying to get into your heart." He frowned then looked down towards the floor.

I had to make a conscious effort to close my agape mouth, because never in a million years did I ever expect something along the lines of that to come out of the mouth of Bentley Jenkins. "What're you saying?" My heart was beating in rapid succession awaiting his confession. Could he really be about to confess that he had the same feelings towards me as I did him?

"Nothing, I'm not saying anything." His tone grew terse as he pointed towards the living room, "No, you know what. If that is what you're wanting… that piece of shit who didn't know what he had in you until he kicked it to the curb, then we can't be friends anymore. I can't allow myself to hold up my end of the bargain any longer." Such intensity behind the words that he said with such conviction had tears springing in my eyes.

I took a step in his direction, feeling my lip begin to tremble. "But you don't understand…I don't."

Bentley wasn't about to let me finish my sentence before he turned on his heel and stormed out of my bedroom. I heard a loud growl come from the vicinity of the living room before I winced when the front door slammed shut.

My feet carried me into the room just seconds after Bentley's departure and the tears that had formed in the corner of my eyes started streaming down my face as I stared blindly at the door, never letting my gaze fully come into focus.

"Well, that was interesting," Travis hissed from the couch.

I pivoted on my heel to look at his outstretched arms draping the back of my couch. Something on the corner of the coffee table caught my attention, and as I dropped down to the edge of the cushion to inspect it, I brought the box towards me and lifted the note off to read it.

**I hope this satisfies at least one of your cravings. I'll gladly help with the other as well, just say the word.**

**With Love, Bentley**

A surge of laughter bubbled up from the back of my throat.

"You still indulge in those sugar infested treats?" he sneered, he never did see the point to my cravings.

The high I was feeling from the gesture and innuendo only Bentley could pull off was obliterated when Travis opened his mouth.

I turned my body so I could face that of my ex-boyfriend. "Yes, Travis." I held up the note. "Some people encourage my indulgence of such fatty snack foods and don't judge. This note and box of *Ding Dongs* mean more to me than anything you ever gave or did for me while I've known you."

Travis leaned forward on the couch, resting his elbows on his knees bringing his face closer to mine. "You mean to tell me the check I wrote is meaningless compared to a box of snack cakes?"

"That was for Gran, that wasn't for me." I inched my face closer to his, showing that I wasn't backing down.

"I beg to differ." Of course he would, everything was all about him.

I placed the box on the coffee table and asked the ten thousand dollar question, "Why are you here, Travis?"

He tried to reach for my hands resulting in me jerking them away immediately. His pride looked wounded before he settled his perfectly perfected mask back in place. "I made a mistake in letting you go."

"And you just came to this realization?" It wasn't like we broke up a matter of months ago, it'd been years since I've seen or even heard from him. He might as well have disappeared because things just weren't said about him.

"No, my decision came to fruition quite some time ago, I was just under the assumption that you'd be taken. It wasn't until I was visiting my parents did I learn that you'd be part of the bachelorette auction. Which, Miri, really? Wasn't that a little demeaning and beneath you? That isn't the Miri I know."

I scoffed, "Doesn't that just solidify that you don't know me anymore at all? The Miri you knew allowed you to use her as a doormat." I looked away from him. "And is now referring to herself in the third person." I wanted to cringe at this entire interaction. I felt as if everything I said and the actions I performed were continuously monitored and judged by Travis. I was so blinded by love and being wanted in the past that I justified his reasoning for putting me in a box. "The only mistake I made was staying with you so long. Let me guess, to further yourself in your career you need a little woman? Someone who will obey and bow down to your every whim?"

"Miri, I assure you that wasn't my intentions," he tried backpedaling, worried that I figured him out so quickly.

"What? You didn't want me as the silent trophy wife who you place in a glass box unable to break free? Unable to have a mind of her own." I objected.

"Miriam…" his voice crept out in a low menacing tone as if he was a parent reprimanding their child.

My averting gaze immediately snapped to his. Who did he think he was talking to me that way? "Travis, I think it's time you left."

He abruptly stood on his feet, "I paid ten thousand dollars for a date with you."

My heart rate was going spastic at the sudden altercation, and I had no idea where this incident was heading. Travis had never raised his voice to me before, but then again, I was always a spineless little girl around him. Now instead of spineless, I was scared, but I tried to portray that I wasn't messing around. "Pretty demeaning, huh? And not to mention, pathetic." I stood tall with my back ramrod straight and lifted my chin to let him know that I wasn't backing down. "I'll say this only once more, you need to get the *fuck* out of my house." His eyes, as well as mine, went wide with my choice of wording, but I stood by it. I bent to grab my cell phone from off the edge of the coffee table where it rested. "I can always let the police handle things from here." I proceeded to swipe my finger across the screen to unlock my phone. "They don't mess around when it comes to harassment."

Before I could even make a move to press the icon that enabled the call feature, Travis had hightailed it out my front door and if he was bright, out of my life.

My feet gave out from underneath me and I collapsed back onto the softness of my cushions and breathed an enormous sigh of relief.

My idiocy knew no bounds and that entire predicament could've gone south at any time. I found myself counting my lucky stars that Travis was still a wimp and loathed confrontation. Although, the mention of police more than likely spooked him. Having 5-0 on your back wouldn't have been very becoming for his career.

Now about Bentley…If he actually had feelings for me like Oliver said he did, then why didn't he just say something? Then again, why didn't I?

All I knew was that his head wouldn't hit his pillow tonight without knowing exactly how I felt. All of my cards would be laid bare out in the open for him to see. Then it would be up to him to decide what he wanted to do with this newfound information. If he was going to embrace my fragile heart in his hands or break it…

# Chapter 23

## Bentley

Once again I ended up at the one place I should be avoiding like the plague. It was as if some higher force knew I needed to drown my sorrows since my heart was practically in shambles. I really needed to find a new place to hang out, this one just brought back constant memories of Miri.

As I made my way towards the bar, I felt as if my heart was legitimately breaking within the cavity of my chest. The knife that was piercing my most vital organ rotated a full repetition once I caught a glimpse of good old Tillie herself behind the counter. Sliding my ass into one of the numerous open seats, Tillie's eyes went wide once she noticed me sitting down.

Her bright pink lips pursed together as she released a high-pitched whistle, "Pretty boy looks like he's been run over by a big rig." She leaned against the counter.

"You're hilarious," I croaked, not even able to come up with a fairly decent retort.

"Well, I may have shown off my stand-up comedy skills a time or two back in my day."

"Can you please spare me the back in the day talk, I'll have a Jack and Coke. Little more Jack and a little less Coke."

She gave me a brief tip from her imaginary hat and went about making my drink. I folded my arms on the table and pounded my forehead against my forearms repeatedly wondering what the hell I was going to do with my life now. I couldn't go back to being the man that I was, it just wasn't possible. That wasn't the fulfilling life that I thought I wanted.

"Now just wait a fricking minute," I heard Tillie say as she slammed down my drink right next to my ear. Next thing I knew she had grabbed ahold of a good chunk of my hair with her talon claws and jerked my head up off of my arm.

Blinding pain radiated through my skull until she finally released her death grip.

"What was that for?" I rubbed on the spot making sure she didn't take a clump of hair with her.

She smoothed her hand along the grain of the wood from the bar. "This has withstood quite a bit, but you didn't need to try to deface property with that big head of yours." She produced a stool of her own and perched herself right in front of me. "Now, who pissed in your Wheaties? Or better yet, left you with a massive case of blue balls?"

Tillie was clearly a sadist who enjoyed seeing other people pained. That had to be the only viable reason that she waited until I took a gulp from my drink to say that. It was awkward as hell seeing a little old woman say the words, "blue balls." I immediately choked on the liquid making it lodge in my throat and threaten to make an appearance out my nose.

"No one has given me a case of blue balls." *Lies, all lies.* "I actually just left your granddaughter's where we had a disagreement." That was the understatement of the century.

She tapped a finger against her mouth and admitted, "Maisie it notorious for leaving men all hot and bothered…"

Was this woman going senile?

"I'm not talking about Maisie."

"Miri? Well, that's new for her." All I could think was that it really wasn't new for her. We had been dancing back and forth with the proverbial foreplay covering as friendship since December.

I proceeded to take another drink, actually finishing off my glass. "She chose Travis. That asshole came to declare his love for the fair maiden after years apart. Trying to whisk her away again after he threw her away. All very poetic actually."

"I really need to set up a tip jar for my valuable time and advice," Tillie muttered under her breath. I wasn't able to ask her what she meant before she looked me dead in the eye and said, "Bullshit."

"Excuse me?" I blinked.

"I call bullshit. Miri may have felt a sense of obligation to go out on a date with Travis since he paid so much at the auction, but that doesn't mean she *chose* Travis."

I decided to forgo the part about the various states of dress I found them in, mainly her. "But he was her first love. He's the better man. Doesn't have the extra baggage that I carry around due to my promiscuity. He can provide a better life for her." Why in the hell I was trying to justify her decision was beyond my comprehension.

"Are you sure about that? Because I can recall a grief-stricken fifteen-year-old girl, who went for her first day at her new school after she was uprooted across the country. She was a depressed mess who would've rather spent the rest of her days hidden in her bed. But she came home with a newfound hope saying that she was going to love Cottage Grove all because of a boy who came to her rescue. And do you know the name of that boy?" Surprised, I pointed to myself and she nodded. "Correct, Bentley Jenkins." I couldn't believe what I was hearing. Miri's entire attitude changed because of our first meeting. Because I extended the nicety that I wanted for myself to a new student. "She fell in love with you that day in her own teenager way and carried on those harbored feelings for ten years until they were ready to grow. So you see, you were technically the first."

I wished that I could say that I was full of hope after what she just enlightened me with, but I couldn't exactly explain what all took place back at her apartment earlier. "What caused this sudden change of heart towards me?"

"Because now I have absolutely no doubt in my mind that you'll do right by my Miri. I told you that she was a rare gem, someone you'll want to cherish, now you're in deep enough to believe it."

"I think I believed it a long time ago, but was just too stupid to get my head out of my ass. Now I'm completely in love with the girl and there is nothing I can do about it."

"Boy, you're lucky that you're sitting across the bar from me and my arms have a short reach or else you'd be rightfully acquainted with the palm of my hand. Quit your bitching and bellyaching and do something about it. Fight for her. Go and tell her how you truly feel, but if you do anything to jeopardize her heart or happiness, I'll castrate you."

The lack of any type of amusement in her voice led me to believe that she was dead serious. I shivered a bit because I honestly wouldn't put bodily harm past her. I peeked up from my stare off with the wood of the bar and saw Tillie looking past me with a smirk on her face. As she slid off of the stool, she chuckled under her breath and traveled off with a limp. "Something tells me you won't have to travel very far. My work here is done. Damn, I need myself a man…"

A warm breath cascaded across the outer shell of my ear before I felt Miri at my side and finally heard her voice, "Do you regret it?"

Leaning back to where I could look her in the eyes, I asked, "Regret what?"

"Falling in love with me?" Her eyes were full of such vulnerability and I knew that I could never deny her anything. Whether she chose to be with Travis or not, it didn't dim the fire that I felt so fiercely inside for her.

"I could never regret falling in love with you, I thought it would be scary, but giving you my heart was the easiest thing I've ever done." I took a perusal of her body and noticed the bag of chips tightly clasped in her clutch.

"What's that?" I asked, nodding towards her hands.

She looked down at the bag and then thrust the Doritos into my hands. "I came bearing gifts for a truce. You brought me my weakness, so it was only fair that I reciprocated by bringing you yours."

I placed the bag on the counter of the bar and quickly grasped one of her hands, "You certainly did. But only now I have a much bigger weakness. One that in particular makes me go weak in the knees whenever I get a glimpse of her or even the slightest thought of her runs through my mind. But this weakness is much more powerful, and the way she looks at me like I hung the moon, I don't ever want that to fade away."

"Bentley Jenkins are you coming onto me?" she joked, her cheeks tinged the faintest of pinks.

"Oh baby, if I'm coming you'll know it…" Miri's face surpassed pink turning several shades of red. "But what about Travis?" I looked around the room for him. "There is a lack of smugness in here, and I certainly don't see him lurking about silently acting as if he's better than everyone else."

"Oh well, he had to run." She shrugged her shoulders not appearing guilty in the slightest. "He learned that things had changed, and I saw him for who he really was; fake and petty."

"You mean you didn't sleep with him?" I carefully inquired.

Her brows furrowed creating deep creases in her forehead, "Tonight? God no…" Understanding dawned on her face. "That's what you thought?"

All I could muster was a single solitary shrug of my shoulder. I didn't want her to think that my insecurities were getting in the way. It wasn't every day that I felt incompetent towards a woman.

"Absolutely not. I actually cussed at him on his way out after he turned up his nose at the gift you brought me."

"Are you kidding me? Did you say fuck? How did it feel?" Another time that I truly missed out on her small slippage of tongue.

She released a breath and nodded her head. "Oddly liberating. Enough about people that don't even matter. I didn't even touch the tip of your presents…Mr. Jenkins, are you wearing Levi's and a ball cap?"

Now it was my turn for my face to turn red, I was actually blushing. I adjusted the hat on my head. "How do I rate on a scale from one to Jason Statham?"

She tipped her head back and released a laugh. "Are you kidding me? You're off the charts. But --" She raised her forefinger. There was always a but… "I really need to see your ass in those jeans to do a fair comparison."

I couldn't help the mental fist bump that I performed, not only because my little present paid off, but I finally was able to complete my challenge. She cussed and it wasn't at me in anger or towards anyone else. I swiveled my chair around until our bodies were perfectly aligned and she took a small step in between my parted thighs. Miri looked up through her lashes and directly into my soul. Her bottom lip quivered as her head descended closer to mine and she whispered, "I love you, Bentley. I think in a way I always have and now that my love is rooted so deep I without a doubt know I always will."

I took the open opportunity to now inch my face towards hers. We looked like all of those lovey-dovey couples that I used to cringe at their open display of affection. But right now, all I saw was Miri, her beauty, her kindness, and love. Everything and everyone else seemed to fade away into the night.

I ran my nose along the side of hers ready to embrace my lips with hers and be the place I craved, the place I could truly consider home. The whole romantic thing was new to me, but I had to venture out of unfamiliar territory and do what felt right in my heart.

"You're my magnum opiate," as soon as the words left my lips I knew they weren't correct, but it was too little too late to reel them back in now. I could only hope that Miri would take pity on me and not rub it in too much. A bit of wishful thinking on my part, but stranger things have happened.

She pulled her face back away from mine just enough to where she could fully look into my eyes. Amusement danced in her brown irises as lines crinkled around her eyes from her smile. "You mean magnum opus?"

"Yeah, that…" I wanted to smack my head and have a whole 'doh' moment. But then I begged her with my eyes to just drop it.

"You're adorable." She was throwing my words from the first night back in my face. Now I understood why she was so offended by being called adorable.

I looked up at the exposed beams along the ceiling, trying to feign a bit embarrassed. "You're not really helping my confidence level here, sweetheart."

"Bentley…"

"I mean I know I have a big ego most of the time, but calling me adorable instead of ruggedly handsome or drop dead sexy really can start messing with a guy's head." I could've kept going all night.

"Bentley…" she warned.

"What?"

"Shut up and kiss me already," She turned the bill on my cap until it was facing backward and was all around pretty confident that I'd comply. Oh, who was I kidding, she asked and I had absolutely no reservations about delivering. I closed the remaining distance between the two of us and fused my lips with hers.

Miri immediately released a mild whimper before her arms wrapped around me and locked behind my back. It first surprised me when she darted her tongue out to seek entrance before it turned me on as she delved into my mouth. I was right, this was where it was at, I was finally home. And it was beyond time for me to take Miri home.

I waited and gauged her reaction before I immediately suggested it. The last thing I needed was for her to think this was strictly about sex. I wanted the whole package. The house, family… Hell, I'd even drive a minivan around town if that's what she wanted. I would fucking rock a minivan.

Being the first to break our connection, I stated, "Miri, we don't have to do this tonight, we have all the time in the world."

Silently I was praying that she wanted to go against my words, but I didn't want to pressure her. It's been a lot longer for her than it had been me, although, for me it was some sort of record.

"Bentley, if you don't do something to ease this ache between my legs you'll be in a fucking world of hurt." She shocked the shit out of me by saying that.

And just like that I had to pick my jaw up off the floor. This woman surprised me at every single turn. Not only did she make threatening bodily harm sound appealing and fan-fucking-tastic, unlike Tillie, but she was also well on her way to a potty mouth, and that turned me on even more.

Miri spun on her heel holding my hand and all but drug me out of Tillie's. This just wasn't going to fly, so I jerked my hand back making her body fling towards mine and bent to pick her up the same way I did when she was drunk. She squealed from the shock and only put up a minimal fight. Being that I wasn't trying to navigate carrying complete dead weight, it was much more fun with her being conscious.

Securing my arm around her back and my other hand under the bend of her legs, I was ready to go out into the night. With an 'oomph' I said, "There that's better."

"For who?" she squeaked. "You know for a fact that I prefer to have both feet firmly planted on the ground," she argued, and another squeal broke free once I sharply turned a corner in the parking lot. "Having my legs sticking out has to be hazardous and not to mention a safety violation."

I brushed my lips against hers just for a brief moment before I reached for the handle on the passenger door of my truck. "Was that to get me to shut up?"

"Now why on earth would you think that? You'd better get used to it because now I can kiss you anytime I want." I didn't think that I would ever grow tired from her kisses. Being able to assault her with my own kisses added with the element of surprise each and every touch of our lips would be an adventure.

I hoisted her up onto the seat finally letting go. Definitely easier when she wasn't drunk and unconscious.

"Oh, is that right?" she snickered with her brows raised.

Using the handle on the interior of my truck, I boosted myself on my running boards and brought my face towards hers once again and kissed her, just further proving my point. Once I released her lips, I stated, "You best believe it. You're mine, I'm keeping you. So therefore I can bestow my kisses upon you anytime and anywhere."

She couldn't suppress her giggle, "Oh, Bentley Jenkins, you're something else."

As I proceeded to jump back down onto the gravel of the parking lot, I muttered to where it was barely audible to her ears, "Just don't call me adorable."

We made it just inside my house and the nervous jitters reappeared. These bastards were becoming a downright nuisance.

I yearned to touch Miri and make her completely mine in every sense of the word, but I didn't know the first thing about going about it. Miri's big doe eyes filled with unshed tears at my apprehension and hesitation.

"What's wrong, Bentley? Are you having second thoughts?" Damn it, I didn't want her to feel badly for my own lack of experience at being in love.

I backed her against the wall in my entryway and cupped her cheeks within the palms of my hands, hoping she would overlook how clammy they were. I wanted this night to be perfect and now my own nerves would possibly hinder the outcome.

"Don't ever think that I will have second thoughts where you are concerned. Without you I'm Bent, on the verge of breaking, but with you, I'm Bentley and haven't ever felt more whole in my entire life. I love you, Miri. I'm just unsure how to go about this. My experience is in being Bentley, the playboy who fucks. I've never been Bentley, the guy who is head over heels in love and actually get to make love for the first time. I want things to be perfect, you deserve nothing less."

She placed her open palm in the center of my chest. "Just do what you feel is right in here." There was absolutely no slowing down my heart, so I knew that she could feel the rapid beat as it thumped wildly against her hand.

With very little coercion, Miri pulled her body off of the wall to my entryway and followed me to the back of my house towards my bedroom.

Walking over to the side table beside my bed, I flipped the switch on the small lamp that resided on its surface, turning it on so a dim light would softly illuminate the space of the room. This moment was many months in the making, and there was no way I would miss seeing a second of it.

The soft glow of the light reflected off of Miri's back as she stood unmoving at the end of my bed. I quickly discarded my boots and with easy, quiet footfalls I moved to stand directly in front of her, our bodies merely inches away from one another.

She tentatively reached out to touch my pecs and brazenly traveled her hands around my body with her feather-light touches. I noticed the slight tremor in her hands. As she swallowed past her nerves, Miri grabbed ahold of my shirt tugging upward trying to pull it free from my jeans, exposing my bare stomach.

Her eyes glanced up to mine, silently asking permission to move forward. If she needed this exploration of my body, I was going to give her all the time she desired. My dick was beyond angry for the slow progression since he normally controlled the show, but I needed Miri fully comfortable with everything that was transpiring between us.

Taking the liberty of raising my arms in the air, trying to get her to take things a bit further, her knuckles grazed my exposed skin as she trailed up my sternum to rid me of my shirt, causing a sharp intake of breath and shiver to run down my spine.

Once my shirt was free from my body, Miri slowly raked her trembling fingertips down my torso towards the top of my jeans with just enough pressure that I was ready to beg for more. It was difficult trying to restrain myself when all I wanted to do was completely ravage her from top to bottom and afterward repeating it all over again.

She peered up at me through her parted lashes and with a breathy whisper divulged, "You're beautiful," before looking back down at my body.

My resolve was drawing near the end of the line, and I could no longer keep my hands to myself. So, I lifted her chin with the curve of my index finger so she had no other choice but to lock eyes with me once more. My thumb caressed down her jawline to her exposed neck, and I traveled to the end of her braided hair that was resting over her shoulder and released her locks from its hold.

Plunging my hands into her hair, my fingers wove through her long strands, the silkiness surrounding my skin, untangling it from her braid until it fell in soft waves down her back. My hands then immediately went for the hem of her t-shirt, where I whipped it off, closely followed by unclasping her bra, freeing her breasts from their barrier.

I couldn't stop another sharp intake of breath after I got my first glimpse of her newly exposed torso. Never being ashamed to admit that seeing her beautiful, creamy, pale skin made my knees go weak and I had to remind myself to release the breath that I was holding. None of my fantasies combined, and there were quite a few, equaled to the pure perfection that stood before me.

"You're wrong, baby, you're the beautiful one. My God, how did I get so lucky?" I didn't know what I did in life to deserve the love of this woman, but there wouldn't be a day that I would take it for granted. "I think you're going to have to make a promise to me now."

Her eyes went wide before she finally replied, "Anything."

"You can't ever leave me, because baby, I'll put up one hell of a fight. I'm never letting you go." My fingers dove back into her hair, this time with a little more aggression, fisting her strands as I hastily descended my lips to hers. I kissed her with several months of pent up passion and reckless abandon. She would not leave my bed without fully knowing just how deep my love ran for her; that my heart beat only for her.

Finally gripping her hips and lifting her up, I moved forward and gently laid her body down on my bed all while our lips still remained firmly locked in place. After releasing my lips from hers, I quickly discarded my jeans as I watched her breasts rise and fall due to her labored breathing. The way her body was positioned, her hair fanned out across my pillow, she was utterly breathtaking, and she had my mouth salivating for a taste.

I meticulously climbed back up her body, careful not to touch any exposed skin, I wanted her to deeply anticipate the next touch, be surprised by where I caressed. Reaching her breasts, I didn't waste any time before I cupped one in my hand and delved forward, latching onto her overly sensitive nipple. She jerked her hips as a loud moan erupted from her once I moved my free hand between our bodies to cup her sex outside of her skirt.

Releasing her breast, I explored her skin, placing open-mouthed kisses down her ribcage, stopping just before I reached the clasp of her skirt. My slow pace obviously wasn't enough when Miri bucked her hips once again, conveying to me that I needed to speed things up. I grinned with amusement when she started trying to rid herself of the barrier between us. My hands moved hers out of the way before I dutifully unbuttoned the top clasp. I was reveling in making her squirm. I proceeded to take the tab of her zipper and with an agonizingly slow sense of torture, drug it down the tines, revealing black lace panties.

My dick was throbbing to the point of pain in my boxer briefs, taking things slow from here on out had to be reconfigured. It wasn't feasible. This went well beyond just mindless teasing, it was teetering on the verge of tormenting, one that would only end by embarrassing this member of the party. My fire for her was burning strong and this barely scratched the tip of the surface. I placed one last open mouth kiss along her pubic bone as I pulled her skirt and panties off of her legs, whipping them to the floor along with my own boxer briefs.

I positioned my dick at her slick entrance and looked to her for confirmation before entering her fully. The "please," she panted, gave me the final urge that I was looking for. Slowly lowering myself into her, I reveled in the feeling of her walls clamping down around my shaft, ready to milk my pleasure if I so chose. Allowing her as well as myself to get acquainted with one another, I had to pause for a brief moment to calm my erratic heart. *Heaven.* No scratch that, heaven mixed with pure fucking bliss was what it was. There was no other place that I could ever want to be. I nipped and sucked at the column of her neck as her arms circled around my back.

With each and every movement, her nails dug in harder to my skin. I knew she was getting close when her moans became louder and more frequent, making me pound into her harder, aching for her to achieve the orgasm we both so desperately hungered for.

"Come on, baby, give it to me," my words breathing into her ear tipped her over the edge granting her, her spin into oblivion. Miri's fingertips clamped down on my back as the walls of her core repeated the same action to my dick. Her eyes rolled back into her head before they squeezed shut as she bit her bottom lip and continued to ride out her orgasm, her back bowing off of the mattress. It was interesting to learn that she was silent during her release and my new challenge was to get her to cry out. I would work night and day fulfilling this mission if I had to.

Her hands went slack along my skin as I felt her heart beating wildly in her chest as she came back down to earth. The gleam in her eyes once they opened informed me that she was satisfied, even before she muttered, "Wow."

Our fun wasn't over yet, though, I latched onto her hips and flipped us over, all while still firmly seated within her, so she was now on top. "Will you ride me?"

Her sated grin slid off of her face as a mask of vulnerability slipped in its place. She was uncertain. My hands ran up the tops of her thighs and curved around to where I could knead my fingertips into her ass. "You've never done this?" I asked, already knowing the answer to the question. But she didn't need to be embarrassed, this was a learning experience for both of us, and I for one was glad that it was me living this encounter with her.

"No," her voice came out small, but she leaned forward placing her hands on my pecs and giving me a lingering kiss on my lips. "But you'll teach me right?"

"Damn straight I will." I gripped her hips in my hands and slowly raised her body up and down along my shaft. After a few moments, she took matters into her own hands allowing mine free roam. A sheen of sweat broke out across my forehead as my eyes fluttered closed from the raw intensity of her being able to control the movements. Her breasts slightly swayed as she took things slowly, her hair fanning around her face as she held onto my chest.

Soon Miri became a bit more brazen, knowing she held all the power in her tiny hands. My hands went to her breasts where I tweaked her nipples with my fingers earning me more moans and groans that slipped through her parted lips. Her speed began to pick up as she grabbed ahold of her hair with one hand, pulling it over her shoulder, and leaned back gripping the top of my thigh with the other, adding a different sensation with her shifting.

"Bentley," she cried as she proceeded to bite on her lip again on her way to garnering another silent release.

My own release was surging forward and I knew it wouldn't be much longer until we'd be toppling over together. "Let go of your lip, Miri. Let me hear you. I want to hear just how good I make you feel." She listened to my plea as she let up on her assault of her plump bottom lip.

Moving my hands to her ass, I gripped hold of it tightly as she screamed, "Ohhh!" Her body rocked even faster and again her walls clamped down around my dick, cumulating just enough pressure to send me over the edge. She threw her head back, screaming my name, "Bentley," in the throes of passion as we both released together. I felt temporarily paralyzed as my eyes rolled into the back of my head and my legs stiffened as I released deep into her pussy. Seconds later I felt her body go completely limp as she collapsed on top of me, she was spent and rightfully so.

"Holy shit," were the only words I could evoke as I was completely rendered inarticulate. Never in my life did I have such an intense connection with someone. Miri and I melded together perfectly as if we were actually made for one another.

A moment after catching our breaths I leaned off the bed to retrieve my discarded jeans and pulled my phone out of the front pocket before throwing them back to their previous position on the floor. I laid back down, tucking Miri tightly in next to my side and lit up my home screen.

"What're you doing?" Miri asked, the confusion clear in her voice.

Hearing her question but choosing to ignore it for the time being, I pressed on my phone a few times getting to where I needed and held the phone to my ear.

After a few rings, my mother answered groggily, her voice laced with sleep, "Bentley?" She inquired, "Do you have any idea what time it is?"

"Ma, you wanted me to let you know if I would be coming into work or not. I'm calling to say that would be a definite no." I felt Miri tense against my side, and I began smoothing my fingers up and down her bare arm as it snaked across my body.

"Bentley!!" she screeched, all signs of sleep long gone. "Does that mean what I think it means?"

I still couldn't believe that I was discussing this with my mother and at some obscenely late time of night. I squeezed the flesh of Miri's shoulder and replied, not being able to hide my smile, "Yes, Ma. Yes it does."

After having to remove the phone from the direct vicinity of my ear from my mother's squeals of delight, I bid her goodnight and replaced my phone on my nightstand before turning off the lamp.

Miri snuggled further into my side, intertwining my feet with hers then suddenly burst out laughing. "Did you seriously just call your mother and insinuate that we had sex?"

"What?" I shrugged my shoulder. "She's excited that her son has finally settled down, I had to put her mind at ease so now she can rest without worrying that I'll end up alone or with dozens of baby mamas."

"Thank goodness for that. I can just picture the headlines now, Bentley Jenkins Is Officially Off The Market,'" she moved her hand in an arch as if she was reading a newspaper word for word. But she didn't hesitate in adding her own subtitle, "'Does this mean total anarchy for the women population of Cottage Grove?' "

I curled to my side, bringing the thin sheet around me and positioning my body over Miri's, planting a brief kiss on her soft lips. "If we're making headlines, then let's give them something to talk about."

And let me just say, that if the walls could talk, they'd have a lot of gossip come morning.

# *Epilogue*

## *Three Months Later*

### *Miri*

You know when you're having an amazing dream, one that outranks any and all form of reality when you are just on the cusp of waking up? Your subconscious is having a great laugh from its playful tease, and it pulls you back and forth in between dreamland and reality. You want nothing more than to snuggle back into your warm covers, fall back into that deep, peaceful sleep, and finish out the remainder of that dream.

In most cases, especially in mine, you feel yourself slipping further and further away from the once in a lifetime dream, and you can only hope that you are able to remember at the very least bits and pieces so you can relive it over and over again while daydreaming.

Once I was finally pulled awake, away from the blissful dreamland, I now fully understood why my sleep was disturbed so abruptly. And let me tell you, my current reality blew any and all dreams out of the water.

Just then, Bentley's tongue surged deep into my core as I clutched onto my sheets to help brace myself for what was to come, because, at any moment, it would be me. I was one lucky lady, with Bentley it was a guarantee, always. He could be extremely arrogant, but he worked magic, especially with his skillful tongue.

It wasn't long before I was hit with the all too familiar sign, indicating that I was close to finding my release. "Oh God," I screamed, practically panting with the intensity of the moment, my toes threatening to curl into the mattress. I couldn't ever be quiet, he needed the verbal clarity and I was all too willing to comply.

All too quickly, Bentley's tongue, lips, entire mouth disappeared. His head peeked up from underneath the blanket with the biggest grin plastered to his perfectly chiseled face. Before I could even form a plea or protest, he said amusingly, "Not God, Miri, just Bentley."

As fast as he came out, he submerged himself back under the covers even faster. This time his lips wrapped around my clit and I was thrown right back to where I was, one lick or suck away from detonating into a mindless orgasm, the only kind worth having.

My eyes rolled back into my head of their own volition and I was almost there, pure bliss was just within my grasp. I could feel the convulsions beginning to take over.

"Oh God," this time the two words slipped by without any heed or warning. And as soon as I said it, he removed himself once again and peeked his head out from under the covers. Not stopping there, he threw back the sheet to where it was now draped on the floor.

"Miri, baby, it's still Bentley. Although, I do have some rather god-like qualities, you keep referring to me in such a way it may inflate my ego." He eyed me with amusement, trying to keep his smile under wraps.

"We wouldn't want that, your ego is already overinflated." I gave the top of his mussed hair a mild shove, hoping he would grasp the not so subtle hint. "Please, Bentley."

"Please what?" he grinned. There it was. That grin, the same one that stopped my heart each and every time he used it, which was often. I loved that grin, even more so the man behind it, but he knew exactly what that grin did to me, which is why it made its play often. "I won't know what you want if you don't tell me."

I flung my hands back on the bed, looked at the ceiling, and groaned exasperatedly. That man better be glad that I loved him because he was completely infuriating.

I heard him chuckle before he thankfully returned to the task at hand. And he was all hands on deck. Bentley inserted two fingers deep into my core and within seconds of him latching onto my clit again I was thrown into a tailspin of orgasms. Stars exploded behind my eyelids as I rode out the wave of something so special that only Bentley could give me.

Coming back down from my high, Bentley had lifted the sheet off the floor and was covering us once more as he rested the side of his head in the palm of his hand.

"Good morning to you, too," I said as I stretched my arms high above my head, trying to work out all the kinks from my slumber and extra-curricular activities. "A girl could get used to waking up like that."

"A girl should get used to waking up like that..." Bentley brushed his lips against my cheek for a quick peck before he hopped up out of the bed, his bed that I've been inhabiting almost every night since we officially became an 'us.' He turned around, halting his hands in front of him, and smiled, "Stay just like that and I'll be right back."

Less than a minute later, he came back into the room with something within his grasp as he ran and took a flying leap over me, flopping back on his side of the bed. As his labored breathing returned to normal, he pressed his hand into the valley of my bare breasts and after pulling it back, there rested a petite black box.

The kind of box that housed a gorgeous pair of earrings, even though my ears weren't pierced. If that's what the box contained, I'd make an appointment today. Or... I didn't even want to think about the alternative because it was too soon, wasn't it?

My heart began racing within my chest as I sat up, allowing the sheet and the box fall aimlessly to my lap. With trembling hands, I grasped the box within my clutch and brought it towards my face. I didn't know whether to inspect it as if it would secretly inform me of what rested inside or actually take a peek.

"Well, aren't you going to open it?" His voice was giddy, and dare I say, adorable. But don't tell him that, it'll bruise his ego and all. Bentley had sat up and was resting on his hand as he faced towards me. The excitement and anticipation on his face made me love him all the more. He was like a kid on Christmas, except it wasn't him ripping into the present.

I didn't know what to think or worse, what to do, but the further I prolonged opening the box, it would only upset him and that wasn't my intentions. My heart raced wildly, like a thousand horses galloping at their fastest pace. I took a deep breath and slowly lifted the hinged lid, hearing it creak until it was fully opened and nestled inside wasn't a gorgeous pair of earrings, but rather a simple round cut diamond solitaire ring. Engagement ring. It was truly stunning. My heart lodged in my throat.

Looking up from the ring to Bentley, I noticed his bewildered expression and a sheen of sweat break out along his forehead. I asked, "What is this?"

He forced out a nervous chuckle, "What does it look like? I'm putting a ring on it."

Bentley, he had a way with words, but it did break the ice a bit, which was his obvious intentions.

I looked back down at the ring, still surrounded by its velvet encasing and blinked, unable to formulate any logical explanation. I loved this man, but this was a major step. Huffing out a large breath, I tried to speak past my heart that currently resided in my throat to no avail. "Miri," he said while tilting my head up to look at him, my eyes now swimming with unshed tears. "I never meant to fall in love. Love was never even on my radar, but there's no stopping it when it's with the one you're meant to be with, it's inevitable. You caught my eye at Baylor's wedding and we had an instant connection, sure at first it was just lust, but there was also something more. Something that at first I couldn't pinpoint and then was too stubborn to listen to. Placing me into the friend-zone was the smartest thing you could've ever done for us. Even though I saw that as a challenge, it led me to actually get to know you." The tears had now toppled over my eyelids and were steadily streaming down my face. "The more I saw you, the more I wanted to know and eventually craved. Then I broke my one rule, never sleep next to a woman. While I didn't actually get much sleep that night," he chuckled, "I think it was truly the first night that I felt my heart giving itself to you. And now that I've fallen in love with you, I can't ever imagine not waking up next to you. I know it's soon, but when you know, then you just kind of know and I don't see why we should prolong our future." He took the box out of my grasp and picked up the ring and raised it between the two of us, it barely resting in between his fingertips. The sun shining in through the window reflected off the diamond making it shine on the ceiling as if it held the same something special that I found in Bentley. Our love was strong and powerful and it could withstand anything. "So what do you say, will you…" He chuckled to himself before he took a big breath of air into his lungs and quickly released it. "Will you be my wife, Miri?"

I completely take back my comment about Bentley not having a way with words. Even more tears were floating in my eyes, and I blinked allowing them to run down my face with the rest of them. He was right, time was only that. I couldn't put a number on our love and if this next step felt right in both of our hearts, then why stand in the way of true happiness. I nodded once before releasing my breath that I'd been holding throughout his sincere and heartfelt confessions and erupted into the biggest smile. "Yes! Yes, I'll marry you!"

The edges of Bentley's mouth slowly curled up revealing the biggest smile I've ever seen from him to date. This. This smile was now my favorite, and the true testament of our love put it there.

*Bentley*

"I don't see why we have to make good on a promise I made to my brother. It's not like he'd expect us to actually show up. This is me we're talking about." I put Miri's car in park once we pulled into Baylor's driveway. We were being subjected to an outing that involved bowling. Yeah, my thoughts exactly. Turning towards Miri, I threaded my fingers into her hair on the side of her head and she instantly leaned into my hand. "I mean look at the alternative, we could still be in bed continuously consummating our engagement." I was totally grasping at straws, but spending an entire day in our bed completely naked as I made love to my fiancé sounded like a helluva day to me. *Fiancé*, I rolled that word around in my head and didn't nearly have the same reaction as I did when we were first dubbed *friends*. Saying the word fiancé made me unexplainably happy. Never in a million years did I think I would ever be lucky enough to fall in love let alone be engaged, but now that it was my reality, I wouldn't change a single thing. Of course, if I had to think of *something*, it would be for her not to accept any invitations from my family, especially ones that involved bowling when we had things to celebrate.

"We're already here, and plus we also promised Norah that we would go bowling with them. It won't be that much of a hardship, I promise. And later --" her eyes became hooded, as she inched her way closer across the console. "If you're a good boy," oh I liked the sound of this. I felt my dick stir to life, apparently he was digging the sultriness her tone had taken on as well. "I'll let you…"

*Tap.*

*Tap.*

*Tap.*

I practically jumped out of my skin and hit my fist against the steering wheel before I turned and saw my darling brother's big fucking ugly mug staring directly back at me on the other side of the glass.

"Baylor, you jackass!" I growled as I blindly grabbed hold of the door handle and whipped it open, not allowing him any time before the door slammed into the front of him. Hopefully hitting him where it counted.

Hearing the instant grunt I knocked out of him and seeing him doubled over, I knew that I had a direct hit on my target. *Bingo.*

Miri rounded the front of her car and ran straight to Baylor's side. "Oh my gosh, Bentley!" she chided. "Was that necessary?"

Shrugging a shoulder I replied, "Meh, seemed like it at the time." I walked up to Baylor and slapped a hand on his back. "Next time don't interrupt me when I'm having a moment."

Taking the time to spit on the ground, he said, "You're a dick, Bentley. I'll get you back on the lanes. You're going down." Oh yeah, I was really shaking in my boots. The sound of his voice faded as we walked in through the front door.

"We're here!" I announced to the entryway and Eden's head poked around the corner from the kitchen.

"Oh good! Bentley, will you run and tell Norah that we'll be leaving in five minutes?"

I made a spectacle of spinning one hundred and eighty degrees around on the ball of my foot so I'd be headed in the direction of my niece's bedroom.

Walking down the hallway, the closer I got to her bedroom the louder and clearer the music she was blaring became. Norah's door, indicated by a sign that stated it was her room, was slightly ajar, and I knew she wouldn't be able to hear me knock over the noise she insisted was music. Kids these days didn't know the first thing about music. So, I prayed to God and basically anyone who I thought would listen that things were exactly how they should be once I took that first step into her room.

No glimpse of Norah, but nothing out of the ordinary either. I took my first step over the threshold and felt as if I was discovering a new planet or being the first man to walk on the moon. My moves were that calculated and precise.

Wrapping my fingers around the edge of the door, I carefully poked enough of my head around to be able to peek at things with one eye. What I witnessed had me literally having to hold my breath in fear for busting out laughing.

My niece, God bless her, was in the middle of her floor, acting a fool, trying to attempt to dance. "Watch Me" by Silento was thumping through the speakers and the poor girl was trying to recreate the dance moves. Stomping on the floor and then waving a hand above her head, it was truly a sight to see. Too bad I had left my cell phone down in Miri's car or else this shit would've been pure YouTube gold. While I wasn't hip enough to know this song, I did have a few dance moves of my own in my repertoire. Without alerting Norah, I barged into her room, her still being too far sucked into her own little world to even notice and started doing a few moves of my own. I closed my eyes and started putting a spin on my own moves, including the Dougie, which I had obviously mastered. It was a prime dance party up in here.

Until Norah noticed me invading her space and socked me in the arm. "Uncle B! What are you doing in here?"

Rubbing away the small sting that she left behind by her fist, I answered, "Eden said that we will be leaving…" I raised my arm and looked at my watch. "Now in two minutes, but you seemed to be having so much fun in your one-woman dance party that I had to join in."

Her lip did this weird curl thing and the look on her face would lead anyone to believe that I just committed murder, she was disgusted and clearly not in the least bit amused. Teenagers scared the hell out of me, they ranked higher on my scare-o-meter than Tillie did and that was saying something. Was this what Miri and I had to look forward to? Jesus, I wasn't ready for this.

We all arrived at Cottage Grove Lanes, Dean and Julia following closely behind us and set the seven of us up on one lane. It would've made it a much quicker game if we split everyone up into teams of two, but who listened to me anyways.

"Wow, I don't ever think I've seen so many balls before," Julia smirked as she looked at the variety of colors and weights they had to offer.

Miri snickered and blushed, we both were well aware that Julia has seen a plethora of balls in her day.

"Just pick one, Julia," Dean whined. I wasn't thrilled that they decided to join us, but I decided for Miri's sake that I would play nice for tonight and be on my best behavior.

Julia's gaze snapped to Dean's. "Babe, there is a science to this. I have to make sure that I choose the right one. It can't be too heavy and my fingers have to fit in the holes just exact."

"I'll show you how fingers fit into holes…" Dean said matter-of-factly with a knowing smirk on his smug face.

"And that's a wrap!" I said as I quickly chose my own ball and ushered Miri and Norah away from their conversation. It was quickly turning into something that my twelve-year-old niece most certainly didn't need to be hearing. Baylor would thank me for such a mature decision as to keeping his daughter away from talk about fingering or whatever roll they were on.

Miri and I took a seat on the bench waiting for everyone else to get their asses in gear. She looked over at me and smiled. "Have I told you today how much I love you?"

"You have, but it's a new hour so I could always hear it again. You could just expand to how much of an amazing guy I am and how much you love my giant…" Her lips sealed onto mine as she placed her hand against my cheek deepening our kiss.

This lasted only seconds until we were rudely interrupted. "Guys, could you please lay off of the excessive PDA for at least an hour or two. Sheesh."

My brother had a way with impeccable timing, let me tell you. I broke our connection and glanced around at our entire group openly gawking at the two of us. Norah's gawking seemed to be admiration, which wiped every impure thought I was having about Miri clean from my mind.

Norah had her chin rested in her hand. "I think it's cute, I can't wait until I have a boyfriend."

"What?!" Baylor squeaked, his pitch going extremely high. "Oh yes, you can. You better not even think about dating until you're thirty."

She jerked her head up off her hand and raised a brow. Oh shit, things were about to get hairy. "But Uncle B isn't even thirty and he has a girlfriend," she huffed. So now the blame was being placed solely on me, what the hell else was new?

If Baylor's voice was a little too high before, now it had taken on a tone that was the complete opposite. Low and left entirely no room for argument, he was putting his foot down and he meant business. "Uncle Bentley isn't my daughter. If you want to see the outside of your room the remainder of the time you are in school, I suggest you break down this little attitude." He quirked a brow to see if she had a rebuttal, but it was clear once she huffed and crossed her arms in front of her chest that he was victorious.

I leaned into Miri's ear and whispered, "No girls. We are only having boys. I don't think I could handle a teenage girl in my house."

Miri's eyes lit up like I just told her she won the Publisher's Clearing House sweepstakes. "You want kids?"

"Of course I want kids…but like I said, only boys," I concurred.

She leaned forward to kiss me again before Julia gasped loudly. "Oh my God!" she shrieked and came over to us and jerked Miri's hand towards her face. "You got engaged?!"

Miri's face turned pink as she tried to shy back into my shoulder before replying with a simple, "This morning."

"Hold on a fucking second," Dean shouted as he pushed Eden and Baylor aside to stand in front of us. "You mean to tell me that you made Baylor and I learn that stupid dance that'll have Julia mocking and ridiculing me for years to come, all for you to propose this morning in lieu of the big scene?"

"Wait a second." Miri placed her arm in front of my body. "What dance?"

"Oh yeah." Dean waved a hand at me having me curse his existence under my breath, "Bozo here thought it'd be great to create a 'grand scheme' to perform in the middle of the fucking bowling alley so he could propose."

"You were going to do that for me?" Miri asked incredulously.

"Yeah, I thought that you would want some big gesture, but then this morning the timing just felt right and what better way for it to be done than just between the two of us," I replied sheepishly.

She smiled brightly at everyone else and then me and released a nervous laugh, "Thank you so much for not putting me through that."

My mouth dropped open, that wasn't the response I thought she would give. "I'm sorry, what?"

She put her hands up in surrender in front of her body. "Don't get me wrong, I love you, but I don't think I could've been subjected to a dance put on by you, Baylor, and Dean."

"Oh snap," Julia said, "In other words, she's saying if you would've done all that embarrassing shit, she would've turned you down."

"No, I just think that other women would be throwing themselves at the three of you, it would be uncontrollable mayhem. So this really saved the three of us women from having to throw down," Eden chimed in, trying to be the voice of reason.

I could not believe what I was hearing.

"Well, it would have to depend on the song they chose…What was the song, Bentley?" If it weren't for the smile that remained plastered to her face, I would think that she was utterly serious.

I stood from the bench and took on a defensive stance with my own arms crossed in front of my chest and said defiantly, "Nope, not going to happen. If you can't be sympathetic to the embarrassing things that I may or may not do due to my overpowering love for you, then I don't think you should get to know what song I picked."

She followed suit in standing from her seated position and taking two steps until she was fractions of inches away from me.

"Was it a, oh say a Roy Orbison song? Or how about Janis, you know how much I *love* Janis."

"Not telling you." I turned my face away, trying my hardest not to smile, but her pout was wearing me down.

"It was the Backstreet Boys, Bentley's favorite band," Norah shouted having me jerk my head in her direction. She had her own smile painted across her face. "Dad just told me," she smirked.

"Bullshit, don't believe everything your dad says. He just told you that you couldn't date until you turned thirty, do you honestly believe that's the truth?" Her smile fell off of her face slowly as the seconds ticked by.

Miri clasped onto my hand as she turned to everyone in our group and said "And that's our cue." She hitched her thumb towards the exit door. "I hope everyone enjoys their game. We'll try this again some other time." She waved and then we hightailed it out of the bowling alley before any blood could be shed.

Once we were safely in the confines of Miri's car she turned towards me and said, "I seriously can't take you anywhere."

"Babe, you know you love me. The sexy, the cocky, and the idiotic. I would just embrace it." I tilted my head with a smirk.

"Bentley Jenkins, you are just too much…"

"I know, Miri. I know."

# ABOUT THE AUTHOR

Amber Nation is a stay-at-home mom and wife currently residing in Southern Indiana with her husband and two beautiful daughters. Amber writes Contemporary Romance, Romantic Suspense, and Romance Comedy novels. She loves hoarding paperback books, shopping, concerts, road trips, and watching her daughters sport it up on the field or in the court. Her personal motto is to always believe in yourself and above all else, be you!

## **Follow Amber**

Twitter @nation_amber

Facebook: www.facebook.com/ambernationauthor

Pinterest: Ber2885

Website: www.ambernationauthor.com.

## *ACKNOWLEDGEMENTS*

First of all I would like to thank you for taking the time to read *More Than A Friend* and delving into the depths of Miri and Bentley's story. Each story that I create takes such time and dedication and I greatly appreciate the continued support and encouragement that comes from each and every reader.

Please consider lending this title or recommending any of my books to a friend who you think would enjoy them. Also, please consider leaving a review. Reviews, whether good or bad, help not just other readers decide to pick up the title, but also helps me build and strengthen my writing.

Jarrod, Alexis, and Olivia- Thank you so much for continuing to stand behind me in pursuing my dreams. It means the world to me that I have such a strong and loving support system. I love the three of you with all of my heart.

Savannah Stewart- My gnomie! 2015 has been a whirlwind of fun together and I cannot wait to see what all 2016 has in store for us! I value your friendship so much and appreciate you always being there for me no matter what. Mad love for you, lady!

Jennifer Hensley- Our friendship has grown so much over these past few months and I appreciate you more than you know! You are my ride or die and my fellow lover of all things Chase. Thank you so much for being you!

Mayas Sanders and Ashley Volk- Thank you so much for always being the first people I come to when I finish a book. I value the fact that you both give it to me straight and let me know if something needs fixed before I show it to the rest of the world. You two ladies are gems!

Enticing Journey Book Promotions- Thank you ladies for being rockstars at what you do! I appreciate all of your hard work!

Najla Qambar- Like I've said before, it all started with a premade cover and has ended with the best covers I could ever imagine! You have such an amazing talent! Thank you so much for your creations!

Silla Webb- Girl, I can't wait to finally squeeze you! Thank you so much for taking on me as an editing client. You rock!

# Other Titles by Amber Nation

## **Brown County Series**

Not Alone

Runaway Love

How To Save A Life

Unconditionally

## **Cottage Grove Series**

More Than A Memory

More Than A Fling

More Than A Friend

Amber Nation

Made in the USA
Charleston, SC
22 June 2016